RUN NO MORE

A SHIFFY P.I. MYSTERY (BOOK 1)

MICHAEL ROBERTSON, JR.

ISBN: 978-1-7360939-3-1

RUN NO MORE

CHAPTER 1

I t had been three days since Alexa Shifflett had decided to change her life.

After being on the run for over twenty years, ever since the day her father had died twisted in his bedsheets in their motel room and twelve-year-old Alexa had been salvaged from the wreckage that had become of her childhood, she felt for the first time a sense of relief at the idea of staying put and starting fresh. But there was fear, too. She'd been running for so long—not from anyone in particular, but from the threatening idea that if she ever slowed down the past would eventually catch up with her, rip open her scars and laugh in her face as the blood began to drip—and now, when she seriously began to think about how to actually attempt to find a home, to start living instead of simply being alive, she would quickly get overwhelmed and feel herself begin to drown in the waters of self-doubt. She'd shake her head, ashamed.

I'm broken. Damaged goods. I don't know how to be anything else.

But then she would remember the people she'd met that

had led her to her decision. Friends that had seemingly come out of nowhere and had helped save her. In fact, they'd all saved one another. She supposed *destiny* was a word you could use to describe what had happened, if you believed in that sort of thing. The memories would reignite her conviction—if not to do it for herself, then to do it for them. Because they'd showed her that she was worth so much more than she'd been giving herself credit for. There was a lot of good in her; buried down beneath all the exterior armor, there was still the woman that the twelve-year-old version of herself would have become had evil not slipped through the door and knocked her off the straight and narrow. She'd never be that woman, but she could be *something*. Something was better than nothing.

I'm going to try, she thought, just as the headlights of her ancient Oldsmobile sedan flashed across the city limits sign of another Nowhere, USA town.

Dammit, I'm going to try.

She'd driven south, after those few days spent with those new friends who had showed her that she could have a future if she wanted, that she wasn't damned to the existence she'd accepted. Never very far, though. Whereas in her previous life she would have downed gallons of coffee and put so many miles behind her each day that she'd often have to ask what state she was in when she finally did stop for the night, these past three days she would only drive for an hour or two, three at the most, and then find a place to stop. She'd grab a bite to eat and find a place to sleep and even go walking around to explore the streets of the place she'd ended up. It had been nice, relaxing. Like she'd been taking a vacation that was decades overdue. Her head had begun to clear, and even though there was still a lot of work to do, she could feel something inside of her beginning to spark to life. A tiny ember glowing warm in her belly, asking to be nurtured, fed. Ready to blossom into fire. Burn bright.

Alexa felt this glowing ember in her soul and found that she loved it, an instant all-encompassing love that was akin to what she imagined a mother must feel the moment they first lay eyes on their newborn child. Her ember was her new life, and along with that love came the desire to protect it, help it grow into what it was destined to become. She even gave it a name.

Lance.

A good friend, maybe the best friend she'd ever had even though they'd only known each other a short while.

She was in Virginia now, somewhere south of Harrisonburg. She'd taken an exit off Interstate 81 close to an hour ago and had followed rural routes ever since. Shortly after her headlights had illuminated the city limits sign, she saw the glowing lights from buildings a mile or so ahead and then passed a big wooden sign on the side of the road, half-obscured by the drooping branches of a pine tree. She hit the brakes, not stomping on them but pressing down abruptly enough that Barlow grunted and scrambled to keep himself from sliding off the back bench seat.

"Sorry, bud," Alexa said as she brought the Oldsmobile to a complete stop. She looked into the rearview and saw the dog sitting up and looking back at her. They shared a silent moment between them before Barlow opened his mouth, freeing his long pink tongue, and started panting. Alexa put the car into reverse and backed up until the sign was back in view. She turned the wheel and drove forward at an angle so her headlights were centered on the half-hidden sign. "I'll be right back," she said, throwing open the door and stepping outside.

There was no traffic. The road was dark except the lights from her car, and silent except for the rattling engine beneath the Oldsmobile's dented hood. The air was cold and crisp, carried winter's bite along with the heavy sent of pine and dirt and melted snow. Alexa shivered and stretched her back, zipped her leather jacket up to her neck. Then she walked toward the welcome sign, the headlights casting her shadow large and looming over the exposed wood. She stood on her toes, her boots sinking slightly into the wet ground, and reached up and pulled the drooping branch aside, worked to tuck it behind the sign. Then she stepped back and read the whole thing.

Welcome to Silent Falls

She stared at the sign for a long time. Long enough for another car to eventually arrive from the long stretch of road behind her. The new vehicle slowed when it reached her, and Alexa heard the sound of a window being rolled down. She turned and found a middle-aged woman poking her head from the passenger side of an SUV. She was smiling, but her voice sounded concerned when she asked, "Are you okay? Need any help?"

Something about the offer of kindness from a stranger caused the ember in Alexa's soul to flash its heat, a pleasant warmth in the cold night. Ordinarily, in her old life, Alexa would have been instantly skeptical of this stranger's attempted intrusion into her business. Her hackles would have risen the same way Barlow's did when he spotted a cat, and she would have braced for impact, prepared for a fight. But tonight felt different.

Alexa made herself smile back and nodded. "Fine, thanks. I just wanted to read the sign."

It sounded strange, Alexa knew that. But it was the truth. She'd told so many lies over the years that she now wondered if the truth would always taste weird on her tongue.

Barlow had his nose pressed to the glass of the back window, staring at the woman in the SUV, his tail thumping back and forth. "Cute pup you got there." A man in the SUV's driver seat leaned forward to be seen around his wife, his face glowing in the light from the dash. He too was all smiles. Radiated kindness. "What kind is he?"

"I have no idea," Alexa said and laughed along with the couple. "But he's the best."

The woman nodded. "Aren't they all!" And then they said their goodbyes and the SUV drove away and Alexa got back into the Oldsmobile.

She started driving toward the lights of the town, looking into the rearview and telling Barlow, "This might be the place."

Silent Falls.

It sounded like a place that could keep secrets.

CHAPTER 2

Before Alexa made it to the larger cluster of lights that must have been the town's center, the pine trees thinned and then vanished from the side of the road and the Oldsmobile was greeted by a long single-story structure on the right—cinderblock walls painted white, a red roof whose color had faded to something like rust mixed with blood. A generic marquee sign by the road announced with plain black letters that the establishment was SMOKEY'S, and that on Wednesday nights wings were half-price. The whole place looked like it'd been tossed here, dropped from the sky and landing in a cloud of dust. There was nothing around it except a bright-burning spotlight mounted high upon a telephone pole and shining down toward the parking lot. It was an outcast of a building, not allowed to play with the others, and Alexa wondered if outcasts were exactly the type of clientele the place catered to. She shrugged and turned the Oldsmobile into the lot.

The parking lot was nothing but hardpacked dirt and

crushed gravel and spanned the entire front of the building. It was mostly full, and an adjacent field held several big-wheeled pickup trucks clustered together like a used car lot that specialized in selling to insecure assholes. Alexa wedged her boat of a vehicle between two other sedans and stopped to think if today was Wednesday, hence the full lot. No, it was Friday. That explained it. Everyone had gathered at the local watering hole to celebrate the end of another soul-sucking workweek. She peered through her dirty windshield and eyed the front of the building. A pay phone was mounted a couple yards down from the entrance door, and several of the windows cut high into the wall boasted neon signs promising beer, billiards, darts, and music. A man was leaned against the wall by the entrance, a cell phone pressed to his ear, waving his other hand around a lot as he talked. Alexa sized him up for a brief moment, a habit she was sure she'd never be able to—nor want to—break, no matter how at peace she began to feel in her new life. He was brawny and his cheeks were red, but he appeared too engrossed in his phone call to even notice, let alone be a threat to her. He seemed agitated, his hand flailing and his voice rising. Alexa sighed and shrugged again. A place this packed couldn't be all that bad.

When she stepped out of the car and stood to her full height, she noticed the police cruiser parked in the grass on the right side of the building. She sized this up, too, pushing away memories and forcing the bile back down her throat that often threatened her with its acidic burn at the sight of a cop. But, the car was empty. A lone deputy or maybe two likely inside, leaning against the walls by the restrooms and hoping that their presence alone would keep anybody from doing anything stupid. Not all cops were bad. Alexa knew this to be as true as her own name, but unfortunately, in her mind they would forever symbolize her father. They were the origin of an entire lifetime of mistrust.

She looked away from the cruiser and then opened the back door and attached Barlow's leash to his collar. The dog jumped out and stretched his legs and then pointed his snout into the air and began to sniff, sniff, sniff. He looked at Alexa and wagged his tail.

"I know," Alexa said, smelling the aroma of meat and grease. "I'm hungry, too." The two of them set off toward the left side of the building, weaving between cars and heading for the open field where the pickup trucks were waiting. Alexa was secretly hoping that Barlow would choose to do his business against one of their tires.

Country music drifted from the side of the building and rolled over the parked cars like slow-moving fog, and as Alexa rounded the corner she saw that a large outdoor seating area had been set up out here: a concrete slab of a patio with lots of wrought-iron tables and chairs. Tall heat lamps burning at all four corners to warm the space. It was all covered with a wooden overhang with crisscrossing white Christmas lights and large speakers mounted in the two corners closest to the building. Only a few of the tables were full, and a waitress hip-checked the side door open and stepped out carrying a tray with two pitchers of beer and four glasses. She dropped the beer and glasses off at a table full of young men who were huddled together over their table in a similar fashion to the trucks in the field, and when she turned to head back inside, she spotted Alexa and then her eyes flicked down to Barlow. She smiled bright, just like the woman in the SUV had.

"Hey there, cutie. Oh my gosh, you're adorable!" The eyes of all four men jumped at her words, all probably secretly hoping she was referring to one of them, and then all their faces fell with disappointment when they followed the waitress's gaze to Alexa and Barlow. They returned to their beer and huddled conversation.

"Okay if he stays with me out here while I eat?" Alexa asked.

The waitress, a short blonde girl who couldn't be more than twenty-one or twenty-two, nodded as if Alexa had just made her night. "Of course! I'll go grab you a menu. Sit anywhere, this is my whole section tonight." Then she tucked the empty tray under her arm and disappeared inside the building, a blast of louder music and laughter and conversation and clacking billiards balls shooting from the opened door like a shotgun blast before getting silenced as the door swung shut. The four guys around their table laughed at something, and Alexa turned in time to see them all quickly look away from her. She was certain they owned the pickups in the field.

Three other tables were occupied, two by couples and one by three middle-aged women whose faces were all saying *Whose idea was this, anyway? We could have stayed home and drunk wine and watched Netflix.* Alexa chose a table along the edge of the patio near the center. She sat with her back to the field, giving her a direct line of sight to the door and a one-eighty perspective of the rest of the outdoor dining area. There was a heat lamp above the door, too, humming and burning a bright fluorescent orange. Barlow sat at Alexa's side for a moment, but then he whined once and pawed at one of the chairs. Alexa used the toe of her boot to slide the chair back from the table and Barlow jumped into it, turning around and sitting like he owned the damn place. Then he looked toward the door as if he were waiting for the waitress to come and take his order.

The waitress came back a minute later with a laminated menu for Alexa and a large salad bowl of water that she placed on the ground for Barlow. Barlow looked down at it, almost as if he were offended she hadn't placed it on the table, but when the waitress smiled at him and scratched his head and said, "There ya go, buddy," he licked her hand once and then jumped down to take a drink. Alexa scanned the menu quickly, ordering a burger and fries for herself and a burger for Barlow. She ordered sweet tea instead of anything alcoholic. One big step she was trying to take in order to keep herself focused on starting new was to keep her head clear, and getting a buzz at a roadside honky-tonk wasn't a step in the right direction. At least not on her first night in town.

The food came and it was good, the meat hot and well seasoned and the bun toasted, the fries crisp. The waitress had already cut Barlow's burger into smaller pieces and brought them out in another salad bowl. This time she did place the bowl on the table, and Barlow, back in his chair, inhaled the food almost before she'd had a chance to ask Alexa if she needed anything else. Both women laughed, and Alexa knew she was going to give this girl a big tip. Barlow was licking the bowl clean of any evidence that a burger had ever existed, like a criminal wiping down his crime scene, when Alexa spotted movement from the side of the building and turned to see the man who had been on his cell phone by the front door headed straight toward her table.

On the outside, Alexa looked calm, kept her face apathetic and her body language neutral. But inside she was tense, her mind calculating the best angle of attack *(go for the balls first, throat second)* should Mr. Hand-Talker deserve a lesson in manners. She had no reason to think this way—the guy had done nothing to her and given her no reason to think poorly of him—but Alexa's past, the entire life she was trying to put behind her, had rewired her dominant trait to be a sort of skeptical cynicism mixed with a healthy dose of assuming everyone was guilty until proven innocent.

Plus, up close, the guy just looked like a cocky son of a bitch.

The waitress, who'd been having a one-sided conversation with Barlow, looked up when the man reached the table, his shadow covering her like a blanket, hiding her away. Alexa saw the look of disgust shimmer behind the girl's features before she caught herself and put her waitress persona back on.

"Hey, Tony," she said. "The guys are still inside at the tables. I think they were waiting for you before they started another game."

Tony, who was about six feet tall and had broad, gym-swollen arms and shoulders beneath a tight black sweater, didn't even look at the waitress. He said, "Thanks, Squirt. Why don't you go tell them to start without me?"

"Don't call me Squirt."

"Colin does."

"You're not Colin."

Tony laughed. "Don't I know it. Hey, why don't you grab

me a beer, and"—he leaned in a bit closer to Alexa, his cologne heavy enough to alter an air-quality reading—"what can I get for you?"

"You can get away from my table," Alexa said. "I already have enough male companionship for the night." She nodded toward Barlow, who was still seated in the chair, his eyes locked onto Tony's, his jaw tense.

Tony looked down at the dog, rolled his eyes, undeterred. "Oh, I can think of a few things this one here can't offer you."

"Doubtful," Alexa started.

"How about I—"

"That you can think," she finished.

The insult crackled across the space between them. The waitress laughed, loud and long. The rest of the people seated at the tables around them were now all entranced by what was happening at Alexa's table.

"She's not interested, Tony. Stop embarrassing yourself," the girl who didn't want to be called Squirt said.

Tony's already red cheeks flushed brighter, and his eyes narrowed. Alexa readied her legs, prepared to push back and spring upward, delivering one solid knee into the guy's groin. That was all it would take to turn this self-described hero into a zero. But it was wasted energy, because Tony settled on simply saying, "Fuck you, bitch," and then turned to head inside. He had his hand on the door and stopped to turn around and yell, "And I still want that beer, Squirt," before he went inside with another blast of noise.

When he was gone, Alexa said, "Nice guy, that one."

The waitress rolled her eyes. "Sorry, he's the worst sometimes. But, oh my God, you totally shut him down. That was, like, the best thing I've ever seen."

Alexa smiled. "I've seen them all before. That one there" —she nodded toward the door—"chump change."

The waitress nodded, an understanding being silently passed between the two women. Then she asked, "Anything else I can get you?"

Alexa shook her head. "Just the check when you get a moment. I'm in no hurry."

The girl who didn't want to be called Squirt went back inside, and Alexa finished off a few remaining French fries, tossing one to Barlow after he'd started a puddle of drool on the ground beneath the chair. He caught it and swallowed it whole. The group of middle-aged women left their table and headed inside with a collective sigh, and the group of guys who'd had the two pitchers of beer started getting louder as the pitchers got emptier. One of them called over to Alexa and asked her if she wanted to join them, but he'd done it in a polite enough way that Alexa simply responded with a "No, thank you," and that had been the end of that. She leaned back in her chair and sipped what was left of her sweet tea, and despite the unfortunate encounter with Tony-the-Worst, she found herself feeling pretty good. She liked the vibe of this place, assholes aside, she liked her waitress, she liked the way the woman and man in the SUV had smiled at her on the side of the road and asked if she'd needed help.

She savored this feeling. Wanted more of it.

The waitress brought out her check and Alexa paid with cash and handed the girl a twenty-dollar tip. It was too much, because Alexa Shifflett wasn't exactly made of cash, but it felt earned. "For being so nice to my dog," she told the girl. The waitress thanked her and assured Alexa that it had been her pleasure. She gave the dog a quick pet and kiss atop his head and then told Alexa to come back anytime.

Maybe I will, Alexa thought as the girl went back inside. *No, I definitely will.*

She reattached Barlow's leash and they headed around the corner of the building and back across the parking lot. As soon as the Oldsmobile started to come into view, Alexa could tell something was wrong. She approached the car and looked down, to where the front driver's side was sitting significantly lower than the rest of the car.

Her tire had been slashed. A long, deep gash that was no accident.

She remembered how Tony-the-Worst had been standing at the front of the building when she'd arrived. He would have seen what car she was driving. *I guess he noticed me after all.*

Alexa looked down at Barlow, who sniffed the slashed tire once and then looked up to her. "Seems a bit much, huh? You'd think a guy like that would be used to rejection by now." She looked to the building, thought about going inside and confronting the guy. But then her gaze shifted over to the police cruiser parked in the grass beside the building. *Not tonight,* she decided. The old Alexa might have decided otherwise, but the burning ember in her soul was telling this new Alexa to take it easy. No sense in starting any trouble your first night in town.

She wasn't going to let a little bad outweigh all the good.

She popped the trunk and shouldered the duffle bag that contained all she owned in this world and then grabbed the burlap tote that held all Barlow owned—some food, his bowl, a few chew toys, and one dirty and worn tennis ball. She slammed the trunk closed and gave the police cruiser one last mistrusting look before she turned and headed for the road.

"Come on, boy," she said, giving Barlow's leash a gentle tug.

They started walking toward the lights in town, and Alexa was proud of herself for leaving all of her anger in the parking lot behind her.

She just wasn't sure she'd leave it there for good.

CHAPTER 3

With her dinner finished and a couple hours of driving behind her, Alexa was enjoying the walk from Smokey's into town. Using the building lights in the distance as their guide, she and Barlow had walked along the dirt shoulder of the road for maybe a quarter mile before the sidewalk had started and then it was smooth sailing. The air was cold but not freezing, Alexa's jacket enough to keep her plenty warm, and the sky was clear and full of diamonds. Barlow's tail wagged as they went, and the dog seemed to want to stop every fifteen yards or so to investigate a smell, which made for slow going, but Alexa didn't mind. There was no timeline to be met.

It felt good to walk toward something instead of running away.

They passed old single-story homes and a tractor sales and repair shop, a used car lot and self-serve car wash side by side, and a small gas station and convenience store next to a laundromat. Closer now, Alexa could see the buildings in town begin to come into view, slowly taking shape in the night sky as the lights help cut their edges and define their features. On her left, the old houses and shops stopped and a large expanse of greenery took their place. Lots of grass and trees and shrubbery, a children's playground in the distance, looking miniature from Alexa's vantage point, like a toy set left behind. A couple basketball and tennis courts were set off to the side, and further away still, Alexa could make out the looming tower lights that would illuminate the baseball and softball fields once the season started. All these things were dissected and surrounded by the dull gray of the pathway that snaked and cut through the grass. The start of the path met her at the sidewalk, accompanied by a bronze sign that welcomed her to Collins Park. For a moment, Alexa considered taking a stroll through the place, stretching her legs a little more before finding a place to stay. But when she glanced at her watch and saw it was nearly 9:30, she thought better of the idea. She didn't know if the park had official hours and didn't particularly want to be caught trespassing. Having a cop shine their flashlight into her face while asking what she was doing out at this hour would not go over well, and she'd likely end up saying or doing something she'd later regret.

New Alexa. New life. Plus—she looked down at Barlow—she wasn't looking out for only herself now.

She chose to keep walking.

A few cars passed in both directions, their headlights moving sleepily across the street, tires humming softly on the asphalt, nobody in a hurry. All of the oncoming traffic was even courteous enough to dim their lights as they passed her by, and Alexa again felt something warm in her soul, an indication that she could definitely work with this place, see if she could mold it into something permanent. She wondered if it was really so much Silent Falls that was making her feel this way, or if it was her own cynicism stepping aside and trying to give the world a second chance. Personal growth, a shrink might call it. Not that Alexa had ever or would ever go to one. But she'd read enough books, seen enough television.

The buildings of what was likely considered downtown Silent Falls were all old brick and stone with flat roofs. Three stories tall at their highest, laid out in what looked like one big square with dissecting streets—the symmetry of the place was enough to give an OCD sufferer an erection. The only anomaly was a large clock tower at the center of the square, a big silver bell hanging from beneath the clock, the entire thing lit up with spotlights, easily seen from any angle. For a place that seemed not to be in any rush, it sure did seem like the city wanted to make sure people knew what time it was. Just as Alexa took a step forward after stopping to take in the scene, the minute hand on the big clocked ticked over, and the bell was drawn back slowly and then released, a single loud *bong!* echoing off the buildings. Barlow jumped and his ears perked up and he stared ahead toward the source of the noise. It was now officially 9:30.

"I guess we better get used to that, if we're going to be staying a while," Alexa said, leaning down and stroking the dog's neck. Barlow looked at her, and then his eyes went quickly back to the clock tower. He gave it a mistrusting look and a small grunt.

They continued straight, heading into the heart of town, the buildings' shadows thrown across them and spilling into the streets. Most of the places of business were closed at this hour—the hardware store, the lawyer's office, a CPA, a karate dojo, an antique store—but a few places were still open—a pizza joint, a sub shop, and a café that had a few people seated at tables with headphones in their ears and laptop computers opened on the tables in front of them as they sipped their drinks. Most of the floors above the ground level had lights on too, and Alexa wondered what was up there above all the businesses. It had to be apartments of some sort, or maybe office space.

Traffic lights went through their patterns at intersections, casting red, yellow and green hues across the ground. More lazy cars came and went, headlights and brake lights joining in the slow disco. A few pedestrians meandered along the blocks, most of them bundled up in jackets and hats and scarves, white plumes of breath popping from their mouths as they spoke with their companions or when they offered Alexa a friendly greeting as they passed. It all seemed so peaceful, so serene. As she walked, Alexa imagined the place throughout the seasons: white snow sparkling in the winter, the firework array of orange and red and yellow that would accompany fall foliage and decorations, the lively green of springtime growth and the rainbow of blossoming flowers, the humidity of summer giving the entire place a shimmer as the heat rolled through.

She found herself wanting to see it all. *Experience* it all.

The prospect of being a part of something after all this time excited her, but she tried to temper her emotions. She was ready for the change, but rushing into something, blindly believing in an unexplored, unvetted future, was not a wise move. Disappointment could lie around any corner, be waiting inside any new place. She had to be prepared for that, had to figure out just how much disappointment was enough to cause concern. This wouldn't be as easy as flipping a switch, no matter how much she wanted it to be. It would require work, hard work on her part. When you finished running a marathon, you didn't just stop and stand still and everything went back to normal. No, you had to keep moving, put your hands above your head and open the airways and work to slow your breathing, calm your heart. There was a cooldown period required. You had to respect it.

That was where Alexa realized she was now, the cooldown period. So the question was, when she got her breathing under control and her heart rate steady, would she still be in Silent Falls?

That warm part of her soul was telling her yes. She wanted to believe it.

When she and Barlow reached the clock, they found benches set up in a small grassy area around the tower, and a two-tiered round fountain sat dormant, shut down for the winter to keep from freezing. The spot was probably a favorite lunchtime hangout for folks working in the surrounding businesses. Alexa and Barlow made their way around the structure, Barlow keeping a wary eye on the bell high above, and then they continued straight.

A few blocks later, the buildings stopped and the land opened up and they found the inn.

The Silent Falls Inn was really just a charming name for a motel that, just like Smokey's, sat by itself off the road, a gap of undeveloped land on either side separating it from an auto garage further down and the small post office on the closer side, nearer downtown. It was a single-story U-shaped building painted a dark blue with a white roof and ten white doors. A glass-doored office capped the end on the left. Cars were parked in front of two of the rooms, a hatchback sedan and a minivan. The neon VACANCY sign in the office's window stared back at Alexa as she and Barlow stood in the parking lot. The building looked like somebody had recently given it some love and attention. The parking area and walkways in front of the rooms were well lit, and the paint appeared fresh. A modern vending machine hummed by the office door, and Alexa spotted three white boxes with small antennas sticking out from them mounted along the roofline. *Wi-Fi*, she thought. *All the comforts of home.*

A car passed by on the road, and Barlow turned to watch it drive away. When the taillights vanished into the night, Alexa walked toward the office. She stared at the VACANCY sign the entire time, and she couldn't shake the feeling that it was trying to tell her something. That maybe there was room for her here, not just at the inn but in the town itself.

She pushed open the glass door and immediately felt the heat inside. Stepping across the threshold was like slipping into a warm bath. The office was small but neat, with a check-in counter on the left and a few chairs along the wall on the right. Framed photos of mountains and lakes—probably local—adorned the walls. A small counter at the rear held a modern coffeepot and a tray of creamer and sugar packets. Barlow began sniffing the air, getting a feel for the place.

"Hello, there." A young black man behind the counter stood from a worn leather recliner and set his Kindle reader on the counter and smiled at her. He had to be in his early thirties at the most and was dressed sharply in dark jeans and a tucked-in blue-and-white button-down shirt, chocolate-colored belt. His face was handsome and his teeth were white and his hair was cut close to his scalp. Well over six feet, he towered over the counter and had to lean down a bit to rest his palms on top of it.

Hello there yourself, gorgeous, Alexa thought.

"Hi," she said. "Is it okay if he's inside?" She gestured down to Barlow.

The guy nodded his head. "Of course. We're pet-friendly. I'd love to have one myself, but I'm here most days. Seems unfair to leave them cooped up in a house alone all the time. Have you had him long?"

Alexa was about to lie. Without even trying, she could tell this guy an entire history of her and Barlow's past life together. Starting with the day they'd fallen in love when she'd found him as a puppy at some shelter somewhere and continuing all through the years until they arrived here at this very moment. And this guy would believe her, too. Because they always believed her. Everybody had their own gifts in life, and one of Alexa Shifflett's was that she was damn convincing when she wanted to be.

No, you're deceitful, the cynical part of her said rudely from the back of her mind.

Alexa didn't try to argue the difference. Instead she tried the full truth. More than she probably should have.

"Nope," Alexa said. "Only a few days, actually. His owner was killed and I took him in. Now he's my new best friend."

The guy's face fell for just a moment as he processed what Alexa had said, and she waited for him to start asking questions. To pry into her past and start judging her and try to figure out if she was the type of person he wanted staying here. Wondering if she was going to cause any trouble, or have trouble come looking for her.

But he didn't. Instead, after that quick flash of concern, he smiled again, but just with his lips this time. No teeth. It was a look of sympathy. "That was very kind of you. Poor guy," he said, looking down at Barlow. "He's very lucky to have had you come along, I'm sure."

Much like she'd felt with Squirt at Smokey's, Alexa found herself really liking this guy.

The VACANCY sign burned in her peripheral.

"So," the guy said, standing tall and clearing his throat, "would you like a room?"

"Please," Alexa said, slinging her duffle bag off her shoulder and setting it on the floor. She pulled her wallet from her jacket pocket. Here came another test. "Cash okay?"

The guy, who had turned his attention to a laptop computer and started punching at the keys, didn't even glance at her. Just nodded and said, "Fine with me." Then he asked, "Can I have your name, please?"

"Can I have yours?" Alexa blurted. It came out harsher than she'd intended, a defense mechanism from her old life. She'd used so many names over the years to hide her true identity that reverting back to her real self seemed like some sort of betrayal. The guy looked up from the screen, and Alexa tried to quickly recover. She smiled and held out her hand. "Alexa," she said. "Nice to meet you."

The guy returned her smile and reached out his hand, his long fingers nearly wrapping all the way around hers. "Ezra," he said. "Call me Ez, and the pleasure is mine. Last name, Alexa?"

He must have seen her hesitate, was witness to the internal struggle Alexa worked to push down and bury. He shrugged. "It's okay. What's the dog's name?"

"Sorry?" Alexa asked.

"The dog. What's his name?"

"Barlow."

The guy leaned down again and typed on the computer. "Okay, Alexa Barlow, you're in room three. End of this block here." He pointed to his left. Then he put a magnetic key card into a machine and punched a few more buttons and then slid it across the wooden surface. He told her the nightly rate and she peeled off some bills and slid them toward him. After the transaction was complete, the two of them stood there for maybe a second or two longer than was comfortable before Ezra asked, "Anything else I can do for you?"

Alexa shook her head. "Nope, I think we're good." She turned to leave but then stopped. "Are you here all night?"

Now Ezra shook his head. "No, ma'am. Herb works the night shift. He's a little, shall we say, rough around the edges, but..." He trailed off, like he wasn't quite sure what to say any further about the guy named Herb. "But he'll be happy to help you if needed. And he knows to call me if something comes up he can't handle."

"Are you the manager?" Alexa asked.

"Owner," Ezra said. "So trust me when I say the Silent Falls Inn guarantees a pleasant stay." He gave her a wink. Coming from somebody else, Alexa might have thought this statement was a euphemism. But from Ezra in the nice clothes and the beautiful smile and the no-questions-asked ... she took it as genuine.

She nodded and walked outside, Barlow trotting dutifully beside her.

Room three had one queen-sized bed and was clean and warm and the carpet and sheets all looked new. The bathroom had been updated recently with modern fixtures, and a flat-screen television was mounted flush to the wall. It looked more like a room you'd find in a chain hotel in the city than anything Alexa had been expecting. She contemplated a shower but decided against it. Instead, she made sure the door was locked and then she stripped down and slipped into the bed and switched on the television. Turned it to ESPN just for the background noise. Barlow jumped onto the bed and curled up next to her. It was a routine they'd quickly developed with each other.

They were both asleep within minutes.

Surprisingly, Alexa slept like the dead. Dreamless and undisturbed until the sheriff's deputy pounded on the door.

CHAPTER 4

At first, Alexa had thought that the knocking sounds were coming from somewhere far away. Another room —maybe the one with the minivan or the hatchback—or maybe another place altogether, a car with a busted muffler waking up the neighborhood as it sped down the road, or a guy using a hammer to fix a fence post or reattach a mailbox after somebody had tossed back a few too many at Smokey's and then decided they were suitable to drive themselves home, thankful that the only casualty had been made of wood and plastic and not flesh and bone. The knocking was a sound meant for somebody else.

But then Barlow jumped from the bed and barked at the door, a single warning shot. Alexa's eyes flew open and the knocking came again, no longer softened by the fabric of her slumber. She leapt from the bed, naked, her body rigid, muscles tense. A voice called from beyond the door. "Miss? I'm a deputy with the Silent Falls Sheriff's Office. Would you mind opening the door so I can ask just a couple questions?"

Alexa found her clothes where she'd tossed them into the

chair the night before. She frantically pulled them on while her mind raced. *A sheriff's deputy? Why? I haven't done anything. I've only been here...* She glanced at the bedside clock, saw it was nearly eleven a.m. *Jesus...* She couldn't remember the last time she'd slept so long, so peacefully. That warm part of her, the part that was burning in her soul, told her that her sleeping so well was another sign that she was making the right choices, that this place was the perfect place to start over.

But the cop pounding on the door said otherwise. Those knocking noises were staccato reminders that Alexa Shifflett's past would forever haunt her.

But still... *I haven't done anything.* Then she corrected herself. *At least not here, I haven't.*

She thought about Ezra at the front desk. She'd only given him her first name—her *real* first name—and she couldn't imagine how that would be enough for him to find a reason to call the police on her. And... *And he was nice. He didn't ask questions.* Alexa shook her head. This wasn't Ezra's fault.

As if he could sense himself playing across Alexa's thoughts, Ezra's voice came through the door, muffled more than the deputy's had been, as if he were standing further away. She could imagine him out there, hands in the pockets of his pressed jeans with that aw-shucks look about him, casually confident. "Alexa, this is Ez, from last night. Look, he's going to make me open the door if you don't. I think if you just give him a couple minutes, he'll be satisfied and then he'll leave. Right, Officer?"

There was a pause, and Alexa could imagine the deputy staring at Ezra, trying to figure out if the guy was trying to play some sort of game. Eventually, the deputy said, "That's right. Like I said, just a few questions. I really am sorry to bother you, but ... well, it's very important."

Alexa had pulled on her pants and shirt and had one of her boots in her hand. She glanced over her shoulder toward the bathroom. There was no window there or anywhere else other than the front of the room. Nowhere to run, even if she wanted to. Plus, she couldn't leave Barlow.

But I'm done running, she surprised herself by thinking. And then again, *You didn't do anything. It's time to act like a regular upstanding member of society for a change. It can all start here.*

She tossed her boot back onto the floor and walked barefoot to the door. She didn't even bother with checking through the peephole. Ezra's voice was enough to let her know that the man on the other side was exactly who he claimed to be.

She pulled open the door hard and fast, for no reason in particular, but it felt good. The deputy jumped back, not much, but enough for Alexa to see she'd scared him. *Good,* she thought. *Now we're even.* She squinted against the morning sun, which was high in the sky and burned everything to the metallic whites and grays of winter. There was no wind, and the air was fresh and cool. All Alexa could smell was the deputy's cologne.

The guy cleared his throat and took a tiny step forward, positioning himself back where he'd originally been standing. He was only a couple inches taller than her, maybe five-nine, and he was thin but fit. Midtwenties at most, with a head full of curly blond hair that went along with skin so smooth Alexa wondered if the guy could even grow any facial hair. He was a kid, she figured, but he was in a uniform, and right now that meant she had to play nice. Alexa watched as he peered over her shoulder while he greeted her, scanning the room behind her, checking for ... *What?*

"Good morning, ma'am," he started. "I'm Deputy Wanamaker." He stuck out his hand. The thought of shaking Wanamaker's—or any cop's—hand made Alexa's stomach roll. Thankfully, right as Alexa was contemplating standing her ground and refusing the handshake, Barlow crept forward across the threshold and started to sniff at the deputy's shoes. Then he saw Ezra standing a couple yards behind in the parking lot, hands—yep, just Alexa had guessed—tucked into the pockets of his jeans, and the dog's tail started wagging and he trotted over to him.

Ezra said, "Hey, boy. Good morning, did you sleep alright?" as he squatted down to pet the dog, but he kept his head and eyes up, never leaving Alexa. He gave her a wink, just like last night.

"How can I help you?" Alexa said to Wanamaker, crossing her arms over her chest. She'd tossed on the T-shirt without her bra, and she didn't need this kid who looked like he couldn't shave getting distracted.

Wanamaker nodded, then visibly relaxed a little, as if Alexa's willingness to engage in his questioning was a relief. Like maybe the tough-guy stuff wasn't exactly in his repertoire, made him uncomfortable. "Thank you, ma'am. Just a couple questions. Would you prefer to talk inside"—he gestured with his chin toward the room behind her—"where it's warmer?"

Alexa uncrossed and recrossed her arms. Leaned against

the door frame. "I think it's a beautiful morning, Deputy. Let's chat out here in the sunlight. Get our vitamin D."

Wanamaker cleared his throat, and Alexa watched as his eyes darted over her shoulder again.

There's nothing in there, kid. Don't make me prove it to you.

"Do you know Anthony Romano?" Wanamaker asked, his eyes locked onto her.

"Nope."

It was an easy answer, because it was the truth. *See? Just a misunderstanding.*

"Uh, he's more commonly known as Tony?"

Shit.

Alexa's mind flashed to the image of Tony-the-Worst aka Tony-the-Tire-Slasher storming through the side door of Smokey's, telling Squirt to get him his beer.

Alexa sighed. "If you're referring to a meathead of a guy with about as much charm as a port-a-potty at Burning Man, then yeah, I've had the displeasure of making his acquaintance."

Wanamaker winced, like her words had somehow sliced open a wound.

"I've, uh, got a witness at Smokey's who claims that you and Mr. Romano got into a bit of an altercation last evening. Would you say that's correct?"

Alexa tried to burn a hole into Wanamaker's face with a deadly stare. She took a deep breath to keep herself calm enough to speak. She only half-succeeded. "Listen here, Dennis the Menace—if you want to know what happened between *Mr. Romano* and me last night at Smokey's, I'll be happy to fill you in. It's a short story, and it ends just like you think it might. I was eating my dinner outside with my dog, enjoying myself, actually, when Tony decided he wanted to try his luck with a few pickup lines. To say that he failed in his efforts would be an understatement, and I was very happy to make sure he understood the uselessness of his endeavor. He wasn't happy that I was unwilling to let him stick his dick in me, and he used a few choice words to articulate this sentiment before he stormed off like a pouty little baby."

From behind Wanamaker, Ezra didn't even try to stifle his laugh. Wanamaker turned and looked at the man, who was still crouched and petting Barlow, and then looked back to Alexa. He stared at her a moment longer, his cheeks growing red. Whether from embarrassment or from the cold, Alexa wasn't sure. Finally, he asked, "And when he stormed off, that was the last time you saw him?"

"Yes. Though I'm pretty sure he slashed my tire." She shrugged. "But I can't prove that."

Wanamaker's eyes narrowed. "The Oldsmobile? That was yours?"

"Yes. How did you know?"

This time Wanamaker's cheeks burned brighter. "It, uh ... it got towed last night after Smokey's closed. There was no note on the car and nobody had told management it was going to be staying overnight. They thought it was abandoned, given the, uh... nature of it." He winced at his own words, then added, "I'm sorry."

Alexa shrugged again. She couldn't care less about the car. The impound yard could keep it, as far as she was concerned. Though ... *It has served me well, that car. It took me to meet Lance.*

Wanamaker swallowed and cleared his throat again.

Stood tall as he asked, "What time would you say you left Smokey's, ma'am?"

Alexa rolled her eyes. "What are you getting at, Deputy?"

"Answer the question, please."

Alexa thought back to the night before, to her walk through town. She remembered the clock tower. "I don't know what time I left Smokey's, but I passed through town about nine thirty and then ended up here. I'm sure he could verify what time I arrived." She nodded toward Ezra, who stood and nodded back.

"Sure could. Got the check-in time in the computer," he said.

Alexa said, "There ya go."

"And you walked, all the way from Smokey's?"

"I did. Slashed tire, remember? It's not that far."

"Did anybody see you?"

"See me?"

Wanamaker shifted his weight from one foot to the other. "What I mean is, can anybody confirm that you left Smokey's and walked straight here to the inn?"

Alexa took another deep breath, uncrossed her arms and braced them, palms out, against the door frame. She pressed hard, the wood creaking beneath her strength. She let her frustration flow through her hands and into the building, letting out a bit of steam.

"Deputy, I've answered your questions, just like you asked. So why don't you do me a solid and tell me exactly why you're here? What is it that you think I've done?"

Wanamaker took a small step back again. "I, uh, I didn't say you've done anything at all."

Alexa waited.

Ezra waited.

Barlow waited.

Wanamaker's head swiveled and he looked all across the parking lot, surveying the building from one end to the other. "Fine," he said. "News is probably all over town by now anyway. Anthony Romano was murdered last night. His body was found early this morning."

Alexa didn't hesitate. "All I did was insult him. I'd hardly call that murder."

Wanamaker blinked at her, his face blank.

"I didn't kill him," Alexa said.

Wanamaker waited a beat, then nodded his head. "Thank you for your time."

Alexa watched as the deputy turned and nodded to Ezra and then started across the parking lot toward where his cruiser was parked in front of the office. He was halfway there when he stopped and turned to call back, almost sheepishly, "Just don't leave town, please. Not until we have some more answers."

Rage burned inside Alexa and she called back, "Hard to leave town without a fucking car!"

CHAPTER 5

After the deputy had driven away, Alexa called for Barlow and the dog accepted one more pet on the head from Ezra and then obediently turned and returned to the room. Ezra stood and stared at Alexa and Alexa stared back, waiting out only a second or two of silence before she stepped back and closed the door, sealing out the world. She leaned down and peered through the peephole. Ezra was already headed back to the office, hands in his pockets, a slight bounce to his step like he'd just asked a pretty girl out on a date and she'd said yes.

Carefree. That was the word that popped into Alexa's mind as she watched the guy disappear into the inn's office. It was an odd demeanor for him to have after just learning that somebody had been murdered.

There's more to him than he's letting on, she thought.

When her mind returned to the conversation with Wanamaker, her anger began to bubble again. She was angry at being accused of a crime she had not committed, sure, but she was even more angered by the fact that she'd been so prepared and willing to begin her new life here. She'd just started laying the foundation to leave her past behind her—as much of it as she was willing, anyway—and everything she'd seen in Silent Falls so far had just felt *right*. As she'd drifted off to sleep the night before, she'd allowed herself a sample of optimism, and it had tasted sweet.

But that flavor hadn't lasted long. Now she was being questioned in a murder investigation. She wasn't sure she was an actual suspect at this point, but Wanamaker's parting words had told her enough. She was in deeper than she wanted to be, that was for damn sure. She sighed heavily, exhaling tension. Barlow had already jumped back onto the bed and curled up into a ball, ready for a midmorning nap after all the excitement. A part of Alexa wanted to join him, to crawl back under the covers and slip away into the blissful sleep state she'd been cocooned in, back when things were still looking up, the future potentially bright. Before Wanamaker's knock.

But she wouldn't give in to the temptation. Her day had been started for her, and she had things she wanted to do. The old Alexa wasn't gone yet.

She went into the bathroom and took a long shower, let the hot water attempt to melt away her uneasiness. She felt better as she stepped back into the bedroom, a towel wrapped tightly around her and water dripping from her hair, Barlow snoring on the bed. She pulled fresh clothes from her duffle bag and dried her hair, staring at her own reflection in the mirror and silently asking herself questions.

Are you sure you want to do this?

Is it really any of your business?

Yes. It had become her business the moment Wanamaker had shown up and started asking his questions.

She pulled on socks and tied her boots tight, then attached Barlow's leash to his collar and grabbed the tote bag with his food and toys. He looked a bit annoyed at being disturbed from his nap, and Alexa told him to get over it— you didn't always get everything you wanted in life. He licked her hand and wagged his tail like he understood.

"I have a favor to ask," Alexa said as she pushed through the inn's office door and found Ezra standing at the computer, fingers a blur over the keyboard.

He looked up from the screen and smiled, stood up straight. "Let me guess, you want to know the best place for brunch?"

"Brunch is for yuppies."

Ezra held a hand to his heart. "I'm insulted. And don't tell me you don't enjoy a good mimosa."

Alexa's lips twitched, threatening to grin. The absurdity of this conversation was not missed. This guy had just witnessed her being questioned in a murder investigation and not only was he acting like it had never happened at all, he was joking about *brunch*.

"What do you need?" he asked, taking a cue from her silence.

"Can you watch my dog? He seems to like you, and I've got to run into town to take care of a few things. I can leave him in the room, I guess, but I just figured ... if you're going to be here. Maybe you both could enjoy each other's company."

Ezra's eyes shifted down to Barlow, who was at Alexa's side and sniffing something on the floor, and then back to Alexa. "I'd be happy to," he said.

And that was all. He didn't ask where she was going or how long she'd be gone. Nothing. He just agreed and that was that. Even for somebody like Alexa Shifflett, who'd worked so hard to protect her privacy and avoid the truth for most of her life, Ezra's lack of inquiry was becoming borderline unnerving. She felt an urge to unpack this with him. Because while on the surface they seemed very different, she was beginning to suspect there were similarities between them, things hidden deep down that they both worked to hide.

"Thanks," she said, sliding the tote bag off her shoulder and setting it on the counter. "Food and toys are in there. He hasn't had breakfast yet." She turned and pointed a stern finger at Barlow. "You be good, okay? I'll be back as soon as I can." She said this not so much for the dog, but to let Ezra know that she wasn't dumping the dog on him and then hitting the road, never to look back.

As she stepped outside, she heard Ezra dig inside the tote bag and ask, "How about you, boy? Ready for brunch?"

ALEXA ZIPPED her leather jacket against the breeze that had developed, but still found the day to be gorgeous. The noon sun was high in the sky and the clouds were absent, letting the rays heliograph off puddles of melted snow and the chrome of passing vehicles. She walked into town and found the place much livelier than the night before—folks hustling and bustling about, in and out of shops and businesses, crossing crosswalks and waving with friendly smiles to the traffic stopped at the lights. They carried shopping bags and gym bags and to-go cups of beverages. Children held their

mothers' hands and were tugged along with bashful indifference. Somebody laughed, a baby cried, a car horn tooted a
polite reminder. The jingling of bells mounted above entry
doors jangled now and again, fighting to be heard over the
din of everything else. Alexa stood at one intersection and
took it all in and was hit with a reminder of that scene in the
beginning of that old animated *Beauty and the Beast* movie,
the one where Belle strolls into town and everyone starts
singing like it's the only thing they were ever meant to do. She
refrained from shouting *Bonjour!* to a young man passing her
on the sidewalk with his earbuds in place and carrying a
large coffee.

*He's probably listening to a true crime podcast and will piss his
pants and try to pepper spray me.*

But the coffee seemed like a good idea, he had that going
for him. Alexa walked another block, passing the clock tower
and giving it a salute. Ezra's computer would definitely be a
more credible source of evidence when it came to Alexa's
whereabouts the night before, but the clock tower had
helped her answer Wanamaker's question quickly and easily.
It felt important, that time. That single strike of the bell
might be the sound of her innocence.

Calm down, she told herself as she stopped outside the
door to the café and looked inside through the glass. *You're
not a suspect.*

But it didn't matter. An accusation from a police officer,
whether for a parking fine, jaywalking, or the grand slam case
of murder, was all the same to Alexa. Unacceptable, intolera-
ble, and disgusting.

She'd been accused of a lot over the years, and yes, some
of them were correct accusations. She'd done bad things,

sometimes out of necessity and survival, sometimes out of spite or malice or, yes, punishment of particular individuals —her own personal flavor of vigilantism. But with those crimes—several of which she'd gotten away with, some for which she'd been caught—she'd always managed to come out mostly unscathed, and they'd *all* been committed by somebody other than Alexa Shifflett, one of the several dozen names and identities she'd been ever since that day when she was twelve and her father had died in that motel.

And she'd never killed anybody. That felt important, too. Despite her flaws and lies and demons, she was not a murderer.

She noticed a small sign taped to the bottom left of the big glass window of the café. It was a FOR RENT advertisement for the second and third floors of the building. There was a headshot of a balding man with glasses and a pointed nose who was the listing agent, as well as the phone number to contact for SERIOUS INQUIRIES ONLY. How pragmatic. Alexa wondered how many people spent their free time calling and asking about rental properties for shits and giggles.

She pulled open the door and allowed a young woman wearing tight-fitting workout clothes and sipping a green drink inside a plastic cup to step out. The girl thanked her and said that she loved Alexa's jacket, called it *vintage* and *totally hip*. Alexa, genuinely perplexed by this, having purchased this very jacket at a thrift store so long ago she couldn't remember, smiled and thanked the girl and then told her that she must be on to something with those green drinks because her ass looked great in those workout pants. The girl blushed, laughed, thanked her, and then scurried off down the sidewalk, giving Alexa a quick glance over her shoulder before she turned left and vanished.

The café was cozy and warm, and busy with Saturday patrons. Alexa stood in line and watched everyone around her without making it look like she was watching everyone around her. They all seemed so at ease, so casual. They all looked like they had no cares in the world. Which reminded her of Ezra, back at the inn. She underlined the mental note to dig into him a little more when she got back.

One thing was for certain, though. Between the looks of the people that had been milling about town and the sense of content palpable inside the café, if news of Tony-the-Worst's murder had gotten out, nobody seemed to really care or be all that worried or upset.

The barista handed her a large Americano and a bag with a blueberry muffin and Alexa headed out, back en route to her destination. She scarfed the muffin down in four huge bites and gulped the coffee. It was too hot and burned her throat, but it made her feel alive at the same time. Before she got to where she was headed, she reached Collins Park. The scene was very different from when she'd passed it the night before.

A police cruiser identical to the one Wanamaker had been in was parked with its right side up on the sidewalk. Yellow police tape was haphazardly strung across the entryway to the park, draped over and attached to the bushes on either side of the path like streamers at a birthday party. A lone deputy was leaned against the cruiser, apparently having been assigned the role of crowd control.

The guy wasn't as young as Wanamaker, and not as thin, either. He was probably in his forties and had the beginnings of a paunch that sagged over his belt. *Ah, the dreaded muffin top*, Alexa thought as she tossed the bag her own muffin had come in into the trash receptacle by the park's entrance. She stopped and looked out over the land, seeing it for the first time in daylight. There was no indication of where Tony's body had been found, which meant either he'd been found further in than she could see, or all the police and medical crews had already come and gone. But judging from the guy leaned against the police cruiser, Alexa bet it was the former.

"Need you to move along, ma'am. Nobody's allowed inside the park right now."

His words lit a fire behind Alexa's eyes. She wasn't going inside the park, had no intention of it, in fact. What kind of idiot would purposely climb over crime scene tape with a police officer watching their every move? Did he think she was that stupid? Plus, no crime had been committed on the sidewalk, and there was no indication that the very spot she was standing played any significance to any sort of ongoing investigation. If anybody was in the way of anything, it was the guy's own cruiser parked on the curb. She took two deep breaths before she turned around. She didn't smile but said, "But, Officer, where am I going to do my naked yoga?"

She walked away before he could find a response.

She was walking the same route as last night, only in reverse. The sidewalk ended and she was back on the shoulder, passing the used car lot and the gas station and the coin laundry. Smokey's came into view ahead, and she was happy to see cars in the lot. She thought it might the type of joint that was open for lunch on the weekends, days when sports on the television would bring in a crowd. She was right.

Even though Wanamaker had told her that the Oldsmobile had been towed, Alexa still looked toward where it had been parked. Found a Jeep Wrangler in its place with snow-boards mounted to a roof rack. It made her only a little sad. The car had been with her for a good while, but just like with the names Alexa had gone by over the years, she'd swapped cars nearly as often. No need to dwell on the specifics or legality of said car swaps.

She crossed the lot and pushed through the front door, her eyes darting to the spot where Tony had been standing the night before when she'd arrived, where he'd been talking to somebody on his phone. She wondered if that had been the last phone call he'd ever made.

She'd think more about that later, but for now she had questions to ask.

Somebody who had been at Smokey's last night had told the police about her and Tony's *altercation*, and somehow the police had known where to quickly find her.

Alexa stepped inside and let her eyes adjust. Just like with her hunch about the place being open for lunch, Alexa was pleased to discover that she was now two for two. She found exactly who she was looking for.

CHAPTER 6

S ure enough, college football was on the televisions mounted above the bar and along the walls, positioned so that, no matter if you were seated at one of the tables in the center of the dining area or in the booths lining the walls, you would have no difficulty seeing whatever it was you'd come to watch. The televisions were all muted, and country music was being pumped through speakers, turned down lower than the night before, barely audible over the murmur of voices and the occasional whoop or cheer that erupted when somebody's team did something worthy of celebration.

Alexa found Squirt off to the right, where the building opened up and the pool tables and jukebox and dartboards and a few vintage arcade cabinets had been arranged. She was standing at a waitress station with another girl, chatting and rolling silverware into napkins, slow work to fill the time when there were few tables to wait on. Alexa stood and waited, and sure enough, both of the girls' trained eyes darted toward the door after a few moments, always on the lookout for new customers, and when Squirt's eyes met Alexa's, she smiled.

Well, that's good, I guess, Alexa thought. But it honestly wasn't the reaction she'd been expecting. Based on assumptions she'd made.

The other waitress made a move to head toward Alexa, ready to seat her and begin the waitress ritual, but Squirt reached a hand out and grabbed the girl's arm and said something and then the girl stayed back. Squirt walked over, weaving between a few of the tables, and said, "Hey! No dog today?"

Alexa had been ready to interrogate the girl, had found herself hardening against the previous good-natured opinion of her, but as soon as Squirt had flashed that smile and had asked about Barlow, Alexa felt herself softening again, realizing that her long-standing and well-practiced defenses had gone up instantly and perhaps irrationally. She wasn't sorry for the reaction, but she was mature enough to realize that it didn't fit well with her plan to start living a different life. She had to stop letting her emotions get the best of her, had to stop going from zero to a million miles per hour with only the slightest provocation.

Squirt must have seen something on Alexa's face, because her own features grew worried. "Are you okay?" she asked. "Do you need to sit down for a minute?"

Alexa shook her head and took a deep breath. Forced on a smile. "I'm fine, really. But"—she nodded toward the left of the room, toward the glass door that led out to the side patio where she'd eaten the night before—"can we chat in private? Just a few minutes?"

For a moment, Squirt looked uneasy, like she was remembering lessons from her childhood, saying no to strangers and all that. But apparently she must have worked out that Alexa wasn't a threat, because she nodded and said, "Sure." Then, "Let me get you a drink, so it looks like I'm working. What would you like?"

Alexa looked toward the bar, scanned the bottles lined on the shelf behind it. "Just water," she said. *New life, remember?*

"Got it. Just a sec and I'll meet you out there."

Outside, nobody was eating on the patio. There were no televisions out here and the sun was coming in at such an angle that Alexa had to squint against its brightness no matter which way she turned. The heat lamps were off now, but they weren't needed. The day was warm enough if you had a couple layers and a little toughness. Squirt pushed through the door carrying a tall tumbler of water and a menu beneath her arm. She handed them both to Alexa and then they both pulled out chairs and sat at the table on the back left of the patio, where the group of young men had been last night. Alexa would swear she could still smell their Axe body spray.

Alexa sipped the water, then took a big gulp. The walk from town had made her thirsty, and she wanted to wash the coffee taste out of her mouth. She set the tumbler back down and asked, "It was you who told the police about my little episode with Tony last night, right?"

Squirt's face did something funny, confusion and disbelief combining into an ugly mess, like Alexa had just performed a magic trick that was more grotesque than amusing. "How do you know that?" Squirt asked. "I mean ... how could you possibly know that?"

Alexa sipped some more water, pleased she'd correctly

guessed who had ratted her out. "Because I was awakened this morning by a cop pounding on my door to ask me if I'd killed him."

Now, Squirt's face went completely blank, like what Alexa had just said had frozen her operating system, the processor struggling to compute. "*What*? You mean it was *Tony* they found in the park?"

Alexa nodded. "So I've been told. You didn't know?"

Squirt shook her head slowly, her eyes still somewhat vacant. She pulled her focus back to Alexa and said, "Colin told me they'd found a body—hell, I'm sure the whole town knows *that* by now. But ... they weren't able to identify it at the time. Apparently it had been..." She trailed off. Cleared her throat. "Apparently it was pretty gruesome, what they found."

"Colin. That's your boyfriend, right?" Alexa asked, remembering the conversation from last night where Tony had said that Colin was the one who had called the girl Squirt.

Squirt scrunched up her face and shook her head. "No. He's my brother. He's the only person I told about what happened with you and Tony last night. He was still awake when I got home from my shift and I thought he'd like to know, that he'd find it funny. And he did, find it funny. We had a good laugh about it."

Now it was Alexa's own processor that was working to keep up. She felt pieces click together, could see the resemblance now that she was looking for it: the smooth skin, the blond hair. They even had the same eyes. "What's your name?" Alexa asked. "I never got it last night."

"Oh," Squirt said. "I'm Clara."

Alexa asked the next question, even though she already knew what the answer would be. "Last name?"

Clara waited a beat before saying, "Wanamaker. I'm Clara Wanamaker."

~

NOT ALL COPS WERE BAD.

Alexa knew this, and she knew it well. It was a pseudo-mantra that she'd constantly repeated to herself over the years in order to try and calm her nerves, settle her anxiety, each and every time she saw or—in those most unfortunate situations—had to interact with an officer of the law. Something as simple as one sliding in line behind her at a fast-food restaurant could sometimes make her lose her appetite. Once, during a particularly bad stretch a decade or so ago, Alexa had found herself so hungry and so tired of sleeping on park benches and next to back-alley dumpsters and, yes, even in a cemetery that she'd capitulated and swallowed her pride and made her way to a local homeless shelter, desperate for just one night's sleep on anything that resembled a mattress, and something to eat that wasn't a leftover scrap. But when she'd rounded the corner of the block late that evening and had seen the cop positioned outside the shelter's door, she'd felt a sinking in her empty stomach, a dizziness threatening to buckle her knees. Horrific and improbable images of what he might do to her once she'd fallen asleep, what sort of favors he might ask for in exchange for the meal she so desperately sought, caused her to turn and run and not look back.

It was irrational. It was fucked up, to put it more bluntly.

She was fucked up. Her father had done this to her, all those years ago.

The wounds which are inflicted on you as a child may heal, but you carry the scars to your grave. Alexa had worked over the years to wear the scars proudly instead of hiding them, to see them and remember what they represented and use them to guide her in how she wanted to live her life. She'd gone on this way for a long time, surviving the only way she knew how. But now ... after meeting those new friends—after *Lance*—she was seeing her scars in a different light. They spoke to her, but in a different language than before.

They were ready for change. Alexa was ready, too.

But change is hard. Ask anybody.

Not all cops are bad.

"Are you okay?" Squirt—now Clara—asked for the second time since Alexa had arrived at Smokey's.

Alexa pushed aside all her self-philosophizing and met the girl's eyes—those *kind* eyes. She smiled at Clara and nodded. "Yes." Then, "At least I will be."

Clara didn't know what to say to that.

Alexa took another sip of water and then continued on with her questions. "So you really didn't 'tell the police'"— she made air quotes—"about me and Tony. You just told your brother, who *happens* to be a police officer, because you thought he'd get a kick out of it, right?"

Clara nodded hard and fast, apparently happy to see that Alexa wasn't trying to blame her for something. "Yes, exactly. He and Tony used to be friends, but like, a looong time ago. Like, elementary school. But then they sorta fell out."

"Why?"

Clara laughed but then quickly caught herself. Put on the serious face again. "They grew up. Had different interests, made different friends."

Alexa clarified. "Tony was trouble and Colin wasn't. That about right?"

Clara grinned. "Pretty much, yeah."

"Tell me," Alexa said, leaning back in the chair and crossing her legs.

"Tell you what?"

"Tell me all about Tony, and why, in your opinion, somebody might want him dead."

CHAPTER 7

Alexa ordered a chicken salad sandwich on wheat with a side garden salad, both because she really was hungry—the muffin had only gone so far, with her having basically slept through breakfast—and because Clara was working and Alexa respected the girl enough not to expect her to just stand around outside chatting and ignoring her waitress duties. More cars were pulling into Smokey's lot as Alexa waited for her food, so she was glad she'd arrived when she had. The lunch rush would make talking to Clara more difficult. Alexa closed her eyes and leaned back in the chair and let the sun warm her face while she waited.

The sound of the door opening and a quick yelp of glee from inside the restaurant jolted her upright again, and Alexa was glad to see Clara carrying her food. The girl set the plates on the table and quickly asked, "Do you need more water?"

Alexa shook her head and took a quick bite of the sandwich. Like the burger the night before, it was very good. She swallowed and said, "No. You're about to get busy, and I just need you to tell me what you know."

Clara nodded but sighed. "I probably shouldn't."

"Shouldn't what?"

"Tell you about Tony."

Alexa cocked her head to the side and absurdly felt like she was giving Clara the same look Barlow gave her when he was trying to make out her human words. "Why?"

Clara glanced at the parking lot, shrugged. "I mean ... if they think you did it ... I don't know, if I talk to you about Tony, does that make me...?" She trailed off, looked back to Alexa.

Alexa understood. While Clara had been inside the restaurant, checking on her other tables and waiting to bring out Alexa's food, she'd had time to think. To really analyze the situation and work to assess her own role in what was unfolding. Yes, the girl had been the one to tell her police officer brother about Alexa and Tony's exchange of words, but that had been innocent. Tony's body had yet to be discovered. No harm, no foul. Just a silly story shared between siblings. But now ... now Tony was a victim of a horrific

("Apparently it was pretty gruesome, what they found.")

murder, and what had started out as a silly story had become a possible motive, a link between victim and suspect. The motive was weak, sure. If every woman who had a bad experience at a bar with a cocky asshole became a murderer, they'd have to build more prisons. But still, for somebody who was probably as squeaky-clean and innocent as her own smooth and unblemished skin, Clara Wanamaker was suddenly finding herself somehow indirectly a part of a very serious police investigation and wondering if the woman with the dog who had left her a big tip was really as nice as she seemed.

Alexa could postulate all this because these thoughts would be the exact same thoughts she would have in Clara's position. She wouldn't fault the girl for her anxiousness or doubts. She could only encourage, and attempt to do so gently as not to spook her. She took another bite of her sandwich and washed it down with a sip of water. "Clara, I get it, this is scary. But you've got nothing to worry about."

"How do you know?"

"Because I didn't have anything to do with Tony's death. All I did was tell him to put his pee-pee back in his pants for somebody else."

This caused Clara to grin, and Alexa saw the girl's shoulders relax a little. A breeze slid under the patio overhang and strands of the girl's blond hair waved in the air before she tucked them behind her ear.

"Do you believe me?" Alexa asked.

Clara closed her eyes and nodded. "Yeah, I do," she said. "It's just weird, you know?"

I've seen a lot weirder, Alexa wanted to say, but instead she opted for, "You're telling me. One minute I'm meeting nice people like you and enjoying a nice bed at the inn, and the next, I'm getting asked if I might possibly have killed a guy. Quite the flip-flop of emotions, let me tell you."

Clara slid out one of the other chairs and sat down, crossed her legs.

"Will you get in trouble?" Alexa asked. "If you sit down and talk to me?"

Clara waved her off. "I'm taking my fifteen-minute break."

Alexa smiled. The girl had made up her mind she was going to talk to her before she'd even come back out with the food. She'd just been getting a better feel for the situation, a better feel for Alexa.

Smart girl.

"Can I ask a question first?" Clara asked, a bit bashfully.

Alexa used a fork to spear a tomato from her salad. "Sure."

"Why are you asking? Why do you want to know about Tony? He's dead now—what does he matter to you?"

"He doesn't," Alexa said, maybe a bit too quickly. It was a harsh truth, but the truth all the same. "But the idea that somebody might think I killed him bothers me. I don't like my name dragged through the mud. I have enough things to worry about on my own without others adding to the pile."

Clara considered this for a long time, then looked at Alexa with genuine curiosity in her eyes. "But still, if you didn't kill Tony—and, yes, I really believe that you had nothing to do with it—then I'm sure it won't take long for evidence or your alibi to prove it. So again, I ask why. Why do you want to know if anybody else might have had reason to kill Tony? Don't you think the police will be able to figure out the truth on their own?"

Damned smart girl.

"How old are you?" Alexa asked.

"Twenty-two. Why?"

Alexa smiled, and the smile became a quick laugh. "You are wise beyond your years, Clara. Far beyond."

Clara smiled back, warmth melting some of the seriousness. "I'm an old soul." Then she shrugged. "Or maybe having an older brother who's a cop has warped my brain."

Alexa would not go down the road of just how warped a

police officer could cause a brain to be, especially when said brain was twelve years old. Not here, not with Clara.

Part of Alexa's new life she was trying to build was going to be predicated on her being more honest. How honest, and with whom she'd exercise this honesty, was going to be more of a play-it-by-ear situation. Fluid, if you will. Clara seemed like a good person to start with, but she would still tread lightly. The girl *was* innocent in all this—just like Alexa—and Alexa wanted to keep her that way.

"It's a good question you asked," Alexa said. "About why I want to know. Here's the short version: I'm not the type of person who takes being accused of something I didn't do lightly, nor am I the type of person who fully trusts the police to get all the answers or do the right thing. No offense to your brother, of course, it's just ... I have a history that has taught me otherwise. So, while the police are off *hopefully* doing their best to find Tony's real killers and exonerate my name, I thought I'd play the game too, if I need to, see if I can find any of my own answers. You know"—she winked, which reminded her of the way Ezra had done the same to her—"just in case I need them."

Clara nodded. "So you're trying to help?"

Several answers popped into Alexa's head, but she settled on a simple "Yes."

"Are you some sort of private investigator, or something?"

Alexa barked a laugh. Clara grinned, confused. "Or something," Alexa said. "Let's just stick with or something."

There was silence then. Alexa ate more of her food and waited patiently, letting Clara start talking in her own time. She was finishing off the small salad when the girl said, "There's really not a lot to tell about Tony, honestly. Nothing that I can imagine would point any fingers to why somebody might want him dead. I mean, other than the women he's hit on, like you said. And, yeah, he was a bit ... abrasive. Always had been. Cocky."

Alexa wiped her mouth with a paper napkin, tucked it under her plate so the breeze wouldn't snatch it away. "You mentioned he was trouble, when he was younger?"

"Oh," Clara said, "Yeah, but nothing crazy. Just your typical rebellious kid, you know? Around middle school, so seventh grade, I guess, Tony started turning into one of *those* kids. You know what I mean. The loud bully in the hallway, picking on the smaller kids. The guy who would get caught behind the gym by the dumpsters selling cigarettes and reading comic books instead of going to class. He'd talk back to teachers, always getting detention or silent lunch. Colin used to come home and tell us all this. Our dad used to always say it was a good thing Colin had 'cut Tony loose when he did,' which I think Colin always resented a little, because if I'm being honest, I think it was Tony who cut Colin loose."

"You said 'selling' cigarettes," Alexa said.

"Hmmm?"

"You said Tony was *selling* cigarettes, not smoking them?"

"Oh, yeah. Tony was a big athlete, you know, when he was allowed to actually play. He never smoked them, but he always *had* them to sell. I guess even then he was business-minded. Supply and demand and all that."

"What do you mean?"

Clara picked up the thread Alexa was tugging. "See, Tony was *smart*, even though he was a troublemaker. His grades were usually garbage, but that was because he didn't try. If he didn't care about it, he didn't do it. But see, one year they had this big countywide math contest. Every month of the school year, every kid in the grade would get this worksheet with three word problems on it. Colin said they were pretty much riddles, and he rarely felt he got any of them right. Well, at the end of the year, the county totaled up the students' results and Tony tied for first place with this kid from East River. The natural reaction was, of course, that Tony had somehow cheated. But the teachers that were able to see him for what he was, beyond his problem with authority, all agreed it was completely plausible he'd won the contest on his own merit. They tried to give him the award at the end-of-the-year assembly, but he didn't show up. My dad actually has that on tape. He'd taken his video camera to the school assembly to record Colin receiving his All-A's Honor Roll award, and when they called Tony's name, you can see everybody's head looking around and hear the murmur of the kids all realizing he wasn't even in the room. The teacher mumbled that she wasn't surprised, which was unprofessional but got a laugh from the kids ... and some of the parents."

"I'm guessing it's pretty much the same story through high school?" Alexa asked.

Clara nodded. "From what Colin has told me, yes."

"Was he ever violent? You said he was a bully—did he get into fights? What about after high school?"

Clara shrugged. "He's gotten into a few shoving matches here"—she nodded back toward the door that led inside— "but I think he's always been more bark than bite. I think he's too smart to get arrested for something dumb like punching the wrong guy."

Alexa considered all this, and also replayed her own encounter with Tony from the night before. From what she understood, the guy had been highly intelligent, but that intelligence had been trapped inside the façade of a muscle-bound hot-head, hidden away more often than not. Shame.

"What does he do now?" Alexa asked. "I mean, what *did* he do ... after he graduated?"

"Well, he was a bit of an entrepreneur."

Alexa scoffed. Too often, she'd heard that phrase thrown around to describe somebody whose Mommy or Daddy had a lot of money and funded their life while they "figured out what they were meant to do" or had lots of fancy meetings at country clubs to discuss their "next big thing" that would make anyone who invested rich.

"So he was unemployed," Alexa said matter-of-factly.

Clara shook her head. "Oh, no. He really was pretty busi-ness-savvy. That's what I meant, with the cigarettes and everything. He got an accounting degree online at the community college and then opened up a landscaping busi-ness with some of his friends. Now some of those guys, *they're* the dumb ones. Probably can't spell *landscaping*, but they can work the equipment and they can follow orders from Tony. Anyway, he started that, and then just a year or so ago he bought the laundromat and the car wash right up the road. Old Merle used to own both and was fit to retire and willing to sell for a low price. Oh, and Tony handles all the books here, of course."

Alexa was about to ask why "of course" when the police cruiser caught her eye. She watched as it slowed on the road and turned into Smokey's parking lot. Alexa felt her heart start to beat faster, and when she looked to Clara, she saw the girl's face had also fallen.

"Oh shit," the girl said, standing from the table. "Do you think they're here to tell him?"

Alexa stood too, because it just felt right. She tried not to sound panicked when she asked, "Tell who what?"

"Tony's dad. *Big* Tony. He owns this place."

CHAPTER 8

Before Alexa could even say anything, Clara was moving toward the door to head back inside Smokey's and saying over her shoulder, "You should go."

Alexa nodded. The girl was right. Innocent or not, Alexa didn't particularly feel like pressing her luck by being seen by yet another police officer, with her right back where the whole damn thing had started. She was now literally standing in the exact same spot Tony had been standing the night before when he'd made his pathetic pass at her.

There was a brief moment in her mind where she experienced what might be considered guilt at thinking poorly of the dead, but it vanished before it could take hold. Assholes in life did not magically become saints in death. More people should take time to understand that.

Alexa pulled her wallet from her pocket and peeled off a twenty, but before she could toss it onto the table, Clara blurted, "Forget it. It's on the house. Go on, I don't want to be seen talking to you."

It sounded cruel, especially coming from such a pretty

young face, but Alexa understood. In a way, Clara was having the same reaction to the sight of a cop as Alexa usually did: one of uneasiness, anxiety and mistrust. Though Alexa suspected Clara had substituted fear for mistrust. The girl's brother was a cop, after all. Clara's reaction to the current situation wasn't based on a lifetime of negative preconceived notions about officers of the law but was a purely instinctive result of the moment: she was having lunch with a possible suspect in a murder investigation.

Alexa called out a quick "Thanks," but Clara was already inside, the door swinging shut behind her. Alexa started moving, reaching the edge of the building and peering around the corner. The police cruiser had parked along the opposite side of the structure, in the same place Alexa had seen the parked cruiser last night. Apparently that was the unofficial cop spot. A man in uniform that Alexa had yet to see today was almost to the front door of the restaurant. He was older than both Colin Wanamaker and Mr. Crowd Control at the park. Tall, with a squared-off jaw and buzzed hair that was gray but looked metallic in the early-afternoon sun. He wore sunglasses with big circular lenses that reflected the entire parking lot and also made it impossible to tell where the man was looking—and for a terrifying second, just as the man reached for the door handle to go inside, his head turned slightly to the left and Alexa was certain he'd spied her spying on him. But then he reached down and plucked from the sidewalk an empty Styrofoam to-go cup somebody had carelessly tossed and then headed into Smokey's.

Alexa took off across the parking lot, not quite jogging but moving at a pace that would make retiree mall walkers proud.

She didn't want to risk moving any quicker, not wanting to draw attention to herself or make it evident that she was, in fact, running away from the police. Because she could already see it adding up, the same way Clara apparently had. What would people say if they found out that, after being questioned at the inn, Alexa had then proceeded to return to the park where the body had been found, then made a trip back to the very place she'd had her encounter with the victim, just to have a friendly chat with the person who had tipped the police off to her in the first place?

People have such a flair for the dramatic. Meaning, it would not look good for her.

After she covered that first quarter mile of nothing but dirt and weed-filled shoulder heading back into town, she slowed her pace when she hit the sidewalk. She stopped briefly once she'd passed the older homes—really nothing more than tract houses—standing in place and swiveling her head to look first at the laundromat on one side of the road and then across to the self-serve car wash on the other, the two establishments Clara had mentioned Tony purchasing after his landscaping business. As Alexa studied both businesses, seeing a single car in one of the stalls of the car wash as a young guy power-blasted dirt off his Mustang, and seeing absolutely zero movement inside the big plate-glass windows of the laundromat, she didn't see how being business-savvy fit into the equation. She didn't see profit here. She saw places that were nothing more than afterthoughts.

But what the fuck did she know? Maybe Tony had been a visionary and could have turned the places around in no time. And why did she care?

A guy was dead, and all she needed to worry about was why.

Do you? Do you really *need to worry about that?* the less-cynical part of her mind spoke up.

And for a moment, Alexa thought she might agree with that voice. Truth be damned—she would head back to the inn and ask Ezra where the closest bus station was and then head out, find a new place to start over, find a new car, a new life. The life she'd thought she might find right here.

But then she remembered the smiling face of the man and woman from the SUV as Alexa had studied the road sign. She thought about Clara and how kind the girl had been to Barlow. She thought about Ezra and his carefree no-questions-asked attitude, and the dreamless sleep she'd fallen into in her room.

She thought about that burning ember in her soul's belly that, despite all the events of the last several hours, seemed to be telling her she was in the right place. Her future was here.

She thought about Lance, and how he'd tried to explain to her one time how he very rarely felt he made any actual decisions for himself, that the Universe always seemed to point him in the right direction of what was to come next in his life. Alexa needed no further proof of this than how she and Lance had come into each other's company in the first place.

She couldn't argue with that.

She'd stick around a little longer.

THE IDEA CAME to her fast, because as she was beginning the walk back into town again, she remembered Mr. Crowd Control, who'd been positioned outside the main entrance to Collins Park, the crime scene tape strewn across the entrance. She hadn't been able to see any police activity in the park from that angle, but she had to believe that if the cop was still keeping people out, there must be a reason. She looked up at the sun, whose bright heat seemed to be encouraging an unexpected adventure on this winter day, and decided it was a good time to explore the town a little more.

She checked both directions for traffic and then crossed the road, walking down the small asphalt pathway that led between the car wash and the used car lot. This side street—if you wanted to call it that—had turnoffs so traffic could enter both businesses, then continued on to wrap around behind each, where it died in an uneven scattering of gravel and grass and tar drippings. The land beyond was all grassy field that dipped down and away from Alexa and shallowed out into a small valley before sloping back up. Across the sea of grass, perched atop the opposite plain, other buildings loomed on the horizon—lots of brick and metal and steel. Industrial. Further up and right, off in the corner of where Alexa could see, sprouting above an outcropping of tall trees, another large brick building was capped with what looked like a turret painted a faded mint green. Alexa stepped carefully down the slope, her boots squishing into the soft earth, and started cutting the corner towards the green turret.

When she reached the flat land of the valley, she turned right and followed a path she believed to be parallel to the sidewalk back up at street level. The ground was even soggier here, where the water ran down the hills and settled into the crevice between, the earth only getting reached by the sun's rays a few rare moments a day. She'd gone a few hundred yards when the land sloped back up, level with the buildings and road, and she found what she was hoping for.

The fence that bordered what she assumed to be the side property line of Collins Park was not the typical ugly and cheap chain-link you'd expect to find. Instead it was a very rustic and charming split rail fence made of rough wooden beams the color of leather. She'd seen similar fences when she'd visited one the U.S battlefields once. Maybe Gettysburg. *How long ago was that?* she wondered as she caught her breath after climbing the steep hill. *It felt like another lifetime ago.*

The same tall trees that hid the turret-capped building from view filled the space on the other side of the wooden fence, creating their own natural barrier between the park and land beyond, working together with bushes and other plant life to create a feeling of isolation, as if the park existed in its own time and space, hidden away from the rest of world waiting outside.

Alexa climbed carefully over the fence, her muddy boots slipping once on the wooden beam she'd used to hoist herself up, and then began weaving her way through nature. Most of the trees' branches were bare, but the air was redolent with smells of earth, and her feet kicked through the skeletons of dried leaves and crunched across downed twigs that had been ripped away in the wind. She tried to be quiet, but it was proving difficult. She suddenly wished she could climb into the trees and swing from limb to limb, traversing the forest without touching the ground like a female Tarzan.

Tarzana, she thought, right before she heard the voices.

They were coming from ahead of her, over to the left, closer to where the turret-capped building loomed over everything.

"You heard from the sheriff yet?" somebody asked, just barely audible.

"Not yet," another voice answered. "I think he's stopping back by here after he talks to Big Tony."

There was silence then, and Alexa stepped forward as quietly as she could, just catching movement past the tree line, where she was able to look out across a low line of bushes and see two uniformed sheriff's deputies standing beside another police cruiser maybe fifty yards away from her. The cruiser was parked outside the fencing of one of the baseball fields, blocking most of Alexa's view of the infield. More crime scene tape sectioned off the lone swinging door in the field's fence, just left of the closest dugout. It looked to be the only official entrance into the ball field.

Alexa was about to work her way further left, hoping to be able to see around the men and the car, when another sound snapped in her ear. She froze and waited, holding her breath, her body rigid and her ears perked. It came again, a quick *snap snap snap* that Alexa instantly recognized.

It was the sound of a camera's shutter.

Somebody else was in the trees with her.

CHAPTER 9

S nap snap snap

The camera's shutter did its jig again and Alexa grabbed onto the sound and followed. She retreated further into the trees, closer to the fence, and started stepping as softly as she could through the leaves and twigs, headed toward the turret-capped building. Whoever was taking pictures had to be close, which was both good and bad. Good because Alexa should be able to find them easily enough, but bad because she didn't know how close *she'd* already come to being discovered. Or if she already had.

She stopped after she'd tiptoed maybe fifteen yards, stood still and strained her eyes to pick up any anomaly in the trees, any sign of human life. Everything was still and silent, a collage of muted browns and grays and greens. She saw nothing.

A new noise came from the direction of the ball field, a low rumble of an engine. Her eyes darted right, and she turned her head just enough to be able to see the ball field while also watching for movement ahead of her. Another cruiser was coming in from the far side of the park, probably from some access road or side parking lot. Its headlights and front grille crested over a small hill like the face of some new creature emerging from the depths. It drove around the back of the ball field, a place where it would have been in danger of a busted windshield or dented hood if a heavy-hitter had been at the plate and the pitch had been just right, and then crawled to a stop behind the existing cruiser and the two deputies who'd been waiting.

Both men stood from where they'd been leaning against the side of the cruiser and waved at the newcomer. The door of the new cruiser opened, and the same guy Alexa had seen walking into Smokey's—he of the big sunglasses and metallic hair—unfolded himself from the driver's seat and greeted them. "Any trouble, boys?"

Both men shook their heads, mumbled some things that Alexa couldn't hear.

"Cleanup crew all finished?" the man asked, lifting his sunglasses and scanning the field before letting them fall back into place. "Looks like it."

Both men nodded. "Yes, sir. Left about a half hour ago," one said.

"Christ, didn't envy them one bit on this one, Sheriff," the other added. He tossed on a nervous laugh at the end that was met with nothing but a deadpan stare and silence from his two companions.

The other officer asked, "How'd Big Tony take the news? I mean ... I guess nobody would ever take it real good, you know ... but..." He shrugged. Before the sheriff could answer, Alexa heard the *snap snap snap* again, just ahead and to her left. And now she *did* see some movement. Just a flash of what looked like those muted grays and browns shifting left to right and then down.

The figure took shape. It was a man, standing a few feet inside the edge of the bushes, half-hidden behind the thick trunk of a tree. He was wearing all camo—some sort of hunting outfit, most likely—but instead of wielding a rifle or a bow, he had a camera with a telephoto lens aimed at the group of men by the ball field.

Snap snap snap.

Alexa felt her pulse start to rise, and she worked to calm it. Took in a few deep breaths and then started tiptoeing again, silently crossing the ground while the man was engrossed in his picture snapping. She was right behind him now, roughly five feet away, close enough to smell him—cigarettes and beef jerky. It made her stomach roll. He had a camo kerchief pulled up over his nose and mouth, so that only his eyes were visible.

Alexa didn't know exactly what her plan was here, but if she had to guess, she'd posit that this camo-clad photographer was not working for the local newspaper or a crime blog, nor did he even have a fetish for men in uniform. No, the cynical and hardened part of Alexa Shifflett was quick to assume that the guy taking pictures a mere five feet in front of her was probably working because of more nefarious motivations to—

A twig snapped under Alexa's foot as she shifted her weight. The guy with the camera pulled his face a couple inches from the viewfinder and then froze. Alexa could see that his shoulders were no longer rising and falling with breath. He was listening, on alert.

Alexa had no weapon—other than her hands and feet,

which had done just fine in the past, thank you very much—
and again, no plan. But ... bad guys are bad guys are bad
guys. So...

"Is that big lens compensating for something?" she asked,
her voice just above a whisper.

The guy's body stiffened, and then he turned slowly to
face her. His eyes were shit brown and they narrowed to slits
when he saw her.

"How do you think the sheriff would feel if he knew he
had a Peeping Tom snapping shots of him and his men? How
about we find out, what do you say?"

The guy stared at her with those brown eyes for what felt
like a full ten seconds, and Alexa could practically hear his
brain trying on his options. But then he did something Alexa
hadn't planned on. She'd been ready for an attack—was
always ready for one of those, in fact—but instead of lunging
toward her or pulling a knife from those camo hunting pants,
the guy quickly pointed his camera at her and snapped one
more shot. Then he took off in a flash (no pun intended), with
no warning, no clever or brazen retort. He'd been caught, so
he ran. Which proved to Alexa all she needed to know. The
guy was bad news.

And now he had her picture.

She started running too, sprinting after the guy through
the trees, her boots squishing and squashing with each heavy
step.

"Hey!" she heard the sheriff yell from somewhere behind
her. "Who's in there?"

Shit!

She couldn't stop, not now. If the men behind her caught
her, so be it, but she was going to make sure they took down

the camo-photographer with her—*he* was the real problem. Her legs were starting to burn, but she was keeping pace with the guy. All that heavy camo gear was probably slowing him down ... or maybe one too many Big Macs instead of salad, or at least a Filet-O-Fish. The trees were thinning a bit, and through their barren branches she could see the brick building with the turret on top taking shape beyond, the earthy floor replaced by the black of asphalt. A huge white pickup truck with a big yellow stripe down the side was parked with its nose pointed toward the building. Black text was printed inside the yellow stripe, but Alexa was too far away to make the words out. The guy with the camera broke through the trees first, but by now Alexa was only a few feet behind him.

"Hey!" she called out, a desperate attempt to slow him just a few paces more, just enough for her to hopefully spring forward in a Hail Mary dive and reach out and wrap her arms around his legs, bringing him down.

But then—just like when he'd snapped her photo—the guy made another unexpected move. Instead of slowing down, he stopped completely. Alexa tried to apply her own brakes but was too slow, had too much momentum going in preparation for her attack. The guy spun around fast and powerful, his arm holding the camera making a big sweeping arc through the air, the heavy plastic base of the camera smashing into Alexa's temple.

The world went instantly black for a second, like Alexa's mind had snapped its own shutter, capturing the moment. The blackness faded, but when the world came back into view it was fuzzy and distorted and sideways.

No, the world wasn't sideways. She was. Alexa was laying

crumpled on her side on the sun-warmed asphalt, tiny bits of pebble pressing into her cheek and her head currently playing host to a marching band of pain. She tried to sit up, but a voice spoke from above her and a hand gently pressed her shoulder back down.

"Don't sit up just yet. You've got a head injury. Ambulance should be here any second."

Alexa knew the voice, but when the person the hand on her shoulder belonged to stepped into view, blotting out the sun like some great eclipse, it was confirmed. The sheriff still had his sunglasses on, and his face betrayed no emotion.

He squatted down next to her again and worked to gently slide a dark jacket under her head, all while taking her hand in his and saying, "Here, let's see if we can at least roll you over, make you more comfortable."

Alexa felt the calloused hand of this looming police officer in her hand, his skin against hers, and in her delirious state of mind she was suddenly twelve years old again, right back in her childhood home, standing in her father's home office while he'd hugged her ... and then his hands had gone other places. It was the day that had irrevocably changed her life. The day that had made her who she was.

The past that had for so long dictated every move and every decision.

Alexa sat up violently and vomited all over the sheriff's shoes.

CHAPTER 10

Alexa didn't apologize, but the sheriff kept saying things like, "It's fine. No problem at all. Don't you worry," as if she had. He offered her a handkerchief from his pocket so she could wipe her mouth, but Alexa only stared at it as if it were made of piss-soaked sandpaper and then used the back of her own sleeve to wipe away the bit of sick that had drooled over her lip. The sheriff didn't react, just shrugged and used the handkerchief to wipe off his shoes before tossing it into a nearby trash bin.

The two of them sat in silence after that, until the ambulance came.

The sheriff told the paramedics how he'd found Alexa— lying blacked out on the asphalt—and they got to work: asking her questions, helping her to the rear of the ambulance, where they could check her vitals and administer their tests. One male, one female, both seemingly much younger than Alexa, they were kind and gentle and in that moment were treating her like she was the most important person on the planet. Alexa was impressed by them, and thankful for their thoroughness, but the entire time they were working, she couldn't take her eyes off the sheriff. He was keeping a respectable distance from them, pacing back and forth on his cell phone by a rear entrance to the turret-capped building, which judging from the

(yellow stripe)

yellow school bus parked by an overhang leading into the building, and the colorful posters and signs she could see taped to the inside of several of the windows, must have been a school. Even behind those big sunglasses, Alexa could tell he was never quite taking his eyes off where she sat.

She wanted to run, just like the camo-photographer had run, but she knew it was impossible. She wasn't guilty of anything, except maybe peeping in on a crime scene, but suddenly up and sprinting away without rhyme or reason sure would make it look that way. No, she'd have to talk to him—give a statement or whatever. And hell, maybe that was a good thing. She didn't have to tell the sheriff *why* she was in the trees, but she'd sure as shit tell him what she'd seen. That she hadn't been alone. That she'd been chasing the proverbial bad guy who the sheriff's own men hadn't been able to notice snapping pictures whey they sat around with their thumbs up their holes. She'd give some version of that, anyway.

The young male paramedic unstrapped the blood pressure cuff from her arm and said, "You're all set, ma'am. We'll give you some meds for the headache—which I'm sure is a doozy—but you don't appear to be concussed."

On cue, the female paramedic handed her a couple of pills that were probably nothing more than Tylenol and a small bottle of water. Alexa thanked them both and swallowed the pills dry before downing the entire bottle of water.

"Try to take it easy the rest of the day," the girl said, a gentle hand on Alexa's shoulder. Then she handed Alexa's jacket back to her and hopped out of the back of the ambulance. The guy nodded to the sheriff, who'd ended his phone call and had been leaning against the school, waiting.

Both the paramedics disappeared toward the front of the ambulance, exercising a routine they'd probably been trained in—help the patient, get out of the way for the cops to do their job. The sheriff ambled over, and Alexa noticed how tall he stood. Not that he was *that tall*—in fact, he had to be a couple inches shorter than Ezra—but how he stood ramrod straight. His posture was that of a line segment. It was a confident look—hell, some might even call it aggressive. But, Alexa had to admit, so far the man had been nothing but calm and kind.

"Looks like you'll live to fight another day," the sheriff said once he'd reached her.

Alexa was still seated on the gurney in the back of the vehicle and moved off it so she could step down and stand. She suddenly didn't like how it felt like the sheriff was trapping her in. He offered her his hand—that calloused hand that had

(touched her other places)

gently encouraged her to stay put until the paramedics had arrived.

"Looks like it," she said, ignoring his help and not stepping but *hopping* off the back of the ambulance, if for no other reason than to show the man that she was completely capable on her own.

"Glad to hear," he said. "Glad to hear." He cleared his throat. "I don't believe we've officially met. I'm Sheriff Brooks Byrd." Again, he offered his hand, and when Alexa again ignored it while also not giving her name, he cocked his head to the side, the sun sparkling off his sunglasses, and asked, "Ma'am, have I done something to offend you?"

Alexa waited a beat, then said, "I'm a germophobe."

The sheriff stared at her, and Alexa could tell he was trying to decide if she was telling the truth or pulling one over on him ... or if it even mattered one way or the other. Finally, he said, "Are you aware the park is closed today?"

Here we go, Alexa thought. *Let's dance, Sheriff Byrd.*

"Is it?" she said.

The sheriff nodded. "Indeed. Up until just recently it was an active crime scene."

"Ah," Alexa said, as if this news suddenly cleared up so many questions she had. "That would explain those police, down by the ball field."

"Indeed," the man said again. "We're keeping it closed until tomorrow, just in case."

Alexa said nothing. If he expected her to ask questions, he'd be waiting a long time.

"Ma'am, can I ask how you managed to get into the park —you see, I've had men stationed at both entrances all day— and why you were hiding in the trees?"

Direct, Alexa thought. *Good. My turn.*

"After lunch, I started exploring," Alexa said. "I just got into town last night and thought I'd check the town out. I found that valley over there"—she nodded back in the direc- tion of the car wash and the used car lot, which you could just make out from up here on the hill and through the trees

—"and started following it this way, on my way back to the inn. I found the fence and then saw the tower lights from the ball field through the trees and figured I wasn't trespassing or anything. So I climbed over. I've got to say, Sheriff, it's somewhat short-sighted of you to think that a criminal—or even some punk kids who got bored and went looking for some fun—would only use the main entrances of the park to get in."

The sheriff digested this insult but apparently found it unworthy of comment. He dug in. "Why did you run? Why didn't you stop when we called after you?"

There it is. The first hint of an accusation.

"Because I found one," Alexa said.

She saw the sheriff's eyebrows dip behind his sunglasses, confused. "Found one what?"

"A criminal," she said. "Somebody was spying on your men, Sheriff Byrd."

What she told him now was mostly all the truth—how she'd heard the sound of the man's camera, how she'd found him dressed in camouflage attire and snapping pictures of the police and the crime scene, and how, when she'd confronted him, he'd run away and she'd chased him. She left out the part where he'd quickly taken her picture before he'd fled, and ended her story with him assaulting her before apparently fleeing in his truck.

"What did the truck look like?" the sheriff asked. "And I don't suppose you got a plate number?"

"No plate," Alexa said. "But it was a bigger than average truck. Maybe an F-250 or F-350. White with a big yellow stripe."

The sheriff had been making some notes in a small notebook while Alexa had talked, and at the mention of the yellow stripe, he looked up. His face was passive, the eyebrows neutral, but he asked, "Yellow stripe? You're sure?"

"Positive."

"Hmm."

"Mean something?" Alexa asked, knowing she would get no meaningful answer.

"You never know," the sheriff said, "which details will matter the most, so it's good to have them all. Anything else you can add about your attacker?"

Alexa thought it was smart of him, to switch gears and focus on the fact that she'd been attacked—making her the victim instead of a suspect in anything.

"His eyes were the color of shit," she said. "That's all I could see. The rest of his face was covered."

"Shit," Sheriff Byrd said, making a show of underlining the word in his little notebook. "Got it."

Alexa was dismayed at herself because she'd accidentally smiled at the joke, but then Sheriff Byrd asked a question that always made Alexa's stomach do something funny, no matter how many times she'd heard it and how easily the lies rolled off her tongue. "And can I have your name please, ma'am?"

She'd already given Ezra her real first name, so lying about that would do no good here. In fact, it would make her look even more suspicious than she possibly already did in the sheriff's eyes if the man later went to the inn to ask Ezra about her and found out she'd given him a fake name.

That's if you're sticking around, the cynical part of her whispered in her head.

Shut up, she replied. *You know I am.*

I am.

"Alexa," she answered.

Sheriff Byrd wrote this in his notebook. "Last name?"

If there was a moment that was going to truly define Alexa's decision to start her new life, to close the door on the past behind her, to step out of the shoes she'd been running in for so long, it was right here, right now.

"Shifflett," she said. "Alexa Shifflett."

The words felt heavy as she said them, like their impact should have knocked Sheriff Byrd off his feet and sent him tumbling to the ground. But all the man did was use his pen to add the last name to the notebook before tucking them both back into his pocket.

"Do you have any ID on you?" he asked.

Alexa did have ID on her, but it was fake, with a fake name. The name she'd been using most recently—Jennifer Smalls.

"No," she lied. "I left it back at the inn in my other pants."

Sheriff Byrd didn't seem to care. Just nodded and reached out with his hand and slapped the side of the ambulance twice, signaling to the paramedics that he was finished.

"Well, Miss Shifflett," he said, "I'm glad you're not more seriously injured."

Alexa nodded.

"Can I give you a ride back to the inn? You probably don't feel much like walking back in your current condition."

There was no way in hell Alexa was getting inside this man's car with him. It had already taken everything out of her to carry on the conversation they'd just had. She shook her head. "No, thank you, Sheriff Byrd. I'll walk. The pills they gave me for the pain are already helping. Besides"—she shrugged—"it's not that far."

She turned and started walking. Not really sure where, but *away* from the ambulance and the sheriff—that was all that mattered.

She'd nearly reached the edge of the school's rear parking lot when the sheriff's booming voice called after her. "Miss Shifflett?"

She wanted to keep walking, wanted not to look back over her shoulder or even slow down a step. Wanted to pretend she'd never heard him.

She stopped and turned, stared at him across the asphalt as the ambulance reversed out from where it had been parked and drove off and around the other side of the building.

"Why did you chase him?" the sheriff asked. "That was a very dangerous thing to do, if you don't mind me saying so."

Alexa thought through several answers, then called back, "I don't like bad guys, Sheriff Byrd."

She turned and walked away.

"Be careful," he added, right before she was out of earshot.

For some reason, Alexa couldn't shake the feeling that with those words came an understanding, that somehow the stand-up-straight, silver-haired, sunglass-wearing sheriff could see right through her.

Knew exactly the sort of person she was.

It sounded like a warning.

CHAPTER 11

Alexa made her way back to the inn, finding another side road a few blocks up from the school and cutting across it to reach the main street of town. The street spat her out a couple blocks from the clock tower. She glanced at it as she made her way around it, hoping it wouldn't choose that moment to give off a strike of its bell and cause the marching band in her head to blow their horns and beat their drums even harder.

She'd lied to Sheriff Byrd, the medication the paramedics had given here wasn't helping much, but she would have said anything to avoid riding in the man's car—or any cop car. No way, no how. The pain was bad enough, a headache that might have brought on nausea if she hadn't already emptied most of her lunch in the school's parking lot and all over the sheriff's shoes, but it was the swelling she could feel around her eye that was bothering her more, a pressure building that threatened to squeeze the eye shut and squish up the side of her face to make her look like a pirate saying *arggh!*

Mercifully, she reached the inn without things getting

worse, and she pushed through the office door wanting nothing more than to collect her sweet Barlow and go take a nap.

If you can even sleep at all, she thought. Which was a good point. The dreamless and deep sleep from the night before, the sleep that had seemed like just another encouragement that this town was going to be her new home, felt like a very long time ago. *I'll never be able to shut my mind off now. Not until this is all over.*

And what did that even mean, when it was *over*?

She was suddenly very tired.

Inside the office, her eyes adjusted to the dim light, and she was expecting to hear the now-familiar staccato padding of Barlow's paws as he excitedly came to greet her, while turning to see Ezra looming tall over the counter. But she saw nobody. No Ezra, no dog. Nothing.

She was instead greeted by a buzzsaw snore coming from behind the counter. A loud rip of air that screamed *deviated septum* and then was choked off as if startled.

"Hello?" she asked, as loudly as she could without yelling.

There was another startled choking sound followed by a gurgling grunt, and then a groggy voice said, "Oh, hello!" This greeting was then punctuated by *"Ooooohhkaaay"* as a man struggled to stand from where he'd apparently been snoozing in the recliner behind the counter.

Where Ezra was tall and thin and lithe, the man currently on the other side of the counter was short and, well ... *portly* was the word that sprang to Alexa's mind. Plump would do in a pinch. Fat if she felt like being cruel, which she didn't because she was too tired. And plus, despite all her flaws and less-than-savory actions over the years,

Alexa had never believed herself to be *cruel*. No, her past was *cruel*, yes indeed—had robbed her of so much—but not her. Though speaking without much of a filter—tellin' it like it is, as the kids would say—sometimes could be perceived that way.

"Are you Alexa?" the portly man asked, using a hand to smooth over what was left of his hair. It reminded Alexa of clumps of seaweed that washed up onto the shore. He wore a plain blue T-shirt that looked to have been washed to within an inch of its life beneath a blue-and-black checked flannel shirt that was untucked and unbuttoned. Blue jeans that seemed to have shared a life with the T-shirt. But, he was smiling (Alexa ignored the yellowed teeth), and he smelled strongly of deodorant and shampoo, and his eyes, now coming out of their grogginess, seemed to have a slight twinkle.

Alexa suddenly remembered her conversation with Ezra the night before: *Herb works the night shift. He's a little, shall we say, rough around the edges, but...*

"I am," Alexa said, trying to sound more polite than she felt at the moment. "And you must be Herb."

Herb winked. "Ez's talkin' me up, is he?"

Alexa nodded. "Something like that. Where is Ezra, and where's my dog?"

"Of course, of course. S'why I'm here, actually. Ez called me up and asked if I could watch the shop for a few while he went to run an errand. He took the dog with him, said he might like the walk on such a nice day."

Alexa felt a tingling of uneasiness start to raise the hairs on arms, wasn't sure what to make of this. Ezra seemed like

(he never asks questions)

good people, clearly, but there was still so much she didn't know.

Can you trust him? That voice again ... trying to rile her up.

He's given me no reason not to.

"Any idea when they'll be back?" Alexa asked.

"No, ma'am," Herb said, shaking his head once, the seaweed on top not so much as twitching, slicked down with some sort of product. "But he said to tell you not to worry a'tall, and if you need somet'in to be sure and let me"—he used his thumb to poke himself once in the chest—"know." Then Herb added, in a sort of bashfully proud way that reminded Alexa of a child showing off the finger painting they'd done in art class that day, "Ez trusts me, ma'am. You can, too."

Alexa smiled, then winced as pain shot through the side of her face, into her temple.

Her discomfort must have been evident because Herb asked, "What happened to your head, ma'am—if you don't mind me askin', o' course."

"I don't mind at all," Alexa said, turning to head out to her room. "I took a tumble on the sidewalk. Wasn't looking and tripped on the curb on my way to lunch. Tell Ezra I'll be in my room waiting for my dog, please."

"Yes, ma'am," Herb said as the office door swung shut.

Ezra might trust Herb, sure, but Alexa could only hand out her trust in small doses, and right now the little bit she was using for Ezra was all she had to spare.

Alexa took another shower, feeling dirty after the trek through the trees and being facedown on the asphalt and spewing her lunch. She made it quick, not wanting to miss Ezra should he come a-knockin' after he'd returned from his "errand"—whatever that meant. She was torn between being perturbed that he would just up and leave knowing she'd left him in charge of Barlow—not mentioning to her about said errand—and being impressed that he was taking the dog-sitting job seriously, taking Barlow with him for a nice walk instead of leaving the dog cooped up inside with Buzzsaw Herb.

She liked Ezra, she realized fully as she toweled herself off, and for the first time since meeting him she understood why.

He reminded her of Lance.

Which was a thing that was difficult to articulate. It was an opinion based more on feeling than adjectives and reason. But, just like Lance, Ezra possessed an air of mystery about him, and Alexa once again wondered about the truth of the man who was playing the role of friendly innkeeper. She wanted to know his secrets, both out of curiosity and also to better understand a man she was developing such trust for. But reaching into somebody else's past only invites the risk of them doing the same.

What would she say if Ezra reached into hers?

Back in the bedroom, she tossed on clean clothes, and as she went digging in her duffle bag for clean socks, she saw it, that flash of amber capped in white. The pill bottle.

Her father's pill bottle.

The amber color of the plastic was still the same, but the label was faded, smudged, the text nearly illegible. The result of all those nights alone, sometimes in a motel room like this, sometimes in places much worse, where Alexa would clutch the bottle in her hand, run her thumb over what was left of her father's name printed neatly near the top of the label, and curse him over and over and over for causing her to have to live this way. She was happy he was dead. She hoped he was burning in hell for what he'd done to her. She would always remember the morning in that motel room, where she'd awakened and found her father dead in the other bed, the sheets twisted around him, the dried vomit on his face—the vomit he'd choked on in his sleep after swallowing his entire bottle of migraine medicine. Twelve-year-old Alexa had stood over her father's corpse and waited, waited to feel something other than relief. No other feeling came. She'd plucked the pill bottle from the bedsheets and tucked it into the pocket of her sweatshirt without fully understanding why, not knowing that she'd still have it all these years later, reaching for it whenever she needed to be transported back to that motel room and that morning, when she needed a reminder that none of this had been her fault...

And why she was the person who she'd become, wondering if she could ever change. Wondering if she even wanted to.

The sound of a car door slamming caused her to jump, and she quickly tossed the pill bottle back into the duffle bag and zipped it closed, hiding away the memories. She peeked out the window blinds, and when she saw the tow truck lugging her Oldsmobile behind it parked outside the room, her brain went all squirrelly for a second, trying to understand.

Ezra opened the passenger door of the truck and Barlow

leapt out with him, his tongue dangling and tail wagging. Ezra closed the door and took hold of the dog's leash. In his other hand, he held a cloth shopping bag alongside the tote bag with Barlow's things. He said something to the dog and then turned and headed for her door while the truck driver got out and began the process of freeing Alexa's car from its shackles.

Alexa beat Ezra to the door, ripping the door open and saying, "What in the absolute *hell* are you doing?"

CHAPTER 12

Barlow darted into the room and leapt onto the bed, his leash trailing behind him like the world's thinnest superhero cape, then did three quick spins around before hunching down and looking at Alexa expectantly, mistaking her agitation as playfulness. Alexa ignored this, her eyes locked onto Ezra, who was standing just outside the motel room door while the sounds from the truck behind him kicked up as the driver pressed buttons and Alexa's car was released. He stared at her for a moment, his gaze flicking once to the side of her head, where the bruise was already growing a deeper shade of purple and her eye was puffy. He set both the bags he was carrying on the floor, just inside the door.

"Can I have the keys?" he asked. "So I can park it?"

Alexa wasn't quite sure why she'd grown so upset at the sight of the tow truck and her car, and was even less sure why, despite her visible frustration, Ezra only remained still and stoic, ignoring her emotions and her injury—*He sees it—oh, I know he sees it. He wants to know what happened, but he never asks any* fucking *questions*—and simply asked for her keys to park her car like they were some long-married couple going through another mundane day together that was completely dictated by comfort and routine.

She wanted to scream. Instead she held his stare a moment longer and then took in one long and deep breath, exhaling it in a show of irritation before turning and grabbing her keys from her jacket pocket and tossing them to him with more force than necessary. Ezra snatched them from the air one-handed with lightning speed and then turned and vanished from the opened doorway. Alexa was standing next to the bed, and Barlow nudged his head under her hand. She unhooked his leash and scratched behind his ear and listened to Ezra and the truck driver's muffled voices and then heard the truck drive away, followed by the familiar sound of her Oldsmobile sputtering to life. A few seconds later, the engine quit, the driver's door screeched open and shut, and then Ezra was back in the doorway. He stood at the threshold, looking at them both. "Can I come in?" he asked.

Alexa wanted to say no, which again she didn't quite understand. She was somehow feeling as though Ezra's noninvasiveness was having the same effect on her as if he were actually being invasive. It made no sense.

He's helping you, the warm ember in her belly seemed to tell her.

I didn't ask for help, the cynical part, the part she wished she could quiet, replied.

That doesn't make it bad.

"Sure," she said. "Close the door, please."

Ezra stepped inside and closed the door as instructed. He stood with his back against it, looking at her as if awaiting further instructions. She let him stand there. "Why did you do that?" Alexa nodded toward the window.

Ezra said, "Because I thought you'd like it back. Benny did me a favor."

Alexa had another thought then, and she quickly strode across the room and peeked out the window blinds. The Oldsmobile was parked directly in front of the room's door. She glanced down to the front driver's side, already knowing what she'd see. She stepped back and asked, "Where'd the new tire come from?"

"Again, Benny. He owns the garage. The tow truck is just a part of the business. Technically it's not a new tire. It's very used, in fact. But it was the right size."

"And Benny did you a favor?"

"He did."

"Why?"

"I helped him out one time."

Alexa considered this, thought about the implications. "Do *I* owe you a favor now?"

Why are you being like this? Why are you trying to pick a fight with him? I thought you were going to be better. I thought you liked *him...*

It's hard, *this is who I am!*

No, it's who you used to be.

"He didn't owe me a favor," Ezra said flatly. "He *did* me a favor. He owed me nothing. And neither do you."

There was silence for a beat, both of them seeming to feel out the moment. Then Ezra nodded and said, "You have a very good dog. I enjoyed his company today." Then he turned around and grabbed the door handle to leave.

"Wait," Alexa blurted without even meaning to. "Don't go."

Ezra froze, turned and looked over his shoulder to her. "Are you sure?"

She nodded.

He picked up the shopping bag that he'd set next to the bag of Barlow's food and toys and pulled out a pack of frozen lima beans. Tossed it to her. With more force than was necessary. She caught it easily, and then the two of them stared at each other, faces blank. He was the first to grin, a small smirk twitching his lips. She followed, letting herself smile and say, "Well played."

"Don't give if you can't take."

She held up the bag of frozen beans. "What am I supposed to do with this?"

"It's for your eye." When he saw her confusion, he quickly added, "Herb called me after you two met. Said you might need an icepack. That was the best I could do in the moment. It's probably half-melted now, but hopefully it helps."

This time, Alexa didn't get upset. She accepted the kind gesture and pressed the bag of lima beans to her face. It was only half-cold now but still felt heavenly against her skin, helped soothe the subtle burn of the wound. "Thank you for picking my least favorite bean. I won't feel so bad for wasting it."

"Speak for yourself," Ezra said, venturing one step away from the door. "I love lima beans. I plan on eating those after you thaw them."

"First, gross. Second, I don't know if I can be friends with somebody who likes lima beans."

"That's okay, I can be friends with Barlow."

The quick retort sparked a laugh from Alexa, and that along with the sweet relief the lima beans were providing worked to give her the first peaceful moment she'd felt since before that morning when Deputy Colin Wanamaker had knocked on her door.

"So Herb filled you in, huh?" Alexa asked, moving to sit on the bed and lean back against the pillows. She motioned for Ezra to have a seat in one of the chairs, but instead he leaned back against the door, crossed his arms.

He nodded. "Herb does well to keep me updated on everything—too many things, if I'm being honest. Said you tripped on the sidewalk."

Alexa nodded. "Wasn't looking where I was going."

"I hate when that happens."

Ask me, she thought. *Ask me what really happened. You know I didn't trip and fall, you* know *it.*

Instead, Ezra said, "I'm really glad you weren't hurt more seriously. Head injuries can be scary."

"Thanks" was all Alexa could think to say, marveling over Ezra's commitment to playing ignorant. Because he *was* playing, she was certain of it. But more importantly, he seemed to know that she knew he was playing ignorant—the way he spoke, that soft but flat inflection of his voice; the way his eyes would linger, conveying meaning that his words did not; and his confident, yet casual demeanor, like he was a man who had both all the answers and none of them at all, depending on what the situation called for.

Alexa recognized these traits because she possessed several of them herself. You might say they were the traits of a survivor.

"Do you know Sheriff Byrd?" Alexa asked, throwing a curveball.

Ezra's only reaction was another shift of his eyes. He'd been watching Barlow, who had balled up on the bed and begun drifting off for a nap, but he quickly flicked a look to Alexa's face, trying to quickly read it before he said, "Not well, but we've met a few times."

Which only caused more questions to grow inside Alexa's mind.

"What do you think of him?" she asked.

Ezra rubbed his face, as if thinking, but Alexa figured he had his opinion of the sheriff locked and loaded and well formed. "He's a straight shooter. I believe he mostly tries to do what's right."

The way he said this last part led Alexa to believe it wasn't as black and white as that. "Mostly?"

Ezra thought again, choosing his words carefully. "He tries to do *his* interpretation of what's right."

Alexa nodded. "Don't we all?"

This caused Ezra to smirk again, and he gave off a quick sound that might have been classified as a chuckle. "Good point." But that was it. He said nothing else. Didn't want to know why she was asking about the sheriff, or how she'd even learned of the man, having only been in town for less than twenty-four hours. These were all questions a normal person would ask—curiosity was human nature.

And Alexa was again pulled into a pool of thought that she and Ezra were somehow very similar. He could perhaps sense that she did not want any questions asked because he himself would appreciate the same courtesy.

But then why is he still standing here? she wondered. *What is he hoping to——*

Then it hit her, hard and fast, just like she'd thrown the keys to him. She thought about the no-questions-asked check-in the night before, considered the retrieved Oldsmobile now parked outside her room with the new (but not actually new) tire, felt what was left of the chill from the not-so-frozen-anymore beans in her hand, and then his words, asking if he could come in only so he could stand against the door as far away as possible.

He wants you to know you can trust him. He wants you to know he's willing to help you if you need it, but...

But he's letting me decide the terms.

Alexa was now absolutely certain that she and Ezra were standing alone in the motel room, both respecting an unspoken understanding of each other.

Survivors, Alexa thought again.

People with secrets.

And she could only ever wonder just how dark his secrets were unless she—

"I need to go relieve Herb so he can catch a few winks before the night shift," Ezra said. But he didn't move to leave, he just stared at her, those eyes doing all the talking for him.

He's giving me one last chance, Alexa thought. *One last chance to tell him the truth.*

She was not going to be the one to give in first. She didn't know why she was being so stubborn, but old habits died hard. Alexa said nothing except, "Thanks again for watching Barlow, and for these." She held up the lima beans.

Ezra didn't wait around to see if any more was coming from her. He just turned and left.

Shit.

He'd called her bluff.

Because the truth was, she'd been serious during that moment in the school's parking lot, where she'd decided that she was going to stick around, try and start over here despite being questioned in a murder investigation and then getting attacked by something as nonlethal and humiliating as a camera. Hell, maybe it was even because of all those things that she was deciding to stay. Maybe she saw it all as a challenge—a rite of passage to earn the right to stay and be a citizen of Silent Falls.

She'd faced challenges her entire life. All of them alone...

Until Lance. Lance had taught her it was okay to need help. It was something he'd had to learn the hard way himself. Lance taught her the value of friends.

Alexa thought Ezra might be exactly the type of friend she needed right now. Just like the vampires in that old Stephen King novel, all she needed to do was let him in.

She rushed to the door and pulled it open. Ezra was nearly to the office, so she yelled out, "Hey, do you like pizza?"

He stopped and turned. Called back. "Doesn't everyone? We're not talking about lima beans here."

"I'll treat you to dinner tonight. As a thank-you for ... well, everything."

He didn't hesitate. Her message was received. "Sounds nice. Your place or mine?" He used one hand to point to the motel's office and the other to point toward her motel room.

"Mine," Alexa said, wanting to keep things on her home turf as much as possible.

"I'll have Herb come in a couple hours early, so we don't have to wait so late. He won't mind."

"Tell him thanks for me," Alexa said.

Ezra nodded. "I look forward to it."

"Don't look too forward to it," Alexa said, grinning. "It's not a date or anything. You're not exactly my type."

"Because I'm black?"

"No, dummy. Because I'm gay."

They shared another grin, both seeming to enjoy the playful banter after the heaviness between them back in the motel room, and before Ezra turned to head inside the office, he said, "See? We're learning more about each other already."

Alexa returned to her room and closed the door.

Yep, message definitely received.

CHAPTER 13

Before Ezra had returned with her Oldsmobile, Alexa had thought that it would be impossible for her to sleep, that the day's events had wound her brain up too fast to be able to relax. Turned out, she was wrong. After she'd scheduled her date-that-wasn't-a-date with Ezra for later that night, she'd returned to her room and found Barlow just raising his head off his paws from where he'd been trying to nap. He gave her a side-eyed look, as if asking her to keep it down so he could catch a few winks, and suddenly Alexa could think of nothing she'd rather do than lie down next to him and catch a few herself. She *was* tired, she found. It had been a busy day. And her head was starting to hurt again, despite the pills the paramedics had given her and the temporary relief from the bag of frozen lima beans that was now soggy and dripping with condensation and tossed into the trash can.

And maybe he's calmed you down a bit, she thought as she pulled back the comforter and slipped under the sheets. She laid her head back and closed her eyes, listening to Barlow's soft snores—yes, he'd already fallen back under sleep's spell, dogs were very good at that—from next to her and realized that regardless of the anger she'd felt when Ezra had first returned with her Oldsmobile, she had felt better once he'd gotten there. Not that she *needed* him for help, or for any sort of protection—she was *perfectly* capable of protecting herself

(except from a fucking camera, apparently)

—or to offer any sort of patronizing comfort, serving up such cliched platitudes as *Everything will be alright* or *It will all work out exactly the way it's supposed to.* But his presence, that stoic confidence, coupled with the underlying certainty that they shared a mutual respect for the pasts that both of them were keeping buried, somehow made Alexa feel very at ease with everything. Not that things were even close to being okay at the moment; she had been questioned in the murder of a man she'd gotten into a verbal altercation with and had then had her picture snapped by a bona fide creeper in the park before he'd smashed her temple with his camera. But there was a part of her, that glowing ember she was nurturing inside her soul, that was trying to be heard over all the noise and tell her that Ezra was exactly the type of friend she needed and...

"And maybe we need each other," she said as the blanket of sleep wrapped her tight.

The phone on the bedside table gave off a soft electronic ring that didn't so much startle Alexa out of her nap but pull her up slowly, like a hand helping you climb out of the deep end of a pool. On the second ring, she opened her eyes, saw that the room had grown dim, and wondered how long she'd been asleep. On the third ring, she snapped fully awake, jerking to her left and rolling over—causing an unapprecia-

tive grunt from Barlow as she kneed him in the ribs—
reaching for the cordless phone in its cradle on the nightstand. She grabbed it and thumbed the button to answer the
call, thinking that the person whose voice she'd hear on the
other end would most certainly be Ezra's, because who else
would possibly have this number.

"Hello?" she said, trying and failing not to sound groggy.

Silence was all she got in return.

"Hello?" she tried again, moving to sit up straighter in the
bed, resting her head against the headboard. Barlow perked
his ears up at the sound of her voice and watched her
expectantly.

More silence this time. Alexa ended the call and replaced
the phone on its base. Watched as the little green light lit up,
indicating the phone was seated correctly and charging.

She smiled at Barlow and reached over to rub his head.
"Must have been a wrong—"

The phone rang again. It was the same soft melody, but
on the second verse it became more annoying than pleasant.
Alexa sighed and reached for the phone again. "*Hello?*"

Nothing but the gentle hum of the dead space between
she and the caller. "Look, if you're speaking I can't hear you,
so maybe there's a problem with the connection or—"

She stopped herself. Pressed the phone harder against
her ear, because she was wrong. It wasn't just silence and the
sound of digital bits and bytes coming through the earpiece.
There was another noise. It was low and heavy, the slow and
rhythmic sound of somebody breathing.

Somebody listening.

She pulled the phone away from her face and punched
the button to end the call. Stared at the phone in her hand,

squeezed it tight as if she could make it talk, spill the truth. Barlow must have sensed something was off, because he crawled over to her and stood, putting his face into hers, his eyes asking, "What's wrong, what's happening?"

A full minute passed, Alexa's fingers turning white beneath the pressure of her grip on the phone. Barlow had settled on lying down again but keeping his chin rested atop her thigh. Alexa took a deep breath, then laughed.

"You're getting paranoid, Shiffy," she said, digging out the old nickname for herself, a name she used when she was trying to make light of something serious, trying to gain control of her emotions. It was a nickname nobody had called her since *before*. Back in that other life, before she'd turned twelve and her father had touched her. A youth soccer coach had started it, because there had been two Alexas on the team and calling out their last names had been easier. For some reason, he'd turned Shifflett into Shiffy—probably because it was easier to yell—and the name had stuck.

Alexa tossed the phone onto the bed and was standing up to head to the bathroom when it rang again. This time, the soft and gentle melody might as well have been a blaring siren for the dread it struck inside her.

And the anger that came along with it.

Alexa snatched up the phone and pressed the button. "Listen here, jackoff, whatever the fuck game you're playing, you can shove it right up your ass because—"

"*Shut up!*" a man's voice snarled from the other end of the line, cutting her off with such ferocity Alexa nearly dropped the phone.

She shut up, but the rage boiled inside her, a pot simmering and about to spill over.

The voice spoke again, the snarl gone but the words still landing a punch. "Leave this alone," it said. "It has nothing to do with you. Leave it, or you'll be next."

The call ended.

~

SHE HADN'T BOTHERED TYING her boots, and the laces flopped against the asphalt as Alexa walked across the parking lot. She walked briskly and with purpose, that bubbling pot of anger inside her combating against the fear that sent a small shiver up her spine each time she replayed that voice

("Shut up!")

in her head. At least out here in the dark parking lot, she could blame that shiver on the winter chill that had returned to the air now that the sun was gone. But she knew the truth of it. Knew that voice would make her shiver even it had been a scorching summer day.

Toughen up, Shiffy, she tried to steel herself. Because why *was* she so unnerved by that voice? Alexa Shifflett was not somebody who was easily spooked, not somebody who feared things. She was a fight instead of flight type of person and had thrived on this mentality, had seemingly craved confrontation at times, if for no other reason than to disperse some of that rage that always seemed to be fizzling just beneath the surface.

As she reached the office door, she realized it might be the uncertainty of it all that had her out of sorts. She'd stepped into something she shouldn't have, but she had no idea what that thing was. All she'd wanted to do was prove she hadn't killed anybody, and now she was getting death threats.

What did the kids say? *Well, that escalated quickly.*

She pushed through the office door, ready to yell, ready to ask Ezra why in hell he didn't think it strange to transfer three back-to-back-to-back calls to her room such a short time apart. That rage needed to go somewhere, and he was all she had at the moment. She got as far as breathing in the big breath of air she'd need to blast him but then cut herself off. A middle-aged couple standing side by side at the check-in counter turned and looked at her. Ezra was on the other side of the counter, his arm extended out, hand holding the couple's room key.

"I've got you in seven," he told them, his eyes staying locked on Alexa for another second before he shifted his gaze back to them. "Right across the parking lot in the far corner. Nobody on either side of you, so it'll be nice and private."

The couple thanked him and Ezra was in full-on host mode, thanking them for choosing the inn and telling them to certainly let him or Herb know if they needed anything at all. Alexa stepped to the side and tried to smile as the couple walked past her and headed outside, and when the man glanced down at Alexa's untied boots, she wanted to tell him to *fuck off* but instead remained silent and still until they were gone.

When the door closed behind them, Ezra only stared at her, waiting. No *What's wrong* or *What happened*, just his standard mode of communication, which was patience. She didn't care this time—she was going to tell him whether he asked or not.

But the sight of him had helped to calm her a bit. Even

though he wasn't speaking, she could see the concern in his eyes—those eyes that said so much—and knew that laying her anger on him was going to be the wrong move here. Instead, she just launched into it. "I just got three phone calls one after another to my room phone. The first two nobody said anything, but the last one was

(*"Shut up!"*)

a death threat."

Alexa watched his face. Saw him swallow once, the Adam's apple in his thin neck bobbing a single time. She saw his jaw flex, like he was biting down hard on one side.

That's his *anger*, Alexa thought. *That's* him *working to keep it down.*

"Tell me everything again, and don't leave out any details," Ezra said, motioning her to come around the counter. He pointed to the recliner and Alexa allowed herself to fall into it, catching a whiff of something she quickly identified as Herb's shampoo-and-deodorant combo from before. It was not altogether unpleasant. Ezra spun an office desk chair on wheels around from where it had been tucked under the counter and sat down, crossing his legs, waiting for her to tell it.

So she did. It was a short story.

When she was finished, Ezra sat quietly for maybe a minute, and Alexa never took her eyes off him. Finally, he spoke, answering the question that she'd been intent on asking (*accusing*) him when she'd first arrived. "I didn't forward those calls to your room," he said. "The phone system has an automated prompt. After you dial the main line, if you know what room your guest is staying in, you can just press the button and you're connected."

He stood and walked over to the computer on the counter. Started clicking and typing. He leaned down and studied the screen, then nodded his head. "Yep, three incoming calls, all to your room only. They didn't hunt and peck."

"What do you mean?" Alexa asked, not following.

"I mean, they didn't just keep trying rooms until they found yours."

Alexa felt the weight of this sink in right at the same time Ezra turned to face her again.

"They know you're here," he said, "and they know exactly what room you're in."

Alexa didn't need him to say any more. She thought about the camo-photographer from the park, the way he'd *snap snap snapped* his pictures. "Which means they're following me," she said.

CHAPTER 14

W*hich means they're following me.*

Alexa's words hung between her and Ezra for what felt like a long time, and then finally, after Ezra rubbed his face with both hands and let out a heavy sigh, as if he couldn't believe what he was about to do, he asked, "Who is *they*?"

Ordinarily—hell, maybe even as recently as twenty minutes ago—Alexa might have made a show of this small victory in getting Ezra to capitulate and ask her an actual question, but that voice

(Shut up!)

from the other end of the phone line was still just over her shoulder, whispering in her ear, dispelling any of her normal dry sense of humor. She said, "I don't know." Because it was the truth.

Ezra tried again. "Okay, you don't know *who* they are, but I suspect you at least have an idea of why they're threatening you."

This wasn't technically a question, but Alexa answered, "Yes, I can at least take a guess."

Before she could fill him in any further, Ezra pointed to the side of her head, to the bruise and the slightly puffy eye. "And I'll take a guess that it has something to do with that sidewalk you tripped and fell on, right?"

See, I knew that he knew. She was happy that she'd read him correctly. She gave him a small grin that said, *Okay, time to lay the cards out.* "You'd be correct," she said. "The sidewalk was actually a guy I found hiding in the trees at the park, wearing all camo gear and taking photographs of the sheriff's deputies who were stationed at the crime scene."

"He attacked you?" Ezra said.

"Yes."

"Any particular reason?"

"I might have made a crack about him having a small penis and then chased him when he ran away."

Ezra stared at her, his face blank, probably trying to decide if she was being serious or joking.

Alexa shrugged a *what-can-I-say?* shrug.

"Why were *you* in the trees at the park?" Ezra asked. "The park is closed today."

Alexa nodded. "Exactly."

"Exactly?"

"It's closed. Because of the murder scene. That's why I had to sneak in the side, away from the main entrances. Which, honestly, was way too easy. It was an oversight on the sheriff's part. I might have mentioned that to him." A beat. "No, I definitely did."

Ezra only stared again, but this time he didn't appear to be judging her seriousness; instead he was shaking his head with a small grin that seemed to be trying to decide if he was impressed by her ballsiness or appalled by it. Alexa didn't know much about the man, other than what her instinct was telling her, which was that they were very similar in a lot of ways, but she was thinking he was leaning toward impressed.

Ezra pulled out his smartphone and started tapping the screen. "Are you okay with veggie pizza? Or do you want to order one with meat?"

Alexa wasn't hungry—a stone of uneasiness sat heavy in her stomach—but she said that veggie was fine. Ezra completed the order and then said, "No reason we still can't eat. But while we're waiting, I'm going to need you to start at the beginning. I want you to tell me everything you did today after you left the inn." Then he added, "Please."

She might not know much about Ezra, but she trusted him. And what was the harm in telling him anyway? Either he could help her or he couldn't, and something about the entire conversation so far had led Alexa to believe that he could.

She just didn't know how.

"Okay," she started. "After I left Barlow with you, I walked into town and stopped to get a coffee and muffin..."

She told him everything after that, about the deputy parked outside the main entrance to Collins Park, about her lunch at Smokey's, when she'd learned about Tony from Clara, who she discovered was Deputy Wanamaker's sister and the reason Alexa had been questioned this morning, and then she finished the story with her excursion away from the main street and her rendezvous with the camo-photographer, which had culminated in her waking up on the asphalt and having to deal with the sheriff and the paramedics before she walked back to the inn.

Ezra listened to all this intently, never saying a word, letting her finish uninterrupted. She appreciated that. She'd met too many men over the years who'd felt the need to interject and mansplain at every small opportunity. When she said, "And you know the rest. You brought me my car back and then I took a nap, only to be awakened by those phone calls. Now, here I am."

When Ezra recognized that she had finished her story, he nodded once and then stood from the office chair, returning to the computer on the counter. "You said the truck the photographer was running toward was white with a big yellow stripe?"

"Yes," Alexa said. "Positive. And there was black text in the yellow, but I didn't get a chance to read it." She liked that Ezra had said "running toward" and not something like "drove away in" in reference to the camo-photographer and the truck. Because technically, Alexa *hadn't* seen the guy get into the truck and drive away. She only knew the truck had been there when she got hit, and it had been gone when she woke up. But anyone could put those pieces together and see the full picture.

Ezra clicked the mouse a couple times and typed a few keystrokes and then stepped aside, pointed at the screen. "Did it look like this?"

Ezra had pulled up a website, and Alexa didn't even have to get up from the recliner to see the truck on the computer screen was the exact same as the truck she'd seen in the school's parking lot. "Bingo," she said, then leaned forward to read the words that were printed on the side. Once she had, she felt another piece of the puzzle fall onto the table, if not into place.

The side of the truck read:

LIL' TONY'S LANDSCAPING

"Huh," Alexa said, leaning back into the chair. "I thought it seemed like the sheriff had a good idea what truck it might have been. Now I know why."

Ezra nodded. "Anybody would. Tony had a pretty good thing going with that business. You see those trucks all over. Hell, I have them on contract to plow the snow here."

"Mr. Camo must not be too bright to have driven such a recognizable vehicle there when he was intent on spying on a crime scene."

Ezra considered this. "Well, you might argue it was genius. Like I said, those trucks are all over. People don't think twice about seeing them anywhere." He shrugged. "The school probably has a contract with them too, if I had to guess. He didn't see any problem, until—"

"Until I showed up and found him," Alexa finished for him. "He wasn't expecting anybody else in those trees."

"Right," Ezra said. "You caught him doing something shady and now he—and whoever else is involved in this, I'm sure—has your picture, and they know where you're staying."

"Yeah," Alexa said, sighing. "I might have made this worse than it needed to be."

"Oh, you definitely did."

Headlights flashed across the front office windows, and Ezra moved around the counter. "Pizza's here."

"Hey, this is supposed to be my treat," Alexa said, moving to stand from the recliner. But Ezra was already to the door. He waved her off.

"I'll put it on your tab."

He stepped outside and then was back with the pizza, carrying it around the counter and heading toward a door in the back left of the office. "Come on," he said. "We can eat back here."

The room was a small kitchenette complete with stove, fridge, microwave and sink. A tiny table was set against the wall, with barely enough room for the two chairs on either side. An opened door on the opposite side of the room revealed a tiny half-bath. The entire place seemed dated compared to the rest of the inn, like it had been forgotten along the way. The only modern thing in it was a small laptop computer on the counter, taking up the sliver of space to the left of the sink. The computer was open and displaying a video feed from a camera back out in the main office space.

Reading her mind, Ezra said, "I know what you're thinking." He set the pizza box on the small table and flipped open the lid. "I didn't see the need to upgrade any of this. It still works, and it's the guests I'm more concerned about. They're the ones that like the nice things, the ones paying for comfort."

Alexa shrugged. "Makes sense to me." She pulled a slice from the box and slid into one of the chairs. She took a bite and the hunger that she'd thought was gone for good for the night quickly resurfaced. She scarfed down an entire slice while Ezra opened the fridge and returned to the table with two small cardboard boxes of water. Alexa eyed them skeptically.

"It's just water," Ezra said. "But the packaging is better for the environment."

Alexa said nothing. Ezra opened her box for her and slid

it across the small table. She sipped it, verified it was, in fact, water, and then chugged half of it. Ezra ate a slice of pizza that nearly matched the speed with which she'd consumed hers, and for a couple minutes they were quiet together, eating and drinking and not saying a word.

After Ezra's second slice of pizza, he jumped back on the question train. "Here's what I don't understand," he said, pausing to take a sip of water. "Just because you found the guy in the trees taking pictures, and then he got spooked and ran away, why is that grounds for these people to call you and make threats? Assuming, that is, that the photographer and the people who called are ... shall we say, on the same side."

Alexa nodded. "You're right. I didn't do anything except call him out for spying on a crime scene, and—"

"And the penis joke, don't forget that part."

Alexa stopped the slice of pizza midway to her mouth, raised her eyes to meet Ezra's. Saw him grinning. "Hey, details are important," he said. "Even the, uh, little ones."

She burst out laughing, and God did it feel good. "Look at you, master of puns."

Ezra's grin morphed into a smile, but then in a flash, the moment had passed and they were serious again. "It would have taken more than that," he said. "Both for them to feel the need to learn who you were and also to threaten you."

"They know I'm digging into Tony's murder," Alexa said matter-of-factly. "They must."

"Is that what you're doing?"

"I..." Alexa trailed off. It was a good question, one that she didn't expect Ezra to understand, mostly because she didn't quite understand it herself. "Yeah," she said. "I guess I am."

"Why?" He leaned back in the chair and crossed his arms,

the same look he'd taken up in her room after he'd brought her back the Oldsmobile, and she saw in that look that he wasn't asking her because he wanted to show her all the reasons she was wrong but because he genuinely wanted to know, wanted to understand.

"I don't like being accused of things I didn't do," she said. "I haven't had the cleanest of pasts, but I'm not a murderer."

Ezra waited. Said nothing. Reached for his box of water and took a sip, his eyes never leaving hers.

"I don't trust police," Alexa blurted. "Some things happened a long time ago and, well ... I'm sure the sheriff's office here does a great job or whatever, but I ... I trust my own results more."

More silence from Ezra. The refrigerator gave off a funny gurgle of air and the compressor kicked on.

"And ... this is going to sound crazy, but I've been on the

(run)

move for a long time. Like, a *really* long time. But some things happened recently and I met some good people and I was just ... finally ready to try and start living again. Then I found this town and something about it, God, I don't know, it just *felt* right, you know? Like, for some reason I really thought that the Universe or karma or whatever you want to call it was trying to tell me that this was the place where I was supposed to make my attempt at starting over."

She rushed through all these words with the sort of desperation in her voice of a person who knows that what they are saying is out of the ordinary but is pleading with their listener to understand, to have sympathy, to be on their side. "Does *any* of that make sense to you?"

Ezra was quiet for a few seconds more, then he uncrossed

his arms, leaned forward, and then thought better of it and leaned back again. "It does," he said. "More than you even know."

And there was something there, something hidden behind the veil of those words, a quick glimpse into whatever past Ezra was hiding, the same way Alexa had been hiding hers. She wanted to peek, wanted to look behind the curtain and dig through his storage boxes, but she didn't dare. Not now.

Alexa felt better, having gotten all that off her chest and, more importantly, having had it be accepted without question or ridicule. She reached for another slice of pizza. She didn't really want it but wasn't sure what to do now, now that their strange truth was out there on the table between them.

"Clara," Ezra said.

"What about her?"

"She's the only person other than me who you've talked to about any of this, right? About Tony? You said she was the one who told you all about him. You told me you asked her if she might know of any reason somebody might want him dead."

Shit.

"You're right," Alexa said, feeling a roulette wheel of emotions spin in her chest.

Before they could discuss it any more, Alexa caught movement on the laptop screen on the counter behind Ezra, and a second later she heard Herb's voice call out, "Ez, you here?"

"Back here," Ezra called back, standing from the table.

Herb popped his head into the room, and when he saw the two of them together by the table, he smiled, and Alexa could see that twinkle in his eyes from across the room. "Wow, Ez, quite the romantic you are. Coulda at least lit a candle."

"Don't worry, Herb," Ezra said. "I'm not her type. Want some pizza?"

"Let me guess," Herb said. "It's that hippie kind you like."

"Veggie, Herb. *Veggie.*"

Herb waved him off. "Same difference. I like dead animals on my pizza like a true 'merican," he said. But he still swooped up a slice and started to eat it.

Ezra motioned for Alexa to follow him back out into the office, telling Herb to take his time eating. Herb mumbled something through a mouthful of hippie pizza and nodded. Back in the office, Ezra went back to the computer and typed and clicked a few things and then turned to Alexa and said, "This might sound forward, but I think you and Barlow should stay with me tonight."

The old Alexa would have refused, and under normal circumstances, the new Alexa might have as well. But she was working hard to distance herself from so many parts of the old Alexa, and it was growing more and more apparent that nothing about this current situation—not Tony's murder, not the threatening phone call, not even Ezra—was normal.

"We would appreciate that," she said. "Thank you."

A few minutes later, Herb emerged from the back room and officially started his shift, telling Ezra and Alexa not to do anything too crazy as they stepped out into the night.

CHAPTER 15

Alexa woke not because of a phone ringing but because of the sun cutting a fan of light across the bedroom and warming her face. She opened her eyes and shielded them from the rays, and as the room took shape around her it took a few disoriented seconds—those disoriented seconds that always seem to follow the deepest of sleeps—for her to remember where she was.

But then the previous night came flooding back to her.

Ezra's. I'm in his guest room.

She sat up straighter in the bed, the comforter falling from her, the cool air prickling her bare skin with goose-flesh. The room was a nice size, outfitted with new and modern furniture that was a stark contrast to the house's exterior. When she'd first seen the two-story farmhouse illuminated in Ezra's headlights as he'd driven his white Toyota crew-cab truck up the driveway the night before, he must have instantly read her mind, the same way he'd known what she'd been thinking when she'd seen the outdated kitchenette hidden away behind the inn's office, because he said, "I wanted the seclusion, and this was the most perfect thing I could find. I spent a lot of time renovating inside. Still have some work to do, but ... she's a good old house."

Alexa hadn't said a word. Only nodded. She couldn't help but wonder—okay, let's call it what it is, she couldn't help but *fantasize*—about what it must be like to have a house like this one all to herself, way out here away from everything. Because even though they'd only driven fifteen minutes or so, Ezra having headed away from town and then made a series of turns where each new road seemed to get narrower than the previous one and any signs of other homes became less and less frequent, when they'd finally made the last turn and headed up the driveway in the dark of night, Alexa felt like they were the only two people left on earth.

Three, if you counted Barlow, who was sitting attentively in the back seat and watching out the window.

When Ezra had parked, they'd all gotten out and Barlow had taken care of business in the grass and then Alexa and he had followed Ezra up the stairs of the porch, Alexa slinging her duffle bag and Barlow's tote over each shoulder, and waited for Ezra to unlock the door and let them in. When the door was opened, Barlow wasted no time, eager to explore his new surroundings. Alexa called after him, but Ezra just shook his head and said, "He'll be fine."

She thought there would be more talk then, maybe Ezra would brew a pot of coffee and then they'd sit at the kitchen table or maybe in a living room or study or whatever you called a room with chairs where people sat these days, and they'd dig deeper into the mess Alexa had apparently gotten herself into. For some reason her mind had quickly flashed to an image of Ezra standing before a giant whiteboard, writing and circling and diagramming as they tried to crack the case.

Crack the case, she thought, then actually scoffed out loud. *You don't even know what the case is.*

"You okay?" Ezra had asked.

Alexa nodded. "Yes, fine."

And she'd been wrong. There was no more talk. Ezra had apparently exhausted his inventory of questions for the time being, or had decided that there was nothing more they could do tonight other than let Alexa sleep somewhere that was, for the moment, safer than the inn.

Unless they followed me here too, she thought and then waited for Ezra to make some comment on this, since he appeared to be so good at getting inside her head. Instead, he pointed to a set of stairs just to the left of the front door and said, "Guest bedroom is at the right end of the hall. Bathroom is first door before that. It should have anything you need."

His voice was flat again, like he was working hard to keep his emotions under control, or that maybe he was regretting his decision to ask her to stay. Alexa didn't want to do anything to sway his pendulum one way or the other. It was getting late, and she knew he'd likely have to get up early to head back to the inn, so she simply thanked him, called Barlow, who came dutifully to follow her up the stairs, sniffing everything along the way, and then got ready for bed.

But sleep had not come at first. Like she'd feared before her nap at the inn, her mind was revved up, incited after talking things through with Ezra as they'd shared their pizza. His last comment, the one about Clara, was particularly worrisome. Because he was right, Clara was the only person other than Ezra that Alexa had discussed her situation with, and therefore she seemed to be the likely culprit to have set in motion the things that had caused the person on the other end of that threatening phone call to make it. Camo-photographer would have had no indication that Alexa was creeping in the woods with him for the very same reason—to spy on a crime scene. And even if he'd thought that, he'd have no way of knowing that she was actively trying to learn more about the murder in an attempt to clear her name instead of simply being curious. Just your average Jane lookie-loo.

On one hand, there was the possibility that Clara had tipped off the wrong person that Alexa had been asking about Tony and that she seemed determined to get to the truth behind his murder. Clara might not have meant any harm by it—maybe she'd just been chatting with that other waitress Alexa had seen her with when she'd arrived at Smokey's and had said more than she should have, and once word got out, it got around, then landed in the lap of the wrong people. Of course, there was also the possibility that Clara's information had been passed along voluntarily and with purpose, with Clara acting as a sort of informant. This was the cynical part of Alexa knocking on the door, looking for deeper, more offensive suggestions.

No, she thought. *She's a smart girl. And she's one of the good ones.*

It was nothing but a gut feeling—*instinct*—but Alexa trusted it. Her life had forced her to get very smart very fast at reading people.

And then there's Colin, the deputy-dawg brother. He'd been the first person who had pulled her into this mess—if you didn't count Tony, that was—by showing up and asking her questions yesterday morning. He'd been acting based on the story his kid sister had told him the night before, just a silly story for them to share a laugh over, and Alexa now wondered if he'd even bothered reporting any of it—the story *or* the questioning—to anybody else at the sheriff's office.

Maybe he was hoping to be the hero, she thought. *The young guy who hasn't really done much except issue a few parking tickets and respond to a few brawls out at Smokey's to tell beer-fueled hotheads to take it down a peg before he had to get serious—which probably sounded ridiculous coming from that baby face of his— suddenly and single-handedly solving the town's biggest murder (hell, maybe its* only *murder) in history. He'd be the shining star, get all the respect he craved without having to put in another decade behind a desk and checking the parking meters and growing a Fu Manchu to make himself look older. If he could* even *grow facial hair*, Alexa reminded herself ... and felt herself finally start to drift away.

But maybe he's crooked, Alexa thought, one of the final thoughts before sleep took her. *Maybe* he's *the one who tipped off the guy*

(Shut up!)

on the phone.

Not all cops are bad, that more optimistic voice reminded her.

I know ... but some are. It only takes one.

Because whether Colin Wanamaker was good or bad, straight or crooked, rookie or veteran, Sheriff Byrd had made no indication he'd had any idea who Alexa was when they'd had their vomit-tainted encounter in the school's rear parking lot. Which meant either he was a hell of a poker player, or he was genuinely in the dark about Alexa and Tony's brief-yet-colorful history and the implications—though farfetched—that could be made because of it.

The bedroom was cool and the sheets smelled of laundry detergent, and as Alexa had lain there on her back with her head nestled into the pillow, eyes closed and listening to the sounds of Ezra moving about down below, she found herself again wondering just who this man was, and whether he was wondering the same about her. Then she was gone.

She'd dreamed she was in the park—not Collins Park, but a park only inside her dreamland—taking pictures of Barlow as he ran around and chased birds and watched butterflies float in front of his nose. The sun was out and it must have been late spring or early summer because the weather was gloriously warm but not hot and she was laughing and everything was perfect ... until she realized that she'd never owned a camera like this, not one with the long telephoto lens, and panic seized her and she quickly pulled the camera away from her eye and saw the spot of blood on the side where the plastic had connected with skin—*her skin*—and she tossed it away into the grass and when she looked up Barlow was dragging something out of some bushes, pulling pulling pulling until the body started to emerge, bloody fingers on the end of a bloody wrist and—

She'd awakened with a small, quick gasp, her heart hammering in her chest, but then sleep had pulled her back down and she'd dreamed no more.

Now, she swung her legs over the edge of the bed and her feet touched down on the cold wooden floor. Barlow opened his eyes and looked at her from where he was curled up on the end of the bed, then closed them again.

"Time to get up, sleepyhead," Alexa said. "It's a school day."

The bedside clock told her it was just after seven, and she had no idea what time Ezra headed back to the inn, but she knew she needed to go with him. She dressed and made the bed and then opened the bedroom door, standing quietly in the upstairs hallway and listening for sounds of life. From down below, she heard movement, the soft clattering and scraping of a fork or a knife on a plate. She smelled coffee.

She found Ezra seated at a white kitchen table, surrounded by white cabinets, eating fruit off a white plate. Even the sunlight that was now coming in through the back windows seemed to be filtered to a white hue, but that much was probably her imagination. Everything was new and modern and spotless.

She stood in the entryway from the main hall, and when he looked up at her she was happy to see that he smiled instead of keeping that flat expression from the night before. "Good morning," he said. "There's coffee and fruit. I also have toast and oatmeal."

"Just coffee, please."

"Ah, I forgot you're more a brunch gal."

She rolled her eyes. "Don't start that again, Mr. Hippie Pizza."

He chuckled and stood from the table and poured her coffee into a (white) mug and she moved to sit at the table across from him.

"It sure is white in here," she said.

He handed her the mug and, instead of sitting back down, leaned against the counter and did that arm-cross thing. "It's the cleanest color," he said. "It's energizing."

She sipped the coffee and tried not to moan over how good it was. "It's very nice .... for an insane asylum."

"I believe the PC term is mental health facility," he said, not missing a beat. "Besides, we're all a little crazy, right?"

"Goddamn right," she said, meaning it completely.

They both turned their heads at the sound of Barlow clopping down the stairs, and he joined them in the kitchen, wagging his tail and sniffing the air to see if breakfast was being served. Ezra greeted him by leaning down and giving him a good rubdown and then Alexa stood and pointed to the back door.

"Can he go out here?"

"Sure, but it's not fenced in."

Alexa opened the door. "He won't run away," she said.

No, because I'm the one who runs...

Not anymore, she reminded herself. *Not anymore.*

She opened the door and Barlow trotted outside. After she'd closed it again and turned back around, Ezra was wearing his serious expression. "You're welcome to stay here today," he said. "As long as you want, actually."

She wanted to ask why he was being so nice to her, why he was offering his home to a stranger, but instead she just shook her head and said, "I appreciate it—and I'm not saying I won't spend the night here again, that bed was heaven—but I'll ride with you back to the inn this morning. I've got ... some things I need to do."

He nodded, as if he had already known this answer was coming. Asked, "Are these things you want to tell me about?"

She shook her head. "Not yet. Maybe the less you know, the better. At least for now."

He did that thing again where he stared at her and his jaw

flexed and she could see him working out the puzzle. In the end, he just nodded again. "Sure, I understand completely." But as he started cleaning up his dishes from the table and carrying them to the dishwasher, he said, "Just let me know when I can help."

When. He said when, not if. She took another sip of the wonderful coffee. *He knows this isn't over. In fact*, she thought, just as Barlow barked from outside to be let back in, *it might just be getting started.*

CHAPTER 16

They drove back to the inn mostly in silence. It wasn't a long drive, but with the morning sun highlighting everything Alexa had missed the night before, it was a much different trip. She took in the trees and the fields and the other homes tucked away off the road, hidden in the trees or perched atop rolling hills with long and winding driveways. She saw the mountains in the distance, dull in color now but surely beautiful in the fall. She thought Barlow would enjoy hiking them with her, when the weather was warmer. She was finding Virginia to be a very pretty state. They passed a gated community about a mile from the inn, and the few houses Alexa was able to glimpse as they drove by were big and bold and screamed high price tags.

Again, Ezra was in her head. "Most people that live there work in East River," he said. "Better jobs there, in the city. It's about forty minutes away." He shrugged. "Too long a commute for me, but I guess those folks look at their pay stubs twice a month and figure it's worth it, that eighty minutes of their life gone each day. It's no wonder the audiobook business is booming. Everyone's trapped in their cars driving back and forth from jobs they hate—might as well listen to something that will let you escape for a while."

This was the most Alexa had ever heard him talk about anything so random. She kept quiet, waited to see if there was going to be more. There wasn't going to be, because he reached down and clicked on the radio and NPR came on. While the radio heads talked, Alexa thought about those big fancy houses again, and the better jobs in East River, and then cast a side-eye at Ezra as the inn came into view about a quarter mile ahead.

Where'd he get his *money?* she thought. The inn renovations, the farmhouse with the modern furniture, hell, even this truck was nicer than anything Alexa had ever ridden in —where had it all come from?

And why is he spending it all here?

Ezra pulled the truck around the back of the office and parked and they all got out. Alexa tucked the toiletry bag and handful of clothes she'd brought with her from the farmhouse under her arm (she'd left her duffle bag with all the rest, because she *did* plan on staying there again tonight) and asked Ezra if he minded grabbing Barlow's tote. He didn't mind, and the three of them walked around to the front of the office and Ezra stopped at the door and asked casually, "What's your plan?"

She didn't mind telling him, but she was still going to leave out some of the specifics for now. "I'm going to go get myself ready and then, if it's okay with you, I'm going to leave Mr. Barlow here in your charge again while I head off on some business."

Ezra nodded and gave her a thumbs-up that for a second

made him look like nothing more than a young teenager who didn't know how to act around the girl he liked, and then said, "Well, you know where to find me," and pushed through the door. Before it swung shut behind him, Alexa heard Herb's snore get startled short and the man say, "Mornin', boss!"

Alexa walked past her Oldsmobile on the way to her room. It had been Ezra's idea to leave it behind and have them ride together because if somebody *was* keeping tabs on her, maybe they'd see the car still there and assume she was, too. Which was assuming they didn't have somebody staked out nearby, watching her every move through a pair of high-powered binoculars (or a camera with a telephoto lens), instead of doing the occasional drive-by.

By *getting ready*, Alexa had actually meant making herself appear different. She pulled a curling iron from her bag and plugged it in beneath the bathroom mirror and then dumped out her makeup. Over the years, part of her survival skills had been an ability to become who she needed to be in any particular situation. When it came to her physical appearance, she could be Plain Alexa, Soccer Mom Alexa, Businesswoman Alexa, Sexy Alexa ... and, yes, Slutty Alexa. Her mannerisms and speech patterns would change with each, of course, and she supposed if she really stepped back and looked at the big picture, she might be considered a con artist. But she really preferred the term *persuasive*.

Half an hour later, she stepped out of the room with her hair curled and wearing sensible amounts of eyeliner, mascara, and lipstick. She'd dressed in jeans and a blue sweater, and she left the leather jacket in Ezra's truck. She didn't look out of the ordinary by any means, could in fact be any woman you might expect to see walking along the side-walks of any street in any town. She put on her sunglasses—one final touch—and then walked Barlow to the office and dropped him off with Ezra (who did not ask any further questions) and headed into town.

Hopefully looking different enough that nobody who might have seen her in passing yesterday would recognize her. One person in particular.

SHE'D ALWAYS HAD a good memory. Even from a young age (from *before*), she'd excelled when it came to learning the multiplication tables and she'd won several local spelling bees. Her dad had been so proud (*Fuck you, Dad*). She could read instructions for cooking microwave dinners or frozen pizzas and then toss the boxes away without ever having to go dig them out of the trash for a quick reminder. The skill had followed her into adulthood (into *after*) and had come in handy often. It was coming in handy now. Because when Ezra had pulled up the website for Lil' Tony's Landscaping on the office computer last night, in addition to seeing the picture of the truck with the words clearly printed inside that yellow stripe on the side, Alexa had also seen the business's corporate address at the top of the page, along with a phone number. She'd memorized both, of course, but the phone number wasn't helpful to her current mission. This mission needed her to be able to see, maybe to touch and feel, if it came down to that. She needed to look people in the eyes. Their shit-colored eyes.

She didn't need a map, because as luck would have it she

had recognized the street name. She'd seen it just yesterday after she'd blown chunks on Sheriff Byrd's shoes. It was the same street the school was on. Sometimes—not often, but sometimes—life

(The Universe)

paid you small favors. She considered this one of them.

Town was quieter this morning than it had been yesterday. A lazy Sunday morning. Businesses opened later, some not at all, and the church doors would be opened wide, inviting all sinners to come and repent, or to come pay their weekly deposit into the Jehovah Bank & Trust. Deposits could be made in good deeds, or by cash and check. Hell, even credit cards, if your particular bank branch was forward-thinking enough.

The café was opened, though, and Alexa caught a glimpse of that FOR RENT sign taped to the window again before she stepped inside. The line was short, but there were several people seated at the tables. She recognized a few of the same heads popping up from behind laptop screens, and she wondered if any of these people lived in those big houses and they came here to squeeze in some extra hours of work for that job Ezra assumed they hated so much. Of course they could also just be dreamers, writing that novel or that screenplay and disappearing into their own imaginations. On this, Alexa was *not* cynical. She truly hoped they were the latter. She ordered her coffee from the same barista as yesterday, and even though the woman gave Alexa the same stock greeting she probably gave hundreds of times a week, Alexa was certain there was no trace of recognition in the girl's eyes. That was good. She left a tip in the jar and then headed out.

She sipped the coffee and strolled along the sidewalk and

made the turn to head north, cutting up the same side street as yesterday. The sun had started to fade, its brilliance reduced by heavy cloud cover that was rolling in and probably meant some snow flurries were on the way. The temperature seemed to be dropping fast and Alexa shivered in her sweater and wished she'd brought her jacket along. She drank more coffee, letting it warm her throat and belly, and shook her head. *No, he might recognize the jacket.*

Today, a new day that was starting to feel like a long time ahead of just last night when that phone call had come in and that voice had hissed at her from the other end of the line, Alexa felt strong. Reinvigorated. The fear—and fear was a word she was ashamed to even use when it came to herself, a word she thought she'd long ago forgotten how to use—had all but vanished today. Now, instead of fear, she felt anger when she replayed that phone call in her head. And with that anger came that deep-seated desire to take action, not to let the fucking bad guys win, that had begun to grow in her when she was twelve and that she had nurtured and fed off and *survived* off ever since. She walked with her head up, confident. Her pace was brisk and she even waved at a couple cars that passed her by, just a normal member of society taking a leisurely Sunday stroll.

But why *were you afraid?*

The question nagged her as she reached the intersection and turned left, walking toward the direction of the school. After a lifetime of laughing in the face of fear, because after what had happened when she was just an innocent twelve-year-old girl, everything else seemed so trivial to her, why had those words last night elicited such a reaction?

The answer came easily, a gentle whisper of a reminder.

Because you were finally ready to start living again.

It was true. How typical—how very *Alexa*—was it that the moment she'd decided that she was going to stop the running, settle down and start fresh, she'd walked right into something that wanted to make her keep moving?

But she would not run. Not again.

Maybe it was the good night's sleep, maybe it was Ezra's calming and confident presence, that underlying sense that he would be a great help to her, but when Alexa had arrived back at the inn this morning, she'd known she was not turning back.

Plus, if something happened to her, at least she knew Barlow would be in good hands.

She reached the school and read the sign out front: **SILENT FALLS MIDDLE SCHOOL**. Beneath this: *Go Eagles!*

In the announcement area in the middle of the sign, Alexa learned that winter break was coming soon and she quickly flashed back to the last winter break she'd ever had. Her best friend, Maggie, had spent the night two nights in a row, something her dad had never allowed before, and he'd made them lots of hot chocolate and popcorn and they'd stayed up late and watched movies and laughed and ... *oh God, did he ever take pictures of her too?*

A sudden and strong breeze whipped in, causing the limbs of trees to crackle together as they danced. Alexa steeled herself against the chill and her thoughts and took two big gulps of coffee. Kept walking. She went another half mile and then the sign for Lil' Tony's Landscaping came into view.

The sign was made of black stone and was slim and tall and reminded Alexa of an oversized gravestone. The name of the business was carved into it, the letters painted a bright white, and while it did look elegant, the building looked less so—single-story and painted a drab gray with lots of metal and a few small windows on the front. Alexa figured this building was not so much a place to *do* business but a place to *run* a business. Curb appeal was lacking. The parking area was crushed gravel, just like Smokey's, and the right front of the building was lined with three of the same trucks Alexa had seen yesterday behind the school. Dirty white things with that yellow stripe with black lettering that suddenly brought to mind the police tape that had been secured across the entrance to Collins Park. The police tape had been a warning, telling all those who came near to keep out. The trucks were having the opposite effect. Seeing them again sparked that fire inside Alexa, and she was here to get answers.

She knew the business was open with limited hours on Sunday (another nugget of info that had been at the top of the website the night before), but as she was almost to the front door of the building with the stenciled lettering and the small silhouette of what she assumed was supposed to be a pine tree but looked suspiciously like a butt plug, she heard voices. Male voices. Coming not from inside the building but from behind it. They were faint, being carried by the wind and wrapped around with just enough juice left to reach her ears, but she heard them all the same and latched on to them like a dog catching the scent of its prey.

Around the corner she went, and the breeze intensified, sending gusts into her with enough force that it almost snatched her mostly empty coffee cup from her hand. Out back of the building, more trucks were parked, along with larger pieces of machinery whose functions Alexa did not know and did not care to know. A large metal bay door was on the left side of the building, probably to drive machinery in and out for servicing. There were large piles of various type of rock along the rear of the lot, and she imagined that, come springtime, there'd be piles of mulch as well, all ready to be hauled off to paying customers ready to make their lawns look more presentable and to try and impress and one-up their neighbors. She guessed a lot of that rock and mulch would be headed toward those big houses she and Ezra had passed on their way in, wondering if any of the café patrons were squeezing in those extra work hours to make sure landscaping fees were going to fit in next year's home budget.

On the left side of the lot, there was a row of five snow-plow blades resting alone in a neat little line. One of the trucks was parked perpendicular to the row and two men were by its side. One was leaning against the driver's door with his arms crossed. The other was leaning forward against the hood. Both wore jeans and work boots along with long-sleeved T-shirts the same yellow color as the stripe along the side of the trucks.

Both were also wearing sunglasses.

Alexa adjusted her own sunglasses, which she'd used as a final cover to keep people from noticing her bruise. The swelling around her eye was almost completely gone today, and the makeup had helped to cover the discoloration, but she didn't particularly want to be walking around all day with people thinking she might be the victim of domestic violence. She had enough to worry about as it was. It was a bad place for a bruise—everybody always assumed a punch.

The guy leaning against the hood of the truck was talking

and he sounded worried. "But I'm serious, dude, do you think we're all gonna lose our jobs now? I mean, this place was Tony's and—"

The guy who leaned against the driver's door with his arms crossed noticed Alexa coming from the side of the building then and swatted his companion's shoulder with the back of his hand. He stood up straight and Alexa watched as his face morphed into an ugly grin. Not ugly in a menacing way, just ugly, because his nose was a little crooked and his lips looked too thin for his face and his skin was pockmarked with old scars that were probably from acne and he needed to shave or at least trim whatever was growing in splotches on his cheeks and chin.

"Help you, ma'am?"

The other guy turned around from where he'd been leaning on the hood and stood up as well. He was better looking, but nothing to write home about, and younger than Ugly Grin. He eyed Alexa and didn't smile, just looked at her unimpressed, uninterested. Almost seemed annoyed, even. Probably because she'd interrupted their conversation.

"I sure hope so!" Alexa said, throwing her voice a little higher than normal. "Is one of you who I might talk to about scheduling somebody to come and plow my driveway this winter?" Behind her sunglasses, Alexa cast her eyes down to both men's hands. The younger one, Mr. Uninterested, was wearing a wedding band. Ugly Grin was not. *Shocking. Who'd want to wake up next to* that *face every morning?* "My boyfriend used to do it, but now that we're, well, now that he's decided he'd rather..." She paused, as if she were trying to gather herself. Cleared her throat. "He's not around anymore, and I'd do it myself, but it's such a *long* driveway and I'd just ... well, I'd rather pay the professionals."

She waited. She only had one real goal to accomplish here, which was to either find or figure out how to find Shit Eyes so she could have a chat with him. The camo gear he'd been wearing yesterday had covered everything else, so the eyes were all she had to go off.

The married guy who'd been leaning against the hood looked at Ugly Grin and asked, "You got this, Griff? I need to head home. Suze will throw a fit if I miss Sunday lunch at her folks' again."

Ugly Grin, aka Griff, nodded and assured Mr. Uninterested he indeed *had it*, and the guy headed off to one of the other waiting trucks and got inside and cranked the engine and drove off, throwing an uninterested wave to them as he left.

"So," Griff said after the sound of the truck's engine had faded away, "you need a good plowing, huh?"

Alexa groaned on the inside.

She gave Griff a sly grin (showing him what a real grin looked like, not the ugly excuse for one he had to offer), as if she actually appreciated the euphemism. "Bingo," she said. She looked up to the sky, examined the darkening clouds. "I know it's last-minute, but with the potential for weather now —well, I was in town and had seen your sign before and thought I'd stop by and see if I could get lucky."

Now Griff grinned again and Alexa wanted to shield her eyes from the result

(The horror! The horror!)

but she remained in character and added, "Plus, I've been thinking about adding a stone walkway leading around to my basement door, and maybe refreshing the flower bed out front." She shrugged. "I've always heard you guys are the best. That you always leave your customers ... satisfied."

Oh God, this was too easy, because Griff was now standing up straighter and puffing out his chest like he was gloating over her compliment/come-on and he actually hitched up his jeans, the key ring he had clipped to a belt loop jingling like Alexa had just pushed through the door to his tiny brain and he said, "Well, to be honest, we're pretty booked up, but ... I'm sure we can work something out. Especially since it looks like you'll be wantin' us to come back for more."

Alexa made a show of relaxing her shoulders and sighing and then said, "Oh, thank you! You're a life-saver. Like I said, it's a big driveway, and well, it's just too *big* for me to handle. You know?"

Another ugly grin. The guy was loving this, and was he *that* dumb?

Desperate, Alexa corrected herself. *The word you're looking for is desperate.*

"Not a problem," Griff said. "Happy to be of service."

Alexa smiled again and reached out and touched his arm. "Thank you again." Griff looked down at where she was touching him and she pulled her hand back and asked, "So what do you need from me? My address, phone number? Do you need me to pay you now, or will you send me an invoice?"

Griff was shaking his head through all of this. "We need to go inside and get all your info into the computer. Janis usually does all that for us, but she don't work on Sunday. It's the Lord's day, she says, but Tony used to always say that if the Lord had a lawn, he'd want us open. Anyways, I'll get you to write your info down and Janis'll work her magic tomorrow morning when she gets in. But..." He trailed off, looked up to the sky and pulled off his sunglasses, as if to study the clouds more closely, like he was a fucking meteorologist. "You're right about it maybe snowin' tonight. So how about this?" He lowered his head back down and looked at her. "Why don't you give *me* your number, and if it snows heavy tonight I'll give you a call first thing in the morning?"

Alexa didn't answer. She could only stare into the guy's eyes. Those *shit-brown* eyes.

Griff was too hot and bothered to have been expecting anything, and Alexa was fast enough that it might not have mattered even if he had been. She dropped her coffee cup and struck out with lightning quickness and grabbed Griff's hand and twisted it hard, putting her other hand on his shoulder and pulling, spinning the ugly bastard around like she was slamming a door shut. Before the guy could even cry out in surprise, she yanked up on the hand she had twisted, lurching it damn near his shoulder blade, and now Griff did cry out. It was a comically high-pitched sound, somewhere between gagging and crying.

"Ah Christ, what the *fuck!*"

Alexa pulled up even harder on that hand and used her other arm to grab a fistful of Griff's greasy hair. She yanked up and then slammed the guy's face into the hood of the truck. The noise it made sounded like thunder. "Shut up right now!" she said, leaning down and speaking close to his ear. "Say one more fucking word before I tell you to and I will snap your arm clean in two, do you understand?"

Griff apparently didn't understand, because just like Tony-the-Worst, he tossed her a "Fuck you, bitch!" before trying to press himself up off the hood of the truck. She applied only the slightest bit more pressure to his arm and he cried out again before slumping back down. But then he tried to be sneaky and kick out at her with his legs, only he was forgetting that his legs were the only thing supporting his weight, and when he lifted one and his body shifted to the side and even *more* pressure got put on his bent arm, he cursed again and then fell still, breathing hard.

"Are you done?" Alexa asked.

Griff didn't speak, just kept panting against the hood of the truck.

"Good. Now, tell me why you were taking pictures in the park yesterday."

It took a couple seconds, but even somebody as daft as Griff Ugly Grin was able to quickly put all the pieces together. "That was *you*?"

He tried to turn his head a little to look at her better, but she reached out and grabbed another fistful of hair and pressed his head flat to the hood. "You don't need to look at me, you've already got my picture, remember? Now why were you there?"

"Hey," he said, his voice sounding lighter, almost more relaxed, like now that the introductions had been made they were just a couple of friends shootin' the breeze. "I'm sorry about having to hit you, but I didn't know what else to do. You were coming after me like a crazy person. I was ... hell, I thought you might have been on drugs or something. I thought you were going to hurt *me*."

Alexa yanked his arm again and held it there. He squirmed against her weight, but this time he did not cry out, only gave off a gargled grunt. "I'm hurting you now," Alexa said. "Answer my question. Why. Were. You. There?"

Griff was quiet for a couple seconds. She let him catch his breath, let his tiny brain try to catch up. When she felt like she'd given him long enough, she said, "Griff, I'm getting impatient." She didn't pull his arm up again, but she did squeeze his hand enough to scare him into thinking she was going to.

"I don't know who they are!" he yelled. "Not exactly. But if I tell you anything, they might kill me! Don't you get it?"

"I might kill you," Alexa said, "if you don't start talking."

Griff actually laughed then. It wasn't very loud, more of a forced chuckle, but he did it and then he tried to shake his head. "No, you won't," he said.

He was right, she wasn't a killer.

With those feline reflexes, she darted the hand that had been pressing Griff's head against the hood down and grabbed the pinky finger of the hand she was twisting. She snapped the finger hard to the right, a single jerk that caused a sound like a small twig breaking.

Griff screamed and his legs buckled, which caused more pressure on his arm, which caused him to scream again. Alexa waited patiently for his fit to be over. He wasn't going anywhere, not getting out of this until he told her what she wanted to know, and the sooner he understood that, the better. She swiveled her head around, surveying the rear lot, making sure they were still alone. She didn't know how much time they'd have before somebody might come along and see them, so she needed to work faster.

"Griff, I will snap every single finger on your hand one at a time. Stop playing around. Who is *they*?"

It was the same question Ezra had asked her the night before.

"I can't believe you broke my fuckin' finger," he whimpered, defeated.

"You believe it because you can feel it. And you're about to feel a lot more if you don't start talking." She grabbed his ring finger.

"Okay!" he yelled. "But if I get offed like Tony because of this, it's on you, do you get that?"

It was a surprisingly deep thought to come from somebody like him, Alexa thought.

"I'll sleep just fine, Griff. Go on."

"Okay," he said, trying to raise his head a little. "I don't know who they are—"

She started to pull his arm up again, but he yelled, "I don't! I was just sitting here in the truck yesterday morning, goin' over my schedule and listening to the radio. Then I look up and this black SUV is driving right toward me. It pulls up next to my truck and the back window rolls down and there's just this guy, just a normal-looking white guy, looking out at me. He's wearing a nice shirt and sunglasses and he starts talking fast. Says that Tony used to work for *them*, says that *they're* the real owners of Lil' Tony's Landscaping, but now Tony's gone because he fucked up. So now they're looking for a new guy to help, and they think I'm that guy. Says there's big money for me if I can do the job."

"What job?" Alexa asked.

"That's what I asked," Griff says. "The guy just says, 'whatever we ask, whenever we ask it.' That and to 'keep my fucking mouth shut.' I was about to ask more questions, because I'm not an idiot"—*Debatable*, Alexa thought—"and because something about this guy seems like big-time bad news." *Duh*, Alexa thought. "But before I can, the guy tosses me a packet of bills through the window. A thousand bucks, just like that. Says that's half what they'll pay if I pass the first test. Says all I have to do is go into the park and take pictures of everyone who comes and goes near the crime scene." He pauses and tries to adjust his weight again. "At this point, I didn't even know that Tony was that body they'd found in the park, but I was starting to put two and two together, and that's when I got scared."

"So scared you said yes?" Alexa said.

She'd meant it sarcastically, meaning to imply that she doubted Griff was thinking of anything at all in that moment except the wad of cash in his lap. But the sarcasm was lost on him. "*Exactly*," he said. "The guy reaches out the window and hands me this camera with a big lens and says all I have to do is turn it on and start shooting. Says not to get caught, and passes me this little slip of paper with a number to call when I'm finished and somebody will come get the camera and give me the rest of my money."

Alexa doesn't need to hear the rest, because she knows how it goes. She lived it. All except the very end. "So after I found you and you ran and then you knocked me out, what did you do?"

Griff didn't even hesitate. "I drove away as fast as I could and called that number and told them what happened. They met me out at the landfill and took the camera and gave me the rest of my cash and that was it. That's the last I've seen or heard from them."

"So you told them about me and then gave them a camera with my picture on it."

"I was only doing what they *asked*." His voice was rising again, getting scared. Then it dropped back down to a whimper. "I didn't want to die."

Alexa knew she'd gotten all she was going to get out of Griff Ugly Grin. For now.

Without warning, she drove her knee into Griff's crotch. She felt his balls compress under the blow and heard him scream like a little fucking girl and she let go of his arm and he crumpled to the ground, rolling and writhing in pain. She delivered a kick to his gut and all the air *whooshed* out of him and she'd swear his eyes rolled back in his head. She reached down quick and grabbed the key ring off his belt and then kicked him one more time for good measure. He was wheezing for air and rolling around like he was on fire as she climbed into the truck with the yellow stripe on the side, found the correct key, cranked the engine, and then roared out of the parking lot to the tune of squealing tires and the sight of the man who had snapped her picture and handed it over to some very bad people rolling around on the asphalt in the rearview.

CHAPTER 17

Alexa might have speeded out of the parking lot of Lil' Tony's Landscaping, but she slowed once she'd hit the road. With Griff still writhing on the asphalt as she made the turn onto the street, she doubted he'd be chasing her very soon, if at all. That blow to his balls had been brutal, and a broken pinky finger wasn't going to help matters much. She briefly wondered if maybe she'd been too harsh with the guy, since he was apparently nothing more than a puppet (*dummy*, more like it) having his newly attached strings pulled by unknown guys in black SUVs who could throw cash around like it was tossing out the garbage. But then she remembered that voice on the other end of the phone call last night, and she remembered that there was a good chance Griff's actions had somewhat helped facilitate that call.

No, she thought. *He got exactly what he deserved.*

The self-defense classes and seminars had been constant if infrequent over the course of her life. She still remembered signing up for the first one only a couple months after she'd escaped that motel room and had been ushered off into her new life. She'd seen the flyer for a women's self-defense class at the local YMCA that was free to all who signed up. She'd scribbled a fake name on the sign-up sheet and had shown up (not even the youngest in the class, believe it or not), and that night had been the beginning of a lifelong goal of being able to keep what had happened to her in her father's home office from ever happening again. To make sure that if anybody she didn't want tried to put their hands on her again, they would quickly realize what a terrible mistake they'd made. After all these years, she was basically a melting pot of self-defense methods and martial arts. She wasn't great at any of them, if she was being completely honest with herself, but she was quick and athletic and she knew enough to be dangerous—ha ha—as the saying goes.

It had certainly been enough to handle Griff.

She'd also gone through a few basic firearms courses and could handle a handgun with enough confidence that she was sure she wouldn't hurt herself, but a person in her position in life didn't do well to be caught with a gun for a number of reasons, number one being it was hard to have a firearm registered to you when you changed names so often. Fortunately, she'd never felt the need to shoot anybody.

She wasn't a killer.

She parked the truck on a side street in town and left the keys inside. Somebody would find it eventually, and she doubted Griff was going to run off and report it stolen. It wasn't a very ego-boosting story for him. Plus, like Ezra said, folks around town were used to seeing the Lil Tony's Landscaping trucks. If it sat there too long unclaimed, somebody would make a call and all would be well again.

She walked down the sidewalk of Main Street and it was a little busier now and people were still smiling and several of them waved at her like they were all just old friends. When she passed the café, she saw the line was nearly to the door and the smell of fresh baked goods almost made her stop for another muffin, but she wanted to keep moving. The inn felt like her safe house right now, especially after committing a couple crimes, and she wanted to tell Ezra what she'd learned from Griff.

But should *you tell him?* a voice asked. She thought about Griff's story and Tony's murder and that damn phone call again and wondered if she should willingly pull somebody else into a situation ripe with the potential for more violence. Maybe the less Ezra knew, the safer he was. She shook her head. *He wants to know*, she thought, remembering last night as he'd asked her to explain it all to him, not to leave out any detail. And then this morning, his words: *Just let me know when I can help.*

He didn't strike her as the type of person who would run away if things got scary. Which, well, they already were.

She got back to the inn without being arrested, which she considered a win, and she pushed through the office door and found Ezra behind the counter. Barlow jumped up from where he'd been snoozing and trotted over to her, tail wagging and tongue hanging out, a big doggy smile.

"I'm glad you're back," Ezra said. "I was just about to order some lunch. Want some?"

"Sure, that'd be great. What are we having?"

How comfortable we've become together, she thought. *And how fast it happened.*

"Chinese?"

She nodded. "Perfect."

Ezra used his phone again to place their order and then looked up at her. "So," he said, nodding toward her, "are you going to tell me why you got all dressed up in your Sunday best?"

"Very funny," she said.

"I'm guessing it's a disguise that's not really a disguise. Am I right?"

He's good, she thought. *He's really good.*

"Bingo," she said. "I paid a visit to Lil' Tony's Landscaping, hoping I could get some info on somebody to come and plow my driveway when it snows."

Ezra nodded. "Did you have any luck?"

"Plenty. Though negotiations were a little ... terse."

Ezra's face twitched up in a quick smile but then he pushed it back down, put on his serious look again. "Tell me."

So she did. All of it. Every little detail, including the sound that Griff's finger had made when she'd snapped it like a twig. When she was finished, Ezra stared at her but was quiet for a long time, and she'd grown to understand this meant he was thinking, processing her words, running them through whatever algorithm lived in his head. "That's very interesting," he said, after a pause so long that Alexa went and sat in one of the guest chairs along the wall.

"I thought so too," Alexa said. "Looks like I might have poked some sort of hornet's nest, yeah?"

Ezra looked at her again, and she saw something akin to worry there.

"What?" she asked. "What's wrong?"

He cleared his throat and crossed his arms and leaned

against the wall. "I found out what they did to Tony. How they killed him, I mean. It's ... well, it's bad."

Alexa didn't hesitate. "Tell me."

ALEXA HAD WALKED around the counter to sit in the recliner and Barlow had curled up at her feet. Ezra leaned against the counter, arms crossed.

"She thought they were Halloween decorations," he said. "The woman who found Tony. She was jogging and when she got to the baseball field and saw it, she said her first thought was maybe some kids were playing a prank."

Alexa quickly threw up her hands. "Wait. How do you know this? Where did you get this information? Was it in the paper?"

Ezra shook his head. "No, but it might be. Tomorrow, maybe. Sheriff asked the *Silent Falls Bulletin* to hold off on printing until they could"—he made air quotes—"'try to get a few more questions answered.'"

Alexa nodded. "So how did *you* find out? You got a secret source at the newspaper or something? A journalist who"—now she made her own set of air quotes—"'*doesn't* owe you a favor'?"

"Yes," Ezra said. "I do."

Alexa said nothing. Just raised her eyebrows and then nodded for him to continue.

"Tony wasn't killed in the park," Ezra said. "They killed him somewhere else and then brought all the pieces to the ball field later."

Alexa felt her stomach do a small flip-flop at the word *pieces*. She swallowed and asked, "How do they know that? That he was killed somewhere else."

"Because there was no trace of fire anywhere at the park, and Tony's head was completely burnt to a crisp. It was sitting on home plate. And there wasn't enough blood for everything else to have happened there either."

Again, Alexa said nothing. Waited.

"His torso, basically everything between the severed neck and the waist, was on the pitcher's mound, naked. His arms and legs had been hacked off and were laid out in a circle around it."

Alexa remembered the two deputies who'd been stationed at the ball field yesterday, the ones that Griff had been snapping shots of, and how the sheriff had asked them if the cleanup crew was finished. *Christ, what a job that must have been.*

She thought about all the bad thoughts she'd had about Tony-the-Worst aka Anthony Romano aka Lil' Tony, and felt a twinge of guilt. Sure, the guy had been cocky and had been an asshole and clearly had needed to take How to Talk Respectfully to Women 101, but did anybody deserve to die the way he had? She had a morbid question pop into her mind: Had he been alive while they sawed off his arms and legs? His head?

She thought about Griff's story again, what the guy in the black SUV had said to him about Tony. How Tony had used to work for them, and now he was gone because he'd fucked up. *What were you into, Tony? And what did you do for this to be the price you had to pay?*

Ezra waited patiently while her mind hopped from one

thought to another. She landed on the mental picture she'd created of the guy's naked torso on the pitcher's mound with all his limbs spread out around him. Deliberate. A macabre art installation meant to be seen ... and interpreted. "Somebody was trying to send a message," Alexa said. "Either that or this town is a lot more boring than I thought and people have got some real interesting ways to pass the time."

It was a lame joke, and it fell as flat as it felt. Ezra's face stayed passive. His arms stayed crossed. "It was a message. Well, maybe more of a calling card or a signature. They wanted people to recognize their work. They wanted the sheriff's office to know who'd done it."

"Why?"

"Because they know that nobody will come after them, and they want to keep it that way."

Alexa shook her head. "I don't understand." Though part of her thought she might, but she wanted to hear it from him.

"These types of killings, with the burnt head and the dismembered bodies arranged out in public, it's something that's popped up all over the state for decades. A little online research will give you a hard and fast confirmation ... but be aware, the pictures you might find aren't exactly kid-friendly."

"So who are they?" Alexa asked. "A gang?"

She'd spent lots of time in big cities where it was easy to blend in, disappear into the hustle and bustle. Places where you could walk the streets and nobody ever really looked at anybody, never remembered faces. You could survive in places like that completely under the radar, everything you'd ever need easily at your disposal—legal or not. She'd seen and heard about her share of gang-related violence in these places. Decades-old feuds that showed no signs of slowing, new members recruited every day. New people killed every day.

A lot of people lived in ignorance of just how scary a place America could be. Alexa Shifflett understood this a lot better than most.

Ezra shook his head. "No," he said. "It's the Abatelli family. They're an organized crime syndicate in Virginia."

Alexa laughed without meaning to, then quickly covered her mouth. "Sorry," she said. "Are you trying to tell me that the *mafia* killed Tony and then threatened me to back off? Is the mafia even a thing still?"

Serious as a heart attack, Ezra said, "Mafia, mob, underworld, the family, it's all the same. Bad news, no matter what you call it. And they're a lot more sophisticated these days than what you might be imagining from those old movies. Technology has changed the game for everybody."

"And they're here, in Silent Falls?"

"No, probably not, at least not directly. They must do work here, have business, if you will. Tony's evidence of that. But they're most likely running things from East River, and I'm sure the big guns are in Roanoke, Richmond, all places within an hour or two."

Alexa saw more puzzle pieces click into place in her mind, but along with the clearer picture that was forming came more questions—ones that might have answers she didn't want to hear.

"Your source," she said. "At the newspaper. You said the paper was holding off on printing anything until the sheriff's office had a few more questions answered."

"Correct."

"So what you're really saying is that the sheriff's office is waiting to find out just how they're going to spin this."

"Correct. At least that's my assumption."

"So the sheriff knows Tony was killed by the mob."

"In all likelihood, yes."

Which would explain why the man had not seemed very interested in Alexa during their encounter behind the school. Even if Colin Wanamaker *had* brought Alexa to the attention of the department as a possible suspect, the sheriff (or at least *somebody* there that was in the know) would have quickly squashed it.

This also meant, thankfully, that Colin Wanamaker was innocent in this, it seemed. Just a young cop trying to do the right thing. So wet behind the ears he didn't know what Tony's murder scene had signified. Come to think of it, it now seemed unlikely that the poor guy had even been given any of the info other than the name of the victim when he'd come to talk to Alexa. Because if he'd known about what had really been found in Collins Park, he might not have been so eager to accept Alexa as the culprit. She'd done her share of bad things over the years, but sawing off limbs and chopping off heads were not among them. For all Alexa knew, maybe the cover-up in this was so big that even some of the deputies didn't know the true nature of Tony's death. Hell, maybe most of them. But something like this ... well, people talk. And...

And the jogger saw it, and Ezra's journalist friend knows and ... will they print this?

"Are they really just going to cover this up?" Alexa asked, feeling that part inside of her that could so easily hate police officers begin to grow again, to overtake that burning ember that was trying to blind the darkness.

Ezra leaned his head side to side. "Cover up? I mean, no, not really. They can't just act like his murder never happened. But they can certainly say they're investigating it when they really aren't. They can wait a while and then say all the leads have dried up and there's not enough evidence and the case will just go unsolved."

"But *why*?" Alexa asked, irritated and incredulous and hating how whiny the question had sounded.

"The Abatellis haven't survived as long as they have without being smart. I'm sure they have allies, have paid the right people, offered protection to the right people." He paused. Looked like he didn't want to say the next part but did anyway. "Done favors for the right people. Bottom line, there's agreements in place. Agreements that keep everybody's world going round and round, and I doubt very seriously that Tony Romano's death is all of a sudden going to change any of that."

Alexa hated how true everything he was saying was. It wasn't a new story for the world. It was only new for her now because she was actively a part of it. Part of her was somewhat relieved, because she knew now that she wasn't a serious suspect in this case—*Thank you for your ignorance, Deputy Wanamaker. Way to ruin my weekend.* But another part of her was angry, because all it had taken was a young deputy's ignorance to cause her to go flying off the handle and sticking her nose where it had no business being and now *she* was the one getting threatened by the mob.

What am I supposed to do now? Walk away, turn a blind eye, just like the sheriff's office? Do I accept that some things are just too big and too powerful? Can I even do that now?

"I don't know," Ezra said, snapping her out of her trance.

"What?"

He cleared his throat. "You asked, 'What am I supposed to do now?' I'm telling you I don't know."

"Oh," Alexa said, not realizing she'd spoken out loud.

"Only you know the answer to that," Ezra added.

CHAPTER 18

When the Chinese food arrived, Alexa insisted on paying, but Ezra said he'd already taken care of it. She cursed him, causing the delivery driver to blush, and then asked if Ezra would mind terribly if she ate her lunch alone in her room.

"I'm not trying to be rude, but it's been an interesting day. Well, an interesting couple of days. I'd just like some quiet."

Ezra said of course that was fine and pulled her food from the bag and handed it to her, Barlow sniffing with his eyes locked on to the food containers. She thanked him, and as she reached the door he called after her. "Hey, don't forget this!"

She spun around and just managed to reach up and grab the fortune cookie he'd thrown to her—slightly harder than necessary. He winked. She rolled her eyes and pushed out the door.

Back in her room—which had been visited by housekeeping at some point since she'd left, maybe around the same time she was pulverizing Griff's testicles—she kicked off her boots and clothes she'd been wearing and swapped them for the sweatpants and the baggy T-shirt she'd worn that morning. The first station she found on the television was playing an older Jim Carrey film, and she sat cross-legged on the bed with her back against the stack of pillows propped against the headboard and started to eat, tried to let her mind drift away for a bit and enjoy the food and laugh at the stupid antics on the screen and just take a breath.

It worked, for a while. The food was very good and she'd been hungry and had to force herself to take her time, to savor the meal instead of wolfing it down like an animal. Barlow might have been offended by this sentiment, but he was too busy sitting next to her and watching her every bite and drooling like he hadn't eaten in days. But eventually she finished the food and Barlow gave up and fell asleep and the movie ended and she found herself using the remote to click the television off. The room was quiet then. Barlow snoring softly on the bed next to her and a car door closing somewhere out in the parking lot. In the new stillness, she lay back and did her best Ezra impression, crossing her arms over her chest. She closed her eyes and took a few deep breaths and slipped into a state of mindfulness. Her brain was spinning up again, her thoughts preparing to mobilize, and she wanted to make sure she kept them in order.

So much had changed, and she needed to unpack it all. Figure out what the next move for Alexa Shifflett was going to be.

"Okay, Shiffy," she said to herself. "Think it through."

She'd arrived in Silent Falls with that warm feeling, her instinct telling her this was the place. She'd finally found her new home—the first home she'd had since she was twelve.

Clara had been wonderful and Ezra was kind and the town was as small and perfect as could be for the type of life Alexa had been imagining she'd live.

But then there'd been that awful knock on her door, revealing an awful image on the other side: a police officer questioning her about a murder. The fantasy of a new life had evaporated in that instant. She'd felt sick to her stomach, had wanted to grab her bag and call for Barlow and jump in the Oldsmobile and hit the road. Leave the town and all its accusations behind.

But she hadn't. She *couldn't.* Because she'd had no car in that moment. So instead, she'd let her anger fester, and then she'd turned that anger into action.

And all you managed to do was learn that you were poking around in the mafia's business and now they're threatening to kill you if you don't back off.

She liked her head exactly where it was, and she'd been never much for baseball or fancy art exhibits.

She could have backed off after that phone call had come in, but she hadn't. Because she hadn't *known.* This morning when she'd woken up in Ezra's farmhouse with her new plan of finding the guy who'd snapped her picture in the trees at Collins Park, thinking he might lead her to some real answers about Tony's murder and thus potentially helping to clear her name, she hadn't known she was stepping into the ring with the *fucking Abatelli family.* She hadn't even known they'd existed. Her temper and her stubbornness had often been a weakness in her life. They'd gotten her into way more trouble than was necessary, which was something she always understood but often failed to remember in the moment.

She'd gone after Griff, which she now realized was probably a mistake. But what's done is done, and who was he, really? Just a mule, a newly minted yet disposable coin in the Abatelli family currency. Plus, she'd heard the fear in his voice, the protests he'd given, begging her not to make him tell her what he knew. He was afraid of these people, and now she guessed she understood why. She figured Griff's fear would keep him from calling his puppet masters and saying anything at all about her little assault.

Because Tony fucked up and now he's gone.

But did any of this really matter to her? Did it *pertain* to her? Was it any of her damn business?

She'd thought it was, in the beginning when Deputy Wanamaker had come knocking. But now ... not so much. The police didn't care about her and the Abatelli family probably didn't either, as long as she stopped digging, because who was *she* really? Nobody, an insignificant bump in the road. She wasn't a threat. It wasn't like she could take down the entire mafia. Even she wasn't *that* delusional. If she convinced herself that the thing with Griff in the back lot of Lil' Tony's Landscaping was the end, the period on the last sentence in her story with all this, then, yes, her involvement was over. She wouldn't be involved anymore in Tony's murder case—not that she'd ever been in the first place, now that she knew Wanamaker had been in the dark—which meant she could just walk away.

But what did that mean, walk away?

Walk away from the situation, or leave town? Would she get in the Oldsmobile and drive away just like she'd felt like doing yesterday morning? The old part of her, the voice she was trying harder to ignore, said to do it. Jump in and hit the road. Nothin' for ya here, baby.

But...

But that glowing ember, that warmth. She could feel it growing, getting stronger. She could keep her eyes closed and slow her breathing and swear she could hear its heart beating.

But, no, that was just her own heart. And that glowing ember, that was her instinct.

She opened her eyes and sighed and rolled onto her side, thinking about her car parked out front and how easy it would be to go, to find another town, another beginning. In that moment, she found herself desperately wanting to call Lance, to ask him what *he* thought she should do. She was just about to reach for her cell phone when something made a crackling sound and dug into her hip. She slid over and reached down and found that she'd rolled over onto the fortune cookie that Ezra had tossed her. She'd forgotten all about it.

She eyed it, almost suspiciously, then ripped open the packaging and broke the cookie apart. Pulled the little tag of paper out and unfolded it. Read it.

Instinct is ignored but never lost. Listen, and be set free.

"Motherfucker...," Alexa said, then burst into a fit of laughter. Barlow jumped up and she tossed him part of the cookie, and when she got her laughter under control, she took his head in her hands and said, "Looks like we're staying, boy. What do you think about that?"

Barlow's eyes seemed to say that would be just fine with him, as long as she tossed him the other half of that cookie.

∾

SOMETHING ABOUT HAVING MADE the decision to stay was lifting Alexa's spirits, making her feel the same way you'd feel after waiting twenty-four hours for a doctor's test results and then finally getting the phone call telling you everything was completely fine. It was a freeing emotion, like letting out a great breath you'd been holding and then filling your lungs with the sweetest of air. She'd thought it all through and was confident in her outcome.

She was not a suspect of the police, and if she left Tony's murder alone and stopped inserting herself (albeit accidentally) into the Abatelli family's dealings, she was positive that Silent Falls and she would have a very fruitful future together. She was excited, for the first time in as long as she could remember, at the prospect of what tomorrow would hold. And the day after that, and the day after that. She had no idea what she would do with those days, but at least now she knew where she'd be spending them. And ... she'd made a friend who would probably help her along the way.

She picked up the cordless phone on the nightstand and scanned the laminated directory for the right button to press. Ezra answered the phone on the second ring.

"I was just about to call you," he said. "But I thought you might be napping or something."

"Not really," Alexa said. "I dozed off a bit, but I was mostly just thinking."

"About?"

"You first," Alexa said.

"You were thinking about me first?"

"No. But way to be modest."

"What?"

Alexa sighed. She much preferred in-person conversations. A lot could be lost over the phone line. "I meant, tell me why you were calling me first, and then I'll tell you what I was thinking about."

"Ah, okay. I was ... well ..." He paused, and Alexa could see him in her mind, the phone tucked between his neck and shoulder while he leaned against the counter and crossed his arms and flexed his jaw while he contemplated the words he would say next. "Can you just come up here, whenever you get a free moment? I'd rather show you."

"Ezra?"

"Yes?"

"My entire life is a free moment. Barlow and I are on the way."

They hung up the phone and Alexa pulled on her boots and leashed Barlow. She led him to a grassy spot by the road so he could use the facilities and then they entered the office. Ezra had music playing from the computer on the counter, something instrumental that Alexa thought she recognized as being from a science fiction film she'd seen a few years ago. He turned it down when he greeted them.

"Welcome back," he said. "How was the food?"

"Really good. Thanks again," Alexa said. "And if you don't let me buy our next meal I'm leaving this place a bad review on Yelp and TripAdvisor."

Ezra grinned and raised his hands in surrender. "Deal."

Barlow walked around the counter and balled up behind the recliner in the corner, having already apparently found his favorite nap spot.

"So what's up?" she asked.

Ezra didn't hesitate, as if now that they were face-to-face again, no longer separated by that mysterious dead zone of the phone line, his nerve had returned. "When we talked last night, you mentioned you might have a belief in, I guess, sort of predetermined outcomes. Like karma, or destiny, or fate." *Or the Universe?* Alexa thought.

"Is that true?" Ezra asked.

"I do," she said. "But only recently. When I was younger I believed, but then for a long time I didn't believe in anything at all. I thought that we were all in this world alone and, well" —she shrugged—"that nothing we did mattered."

Ezra nodded. "But you changed."

"I did." She remembered how, when she'd asked Ezra if what she'd told him last night had made any sense, his face had very turned serious, and he'd answered that it did. More than she would know.

"Because of those friends you met?" he asked.

Alexa nodded.

Ezra reached out and slid a small slip of paper across the counter toward her. She recognized what it was instantly, because she'd only just recently held one exactly like it. It was his fortune that he must have pulled from his own cookie. Alexa didn't touch it but looked down and read the words printed there.

Cherish your new friends.

Alexa felt a chill run through her, and she couldn't suppress a shiver.

"Spooky, right?" Ezra said. He acted like he was making a joke, but she knew he was only trying to hide some of his own emotion.

Alexa cleared her throat and followed up with a defensive joke of her own. "It's plural," she said. "So who's the second friend? Should I be jealous?"

Ezra looked at her with eyes that were asking *You really don't know?*, and when she only stared in return, he simply raised his hand out and pointed behind him to the corner. The place where Barlow was curled up and resting. "Man's best friend," he said.

This time, Alexa's arms broke out in gooseflesh and another chill shook her.

Neither of them seemed to know what to say after that. The room stayed silent while the tiny slip of paper with the tiny words that carried big meaning sat on the counter between them. Alexa thought that the paper seemed to signify that what she'd been feeling about Ezra—that notion that there *was* a connection linking them—was real, and not just a fantasy she was perpetuating in her head. Her own slip of paper, the fortune she currently had tucked away in the pocket of her sweatpants, coupled with Ezra's to unlock the unspoken truth. Or maybe to validate it.

Because we both know, she thought. *We both know there's something here.*

Alexa was about to reach into her pocket and pull her slip of paper out and line it up neatly next to Ezra's on the counter. Was going to say something witty as Ezra read it in an attempt to help lighten the thick air of importance that seemed to add weight to the room's atmosphere.

But she never got that far. Because movement outside the office window caused both of them to turn their heads, and they saw the police cruiser speed into the parking lot and park crooked outside the door. The driver's door was flung open and Colin Wanamaker jumped out, not bothering to close the door behind him before he stormed up to the office and rushed inside.

Barlow jumped up at the noise and let off a defensive bark, but Ezra was able to reach down and gently grab him before the dog could round the counter. Deputy Wanamaker's eyes were tainted with worry and rage. His face was red and Alexa thought she saw the traces of dried tears on his cheeks. He looked her directly in the eyes and said, "You need to tell me exactly who the hell you are."

.

CHAPTER 19

It was Ezra who answered first.

"Deputy, what exactly is the problem here?"

Colin Wanamaker eyed him but said nothing, let his gaze find Alexa again and he stared daggers into her. "Answer me."

Alexa's heart was beating fast, but not because of fear. It was thumping because of anger. Less than two minutes ago she'd been awash with such a sense of relief, a sense of *happiness* that she was going to be able to put everything behind her and start new. And now once again, before she'd even had an opportunity to relish that feeling, here was the same sheriff's deputy that had started all her problems to begin with, trying to ruin her day again.

Ezra had let Barlow go after the dog had settled down, and now he trotted next to Alexa and sat at her side, playing the role of guard dog. He stared his own daggers back at Wanamaker, breathing heavy.

Be nice, the wary voice in Alexa's head whispered. *He's upset, but you didn't do anything.*

Except assault Griff and steal his truck.

No, that idiot wouldn't report you. Not to the mob and certainly not to the local police.

Then why is Colin here?

"Deputy, you know who I am," Alexa said. "We met just yesterday morning."

"Don't play dumb with me, okay?"

"Fine."

This answer seemed to shock Wanamaker. Like he'd gotten himself all prepared for a confrontation and now didn't know how to react. "What do you mean?" he asked.

"I won't play dumb," Alexa said. "If you remember our conversation from yesterday morning, you'll recall that I'm pretty much a straight shooter. I'm allergic to bullshit, you might say. So, what is it you're really asking me here?"

She watched as some of the adrenaline began to drain from the man. He'd obviously gotten very worked up over something that had caused him to speed over her like a bat out of hell and come stomping inside like a man intent on violence, but now that he was here, facing her, and with Ezra watching from the opposite side of the counter, he was realizing he might have played this all wrong. But to his credit, when he spoke again he kept his voice strong, full of authority.

"What's your relationship with Clara Wanamaker?"

Oh no.

Alexa's heart kicked up even faster. The cynical part of her, the part that had guided her for so many years and had helped her fight her way through so many things, was already putting the pieces together, showing her the image it was building and pointing at it and saying *Look what you did ... this is all your fault.*

She took a breath to calm herself. The way Colin had phrased his question, it was apparent he didn't know that Alexa knew that Clara was his sister. Alexa wanted to change that, wanted to appeal to his more personal side. Thought maybe if she was sympathetic to whatever he was about to say that this would go more smoothly for everyone.

"You mean your sister?" she asked. "We met at Smokey's and we've chatted a few times. She's very sweet." Then, to throw more of her cards on the table, she added, "And it's okay, Deputy. I know she's the reason you came by here yesterday asking me about Tony. I'm not upset about that." *(Yes, I am.)* "You were only doing your job." *(Because you're the new guy and don't know shit about the real world yet)*.

If Colin thought his secret about Clara being his sister was somehow giving him an edge in the conversation, it all went right out the window. Alexa saw it all play out on his face, how it had gone from hardened (as hard as that baby face could be) to crestfallen as the words had hit him. This new look brought attention back to those traces of dried tears on his face, and as Colin spoke again, he appeared completely deflated, new tears forming on the brim of his eyes.

"Clara's in the hospital," he said, voice cracking. He caught himself, though, managed to clear his throat and quickly wiped his eyes and said, "She's refusing to talk to anybody but you."

And there it was. The truth that Alexa had known was coming.

This is all your fault.

~

EZRA HAD OFFERED to join them, but Alexa had shot him down. She didn't want it to appear to Colin that she needed anybody to come along with her. She was perfectly capable of handling this on her own. She'd rather Ezra stay behind to hang out with Barlow. Plus, she was confident that if she hadn't returned to the inn within an hour or two, Ezra would start digging on his own, trying to track her down and find out what happened. It didn't need to be said.

The fortune cookies had said it all.

She didn't ask but told Colin that she would follow him to the hospital in her own car. He offered (more like strongly suggested) to give her a lift himself, but fuck that. Alexa calmly and politely declined, stating that unless she was under arrest, she would drive herself, if he would only kindly lead the way. She said it all with a smile that she hoped did not seem too out of the moment—sympathy, remember?— but was prepared to firmly stand her ground and argue if needed. But it wasn't needed. Colin just stared at her for a beat and then nodded his head and got into his cruiser.

They drove.

Back into town and then a left turn and into residential streets cluttered with modest houses. A few yards had small signs perched near the street that read PROULDY MAIN-TAINED BY LIL' TONY'S LANDSCAPING, and Alexa felt her stomach roll.

Fucking Tony ... fucking Griff.

Why couldn't she have rolled into town and dinner at Smokey's one single day later? That was all it would have taken to avoid all of this. Her timing had been terrible.

Or maybe not.

It was Lance's voice she heard speak this thought.

Then it was Ezra's. *"When we talked last night, you mentioned you might have a belief in, I guess, sort of predetermined outcomes. Like karma, or destiny, or fate."*

Alexa sighed. She didn't have the mental bandwidth to focus on any of that right now. All she could think about was Clara Wanamaker and what a sweet and nice young woman she was. Smart, too. Capable of anything. And now she was in the hospital.

"She called me first," Colin had said in the inn's office. "Told me somebody had hurt her. I'm the one who called the ambulance. When I asked her what happened, she only told me she needed to talk to you. That she wouldn't say a word more to anyone until then." He'd gotten angry again then, and Alexa couldn't blame him. She'd be angry too, if the roles had been reversed. Colin's face had gotten red and he'd just looked at her for a moment or two and then shaken his head and sighed and said, "So let's go."

"Where was she?" Alexa asked before she'd moved to head toward the door and follow Colin out of the inn's office.

The deputy had stopped and turned, and at first Alexa had thought his anger was going to win out and he would respond with something snarky, like "What do you care?" But instead, he was honest. "She called me from the middle school. She said that's where they dumped her."

The words *dumped her* had sent Alexa's own adrenaline spiking. *That poor girl. Whatever happened, she didn't deserve it.*

The hospital was small, like the town, and built on the corner of two residential streets. A two-story building with a dark black parking lot sitting on a three- or four-acre square of land and surrounded by homes. The hospital's entrances were spruced up with small trees and bushes and flower beds that probably bloomed into color in the spring, trying to make an otherwise grim place appear welcoming, and Alexa would bet the Oldsmobile that Lil' Tony's Landscaping was responsible for the upkeep.

Colin pulled his cruiser under the EMERGENCY overhang and parked and got out. Alexa found a regular parking spot nearby and then got out and headed toward him. They walked through the automatic doors of the emergency room waiting area, and Colin smiled and greeted a woman at the intake desk. She pushed a button under her desk, and another set of doors to their left *whooshed* open and Colin headed through them. Alexa followed, trying not to make eye contact with anybody. She could already hear their hushed chatter in her mind, all the nurses and waiting room patrons wondering who she was and why she was with the police officer. She wished she'd still been wearing her other clothes— her Sunday best, as Ezra had put it—instead of the sweatpants and T-shirt.

The emergency room was slow and quiet. It smelled of antiseptic and all those other hospital smells, sterile things that somehow made your skin crawl, and the soundtrack was all soft voices and the clicking of keyboards and the random beeping of various machines. An overhead speaker boomed to life and paged a Dr. Rhodes to please come to the second-floor nurses' station. Clara Wanamaker was in the exam area in the back left of the room. The curtain was half-pulled open, and Alexa could see the girl's sneakers dangling from the bed. Colin stepped into the exam area and pulled the sheet open wider so Alexa could join them.

When Alexa saw Clara, her heart dropped to her gut.

The girl's right eye was purple and swollen, and there was

a yellow bruise across the bridge of her nose. A few bits of dried blood were still visible just beneath her nostrils. She was fully dressed in her uniform from Smokey's, which Alexa considered to be a good sign, hopefully meaning she was seeing the extent of the damage done. But there was something else ... the pinky finger on Clara's right hand was in a metal splint and taped to her ring finger. The swollen eye and the bruised nose looked worse, but it was the finger that Alexa couldn't look away from.

"Okay," Colin said, not waiting around for introductions or pleasantries. "She's here. Now talk."

It was almost funny, really. He wasn't speaking like a cop demanding answers. No, there was a subtle difference, one that most people might miss if they didn't know the full situation. He was speaking like a big brother, one very irritated with his younger sibling. If Clara didn't start talking soon, Alexa had a feeling Colin might stoop so low as to say "I'm going to tell Mom!"

"Not to you," Clara said. "I'm only talking to her. You need to leave." Her voice was flat. She sounded tired. She hadn't yet met Alexa's eyes. She just looked down at her sneakers.

"No way," Colin said.

"It's what they said, *Colin*." That little sister voice. "They said to only talk to her, that if I ... if I told anybody else what happened, they'd..." She never finished speaking, but she might as well have.

Alexa saw Colin's fists ball up and then relax, ball up and then relax, as he tried to stay calm. "Clara, you can trust me. I'm your brother. Whatever you say here ... if after you're done you still don't want anybody else to know what happened, I promise I won't say anything to anyone."

That's a tall order for an officer of the law, Alexa thought, but she said nothing. This was between the two of them, not her.

"Oh, really?" Clara snapped. "You sure didn't wait long to go and accuse her of murdering Tony after I told you how she shot him down when he hit on her."

Colin didn't know what to say to that.

"Hell, Colin. Now that I think about it, this is probably all *your* fault." Clara's voice was rising now, and Alexa reached out and quickly slid the curtain closed, like that would do any good. "In fact," Clara continued, "why don't you just go ahead and get the fu—"

"Clara?" Alexa reached out and laid a gentle hand on the girl's arm.

The girl did not pull away. Only met Alexa's eyes with her own for the first time.

"It's okay. It's not your brother's fault. He only wants to protect you." Alexa said. "I wish I'd had a brother like him growing up. Maybe things would have turned out differently for me."

She wasn't going to elaborate any more on that subject because that wasn't why they were all here, but she saw Clara's body relax a little, some of the tension releasing. The girl sighed and looked back to her brother.

"I mean it, Colin. Not one word to anybody."

"Not a word," Colin said, too quickly.

"I don't care if it gets you employee of the quarter or some shit, either. One word and I'll never forgive you. Hell, you might never forgive yourself. Got it?"

"Jesus, Clara, I got it."

Clara stared at him then, and something that could only happen between siblings must have happened, because

Alexa watched as both of their faces seemed to be hit with a mutual understanding, a realization that they were now in the same place, playing on the same field. It was trust.

Clara started talking.

"I know this is going to sound very *classic victim* or whatever, but it's true—everything just happened so *fast*."

Alexa and Colin said nothing. Let her go at her own pace.

"I had just started my break. I was getting thirty minutes before the dinner shift. Sunday nights are big, because of NFL games. A lot of us park around back on the weekends, to keep the lot clear, so I had just stepped outside and the first thing I noticed was a black SUV parked just to the right, over where we drive through from the front, around the side of the building. But before I could really get a *good* look, somebody threw a black bag over my head and punched me in the stomach and then picked me up. All the air had gotten knocked out of me, so I couldn't even scream. I tried to fight back, but I couldn't breathe and whoever had me was strong. I tried pounding on them a little, but it was all solid muscle, you know? It was pointless."

There was an opened can of Pepsi on the small table next to the bed and Clara reached for it. Took a long sip from the straw sticking out the top. "Sorry," she said. "Throat was dry. I think it's the air in here. I hate hospitals, by the way."

"Don't we all," Alexa said.

"Anyway, they threw me into the SUV and somebody else grabbed me and zip-tied my hands together. Then my ankles. I was just starting to get my breath back, and when I started to yell, somebody punched me in the face and it felt like my head had exploded and all the fight went out of me. I could feel the blood dripping down over my lips. A hand clamped over my mouth and somebody told me to—

(Shut up!)

shut up or nobody would ever see me again. I think that part was meant to give me a little bit of hope. Like maybe everything that was happening would all work out in the end as long as I played their game." She shrugged. "Either way, I shut up."

Colin didn't know what to do with his hands. He tried his pockets, then tried crossing his arms, and then clasped them in front of him while he leaned against the wall. His shiny shoes squeaked and the items on his belt jingled a bit with each movement. It was unnerving.

"We didn't drive for long," Clara said. "Just a couple of minutes. But then we stopped and I heard the sound of a door opening. Like, not a car door or anything, but something bigger, maybe metal or on a chain. It was motorized. When the noise stopped, we drove forward again and then stopped and then that noise came on and I knew the door was closing and that's when I really got scared.

"Whoever was driving shut the engine off and then everything seemed really quiet. Too quiet, like they say in the movies." She laughed, but Alexa could see the fear in the girl's eyes, the pain, as she relived these moments in her head, the wounds still fresh. Both literally *and* metaphorically. "Then that guy's voice, the one that told me to shut up. They were right next to me in the back seat. 'You should choose your friends more wisely,' they said. 'You could have avoided all this.'"

Alexa felt a coldness flush through her.

"Then they opened one of the car doors and dragged me

out. Told me to stand up and not move, like I could go anywhere with my ankles cuffed. I tried to tell where we were, but inside that hood was like staring into nothing. But I could smell, and it smelled like gas and oil. So I thought maybe it was a mechanic shop. But before I could think much more about it, that voice called out again. 'Okay, here's your shot,' they said to somebody else. 'Send the message, just like we talked about. Do this, and we know we can trust you.'

"I heard footsteps coming closer, and then somebody grabbed my wrists and pulled my hands up. Held them that way. Whoever else was there must have hesitated too long because the voice said, 'I'm running out of patience,' and then another voice said, 'Okay, okay!' and then somebody grabbed my pinky finger. They snapped it to the right and I heard it crack and I tried to scream but that hand clapped over my mouth again. Everything went dark—like, dark *inside* my head, you know?—and I must have fainted because next thing I knew I was back in a car and we were moving again. Then we stopped and the door opened and somebody dragged me out again and cut my hands and legs free and they grabbed my head and pulled it close to theirs. 'Tell Alexa we're even now, but this is her last warning. If you speak a word about what happened today to anybody but her, they're going to find *you* in the park next.'"

A nurse poked her head in, but when she saw the look on all three of their faces she must have decided that whatever she'd come for could wait, because she vanished with a quick apology for interrupting.

"They told me to count to a hundred before I took the hood off," Clara said, "and I did. It felt stupid, standing there and just counting, especially after I'd heard them drive away, but my head was still swimming and my finger was on fire and honestly, focusing on the counting might have been the only thing that kept me from puking.

"When I finished counting, I pulled off the hood and I was in the back parking lot of the middle school." She looked at Colin. "You were the only person I could think to call, even before 911. I'm sorry if that put you in a weird position."

Colin shook his head and moved to sit on the bed next to his sister. He put his arm around her and she leaned her head into his shoulder and he said, "Weird position? Are you kidding me? You're my baby sis. You've been pissing me off since the day you were born—why stop now?"

The two of them shared a quiet laugh together, and Alexa suddenly felt like she was the one intruding and wanted to go join the nurse.

Clara looked up and asked Alexa, "What did they mean, about being even now?"

Keeping with the pattern of trying to be more honest in her new life, especially with good people, Alexa said, "I did something stupid and pissed off some bad people. They took it out on you. I'm so, so sorry."

"Who? How? Does it have to do with the people who killed Tony?" asked Clara, who had perked up, like suddenly the prospect of some bigger picture was exciting her.

Colin shot Alexa a look.

"Why don't we get out of here?" Alexa said. "I'll wait for you two outside."

She pulled the curtain open and then walked out of the emergency room and the waiting area and leaned against a brick pillar that was supporting the entrance overhang outside. It was almost full dark now, and the yellowish lights of the parking lot hummed.

Fuck!

She cursed herself. Because she'd been wrong. Griff, that pathetic bastard, *had* squealed on her. The broken pinky was all the evidence Alexa had needed on that front. A tit-for-tat situation. Message received. Plus, Clara had mentioned the sound of a big metal door on a motor, the smell of gas and oil. It hadn't been a mechanic's shop, it had been the big bay door out back of Lil' Tony's Landscaping—Alexa would bet her life on it.

A few minutes later, Clara and Colin came out the electronic emergency room doors, and Alexa wondered just what in the hell she was going to do now.

Tell Alexa we're even now, that voice had told Clara.

Alexa Shifflett did not play to be even.

She played to win.

CHAPTER 20

Alexa could only guess as to what sort of conversation had happened between Clara and Colin after she'd left them alone in the emergency room, but from the look on Colin's face as the two of them emerged from the electronic doors, she'd bet money that it hadn't gone exactly as smoothly as the brother had planned. The siblings walked past Colin's police cruiser and headed toward her. Alexa was hugging herself and rubbing her bare arms for warmth. With the night sky had come the cold, the first real cold, it seemed, since she'd arrived in Silent Falls. She wished she'd at least remembered to grab her jacket from Ezra's truck before she and Colin had left for the hospital, but in that moment all she'd been able to think about was Clara, imagining all the terrible things that might have happened to the girl.

Alexa wasn't sure how this particular scene was going to play out. She knew Colin was still wary of her—both as a big brother and as a sheriff's deputy—and Clara, despite her bruises and broken finger, almost seemed to be walking with a bit of a pep to her step, her eyes vastly more alive and alert than they'd been when Alexa had first seen the girl sitting on that exam area hospital bed and staring down at her dangling sneakers.

She feels better now that she's talked about it, Alexa thought. *And she's alive ... that part is now sinking in.*

Alexa knew that feeling, that euphoric rush that can sometimes follow those terrifying moments where you think *This is it, this is the end*, but that doesn't turn out to be the case. Your lease gets renewed and you're free to go and live another day. It's impossible to fully explain if you haven't lived through it. And Alexa, over the course of all these years, had experienced it more than enough times.

I should write a book one day, she thought, then failed to suppress a small smirk as Colin and Clara reached her.

"Something funny?" Colin asked, his voice full of irritation, trying to sound authoritative again. Honestly, it just didn't work on him. Maybe some sunglasses like the sheriff's would help.

"Sorry," Alexa said. "I was just thinking. My mind wanders sometimes." She looked to Clara and asked, "Are you okay? Like *really* okay? And I'm not just talking about bumps and bruises. I'm talking about up here." She tapped her finger against the temple.

Clara nodded. "I am. I mean, sure, it was all terrifying, but it's over now, right? I shall live to fight another day."

Alexa smiled. "Right. Good, I'm glad." But she wasn't completely convinced, thought the girl might be putting on a show. Thought that when Clara got home, she'd lock every door and check every window in her parents' home and then go take the longest shower of her life, maybe until the hot water was gone and the cold forced her out. Then she'd crawl into bed and hide under the covers and cry herself to sleep and somebody would have to come check on her in a day's time, make her eat something, make her rejoin the living.

No, Alexa thought as Clara returned a smile of her own. *She's way stronger than that. She's a fighter. She reminds me of Leah.*

Leah. Another of those new friends, the ones who'd helped open the door to Alexa's search for a new life.

"Can you give me a ride home?" Clara asked Alexa, and Alexa saw Colin roll his eyes.

"Clara, I *told* you I could—"

"I know what you *said*, Colin, but it's fine. Go back to work, do your job. I'm fine." Colin did another eye roll, and Clara sighed. "*Really*. It's not like it's even that far. I could walk if I wanted to."

"No," both Colin and Alexa said in unison, and they locked eyes for a moment, agreement passing between them.

"You can't tell me what to do," Clara said, sounding every bit the annoying little sister. "I'm an adult, in case you forgot."

Alexa laughed, which caused Colin's face to turn red. He stared at his sister, and Alexa understood his dilemma. But Clara was right—she could do what she wanted, and Alexa would be happy to take her home. She was hoping for some time to talk to the girl alone.

Colin sighed and looked around the hospital parking lot, scanning it from side to side, maybe looking for signs of a black SUV, maybe just looking for somebody to be on his side. When he spoke, he didn't look at Clara; he looked directly at Alexa. "Straight home," he said.

Alexa raised her hand, stuck up two fingers. "Scout's honor."

This caused Clara to giggle, which caused Colin's face to turn red again, and Alexa suddenly felt bad. She wasn't trying to poke fun at the guy, and she was internally applauding him for the care he was showing for his sister. She pointed to the Oldsmobile, which sat alone in the parking lot now, like a sunken ship at the bottom of the ocean, and said, "Go ahead and get in. It's unlocked. I want to talk to your brother for a second."

Clara looked apprehensive at first, like maybe she would put up another fight, try to pull the adult card again and say that anything Alexa had to say to Colin, she could say in front of her. But in the end the girl just nodded, turned and pecked her brother on the cheek and then ruffled his hair before almost skipping to the Oldsmobile while Colin's face flushed again and he smoothed his hair down.

He shook his head. "I swear, that kid."

"She loves you," Alexa said, not really even meaning to. But it was her first thought, and she'd just blurted it out. She'd enjoyed watching the two of them interact with each other, seeing the loving relationship up close. She'd been serious in the exam area, about being envious of Clara for having a big brother to watch out for her. If Alexa's own mother hadn't run out on her and her dad...

There was no sense in contemplating the what-ifs in life. The only goal now was to stop asking them as frequently.

What if I started to live?

That was the only one that mattered now.

"Yeah," Colin said. "I know."

"She's smart," Alexa said.

"Smarter than me," Colin said. "A lot smarter. She'll do something big one day, once she's ready." Then, as if he suddenly remembered who he was talking to, Colin cleared his throat and stood up straight. The harsh lights burning under the overhang revealed the faintest whisps of peach fuzz on his chin. "She doesn't want to even report it. She's completely serious about that."

Alexa nodded. "She believes them. About what they said they'd do."

Colin closed his eyes and pinched the bridge of his nose. Looked back up at her. "You know who 'they' are, don't you?"

"I only just found out earlier today. If I had known, I would have never gotten involved, and certainly never gotten Clara involved. I hope you know that. I thought I was just asking some innocent questions."

Colin studied her for a second. "Why *did* you start asking questions?"

People keep asking me that.

"Because you pissed me off. I don't like being woken up and having it implied I might be a suspect in a murder case." Before Colin could get himself worked up again and defend himself, Alexa held up her hands. "It's okay, I'm over it. You didn't know. You thought you were doing the right thing, even if it *was* a bit of stretch."

Colin was quiet again. She saw the understanding spread across his face. He nodded. "Sorry. It felt like a lead and, well..."

"First murder since you became a police officer?"

He nodded.

"And you only found out later about..." For some reason she didn't want to say their name out loud. Had a silly feeling that somebody might be listening.

Colin nodded again and once more looked around the parking lot, like he was thinking the same thing she was. She didn't know if Colin had found out about the Abatellis from somebody else at the sheriff's office or if word had simply started to spread, the ritualistic display of Tony's body gaining a louder and louder voice through town. The message being delivered. She thought it was likely the latter. He seemed too green and innocent to be brought into the inner circle of the department just yet.

"What did you do?" he asked her. "Why did this happen? With Clara, I mean. The finger, all of it?"

"It's better if you don't know, wouldn't you say? One less thing you have to keep under your hat. I went digging when I shouldn't have, plus a bit more. But you heard what they told your sister. We're all even now. The score is settled. It's over. I'm done."

Colin considered this, and she knew that he would see her point. It would eat him alive not to be able to report and go after the guys who had hurt his sister—why pour more fuel on the secret fire? But still, he eyed her with slight apprehension.

"I'm not dangerous, Colin. I promise. Your sister will be safe with me."

Colin glanced at the Oldsmobile, then darted his eyes back to Alexa as he turned to leave, apparently understanding there was nothing more to be said here. "Straight home," he said again. "You might not be dangerous, but *being* with you might be dangerous enough."

"So what did Colin have to say?" Clara asked after telling Alexa to make a left out of the hospital parking lot.

Alexa waited for a minivan to pass and then made the turn. "He's just worried about you," she said. "Wants to make sure nothing else bad happens to you."

Clara sighed, traced her finger along the window. "Sometimes he treats me like I'm still a kid."

"You are."

"You know what I mean."

Alexa nodded. "I do. Where am I going?"

"Make the second left."

Alexa drove, being very mindful of the twenty-five-miles-per-hour speed limit through the neighborhood. "Clara, I'm so sorry about what happened to you. I didn't know what type of people these were."

Clara shrugged. "It's okay. You aren't the one who broke my finger."

Indirectly, I did, Alexa thought.

"So who are these people, anyway? The ones who jumped me."

Alexa shook her head. "They're bad and that's all you need to know. But they're the type of people who I think *will* keep their word. They won't bother you anymore as long as I stop bothering them."

"Really? You're not going to tell me?" Clara held up her hand, the one with the pinky in the splint. "I mean, I'm about as much a part of this as I can be, wouldn't you say?"

"This isn't up for discussion," Alexa said, flipping on her turn signal and making the left. "Same thing I told your brother: the less he knows, the better off he is. He won't have to lie to anyone, and he won't accidentally say something he shouldn't. Even with as mad as he was and as upset about you getting hurt, he was smart enough to understand that. I'm not his favorite person in the world right now, obviously, but we were in agreement on this. Besides, I'm sure you'll hear more about it soon. Ezra says more of the details might be in the paper tomorrow, but people in town are already talking, putting the pieces together."

"Ezra? That's the guy that bought the inn, right?"

Alexa nodded. "He owns it, yeah."

"You two know each other?"

"Just met, but he's been very friendly."

"He's kinda hot," Clara said. "But he's kinda weird, too."

"How so?" Alexa glanced over to the girl, curious.

Clara shrugged. "Like ... nobody really seems to know much about him. About a year ago, he just sort of showed up. Bought the old inn and started fixing it up, made it real nice. Lives all alone out there in the middle of nowhere..." She trailed off, shrugged again. "I guess weird isn't the right word. More like *mysterious*."

You got that right, Alexa thought.

"Next right," Clara said, pointing ahead. "Go to the cul-de-sac and I'm the house on the left."

Alexa took in the houses lining the street, more yards, more backyard fences, more established lives. Slowed to make the turn. The Wanamakers lived in a two-story brick home with a big front yard that sloped down toward the street. There was a lamppost burning at the edge of the side-walk leading from the driveway to the front door and a big attached two-car garage on the right. It was one of the nicer homes Alexa had seen on their drive, and she could see why Colin and Clara might both still want to live at home with their parents. She hadn't exactly seen any apartment buildings around Silent Falls yet. She carefully drove the Oldsmobile as close as she dared to the garage doors and parked.

Clara did not move to get out. She looked out the windshield and stared at her house for several seconds before eventually shaking her head and saying, "I'm going to have to make up a story. To tell them"—she nodded toward the house—"and to tell my boss at work."

How many stories had Alexa told in her life? Countless, almost all of them made up. She felt another pang of guilt. "I'm sorry you have to lie to them because of me."

Clara waved her off. "Please. It won't be the first time I've given them a more palatable version of current events." She smirked. "You think *Colin* treats me like a kid ... well, you should meet my dad."

I'm sure he's better than mine was.

Clara still did not get out of the car.

"Clara?"

"Yeah?"

"What's wrong?"

The girl sighed. "You're going to think I'm crazy."

"I won't."

Clara looked at her. Studied Alexa's face. "You know, you're right. You're..." She paused, thinking. "You're cool."

I'm a mess, Alexa thought, but she said, "I think I'm just very realistic."

Clara shrugged again, and each time she did, it reminded

Alexa of just how young she really was. "Everything that happened," she said, "it was totally terrifying. Like, the whole time in the back of that SUV I just kept imagining what they were going to do. Rape me? Kill me? Both? It was like being stuck in a nightmare of waiting, under that hood with nothing but the blackness and my mind. But after ... after they let me go, I wasn't afraid anymore." She looked at Alexa, and Alexa recognized what she saw in the girl's eyes before Clara even spoke. "I was *angry*," Clara continued. "Instead of calling Colin or 911 or calling *anybody*, for a few crazy moments all I could think about was getting revenge. In the span of just a few seconds I could already see it playing out in my head. My dad's got a gun safe and I know the code. He doesn't think I do, but I do. I could get one of his guns and then try to track down that SUV and..." She trailed off. "It's nuts, I know. I couldn't do that, not really. And how would I ever find those people? I never even saw their faces. Now, I see how dumb it was, but in that moment, it was like that feeling—"

"Consumed you," Alexa finished for her. "It was all you wanted. You were seeing red."

Clara nodded. "In that moment behind the middle school, I would not have hesitated to kill the people who did this." She held up her splinted finger and pointed to her bruised eye. "It felt right, at the time, but now I'm almost afraid that feeling will come back. I might be more afraid of that than if the SUV showed up again."

Alexa wanted to reach out and wrap the girl in a hug, but instead she only said, "You're not crazy. What you experienced, that's a completely normal reaction to have. In fact, I'd say it's a good reaction to have. I'd rather be brave and confident than afraid and cowering. It means they didn't break you. You're winning up here." She tapped her index finger against her temple, the same way she had in the hospital parking lot beneath the emergency room overhang.

They were both quiet for a few seconds. The Oldsmobile's engine did something funny, gave off an odd clanging sound, but it kept running. "See?" Clara said. "I told you you're cool."

"Let me be clear," Alexa said, almost laughing at how much she sounded like a mom, "if you happen to get that feeling again, that seeing red feeling, you are *not*, under any circumstances, to act on it in any way. You got it?"

Clara waved her off again. "Yeah, I know."

"In fact," Alexa said, "if you feel that red feeling coming on again, give me a call. You got your phone on you?"

Clara did, and Alexa gave her the cell phone number for the current pay-to-use cell phone she'd been using for the last few months. The girl punched it in and saved it and said, "Thanks."

"I'm serious," Alexa added. "Call me anytime. Tell me how cool I am."

Clara actually laughed now, and she nodded. "Will do. And thanks for the ride. I should probably get inside." But before she left, a small glint of fear finally darkened her eyes.

"You'll be fine," Alexa said. "Now go on. It's time to lie to your parents."

Alexa watched the girl walk up the sidewalk and push through the front door, warm light spilling out and bathing the sidewalk in a slice of gold. The door hadn't even been locked. As Clara gave a final wave and closed the door, Alexa felt something stir inside her.

An anger of her own. That red feeling.

Colin's words about his sister: *She'll do something big one day, once she's ready.*

Alexa believed it. The girl was special. As good as they came.

How dare somebody think they could hurt her and get away with it?

CHAPTER 21

As Alexa drove back to the inn, she thought more about how it came to be that the Abatelli family had known that she and Clara had chatted about Tony. The more time she spent with Clara, the more unlikely Alexa was finding the possibility that the girl had gone into detail with anyone about what they'd been talking about, especially now that Alexa knew that Tony's father, aka Big Tony, owned Smokey's. Alexa didn't know how the scene had played out when Sheriff Byrd had come by to tell Big Tony the news of his son's murder, but unless Big Tony had a heart made of stone, she couldn't imagine that the man would have taken the news well, and Clara certainly wouldn't have decided to say anything along the line of *I'm sorry for your loss, but hey, by the way, I just told that new woman in town all about your dead son*, or even mention Tony's name in possible earshot.

But ... she was just a kid. Okay, not really, but young enough in Alexa's rearview mirror. Tony's murder was the hot talk of the town, and Clara worked at one of the busiest restaurants around. Gossip would be had, no question. Alexa drifted back to her original thought she'd had before, about how maybe it had all been as innocent as Clara telling her waitress friend what she and Alexa had been talking about. Alexa could see this playing out very clearly: after Alexa and Clara had shared their conversation in the outdoor dining area, Clara had gone back inside to work—just as Sheriff Byrd was arriving to drop his bomb on Big Tony—and the other waitress, having been watching with curiosity this whole time, leaned in close to Clara and asked, "So, what was that all about? Who *was* that woman?"

Alexa shook her head, her headlights lighting up the rear side of the inn as the Oldsmobile rumbled toward it. It just didn't feel right, blaming Clara for what had happened, whether her mistake had been innocent or not. It didn't add up in Alexa's mind.

Her instinct simply wasn't accepting it.

She pulled into the inn and noticed that Ezra's truck was gone, missing from around back, where he usually kept it parked. Instead of driving up to her own room, Alexa parked the Oldsmobile in front of the office and killed the engine, sat in the quiet for a long time, the occasional clang and drip from the engine almost soothing, meditative. Through the office door's glass, she could see Herb's head above the counter, looking down at something, a look of intent she'd not seen on the man before.

Turned out, he was playing solitaire. When Alexa pushed through the office door, Herb didn't even look up from the cards splayed across the countertop at first, just said, "You know, I've been playing this game my whole life, and I can confirm it is the most frustrating pastime, second only to those hippie Sudoku puzzles." He did look up now. "Have you tried those? It's like going back to math class, only it's supposed to be *fun*."

Alexa forced on a smile and shook her head. "I haven't. But I'm a solitaire expert."

Herb shook his head. "No such thing." Then he grunted a laugh and answered before Alexa could even ask the question. "Ez took off with your dog. Called me in a bit early so he could head home to 'take care of a few things.' That's all he told me. Said you'd understand, and to tell you to head on out that way whenever you were ready. Said he figured you could find the place. Said you were the observant type like that."

At first, Alexa found herself annoyed by this—Ezra assuming he could just take her dog with him and tell her to come back to his house for the night. What if she hadn't planned on staying in town? What if what she'd learned from Clara had been the last straw and she'd finally been ready to grab Barlow and head out? What if she'd been tired and just hadn't felt like fucking driving out to Ezra's farmhouse? Had ordered a pizza and had planned on plopping down on the bed in her room and watching old movies and trying to forget everything that was happening, just like she'd tried to do earlier when she'd been eating Chinese food and had then found...

The fortune cookie.

And Ezra had found his.

Truth was, Alexa was happy to head back out to Ezra's. Was happy the man was taking such good care of Barlow instead of sticking the dog back inside the motel room to wait. And, when she boiled it down to the bone, he was taking care of her too. Not in a pushy and commanding way, not like he was trying to play the role of protector and provider, but more like the two of them had become partners.

Partners in what? Alexa had to ask herself as she thanked Herb and wished him good luck in his game and then stepped back outside.

Much like Ezra, Herb didn't ask any prying questions. No spoken curiosity about what exactly was going on between her and Ezra. Alexa thought that might be a big reason why Ezra liked the guy.

She fired up the Oldsmobile, and the headlights splashed across the front of the inn. When she drove off, she saw Herb looking back down at his cards and shaking his head.

Alexa laughed.

ALEXA ONLY MADE one wrong turn on her way to Ezra's, and it was early going. Once she got deeper into the back roads, the easier the trip seemed to come to her, memories from the night before playing out in her head like a built-in GPS. Despite the familiarity of the trip, however, she was again hit with the feeling of isolation growing larger the longer she drove. This feeling was intensified even more when she parked the car next to Ezra's truck in the driveway, warm light burning from the front windows in a way that reminded Alexa of the light that had spilled from Clara's home's front door as the girl had slipped inside, and then shut the car's door and stood in the silence of nature.

I could scream for my life out here and nobody would ever hear me. The thought gave her an unexpected chill, and she hurried up the front porch steps. Ezra had one of those camera doorbells, and instead of ringing it, Alexa simply knocked softly on the door, a quick one-two *rap rap*. From inside, Barlow barked once and she heard his paws scurrying toward the door. She smiled, peeked through the window next to the door and saw the dog wagging his tail and spinning around impatiently while Ezra made long strides up the hallway and then unlocked and opened the door. He was still wearing the same clothes from earlier, though he'd taken his shoes off, and the smell of pizza came wafting out of the house.

Alexa fought the urge to say, "Honey, I'm *home*." Instead she just said, "Hi." Ezra waved her in.

"I made pizza," he said. "Well, let me clarify. I baked a frozen pizza. Set your expectations low. I live alone, remember?"

"Pizza two nights in a row? Ugh!" she joked. "Just kidding. It smells great," Alexa said, reaching down and giving Barlow a good rubdown as he panted and wagged his tail fiercely. She and the dog had only been together a short while, but there was no denying the love they had for each other.

And there was no denying the level of comfort she and Ezra had fallen into. Somehow, arriving back at the farmhouse and seeing these two had been unexpectedly like slipping into a warm bath after spending all day out in the cold. It was such a foreign feeling to Alexa that she found herself almost trying to squash it, to ignore the reality of it, push it away.

But why? that burning ember in her soul asked.

Because I'm still here, the cynical part of her replied, although with a tone more somber than normal. *I'll always be here. You're just going to have to learn when to tell me to shut up.*

Half the pizza was left on a metal pan on the stovetop. "You might need to microwave it," Ezra said. "I wasn't sure when you'd get here, and I was hungry. It hasn't been sitting out too long, though."

Alexa walked over and scooped up a slice, took a bite and started chewing. It was chewy and a bit cold, and veggie. She could already see Herb rolling his eyes. "It's fine," she said. "Cold pizza can be the best pizza."

Ezra nodded, but it didn't look like a nod of agreement. He pointed toward the coffeemaker on the counter. "I was about to make some coffee. Want some?"

Alexa swallowed another bite and nodded. "Would love some."

And the coffee made her think of Lance again, which made this moment seem all the more perfect. Like, by standing in Ezra's kitchen in this farmhouse way outside of town, she was exactly where she was supposed to be.

Ezra brewed the coffee and Alexa finished off the pizza. The Chinese food they'd had for lunch felt like a very long time ago, and she was starving. Barlow sat obediently at her feet, eyes never leaving the food in her hand, and she eventually tossed him a small bit of crust, which you would have thought to have been filet mignon by the way he greedily caught and swallowed it whole, like his life depended on it.

"I did feed him," Ezra said, pointing down to Barlow's food and water dish on the floor by the back door. "And your toiletry bag and clothes from earlier are upstairs. I hope you don't mind, I went into your room at the inn and got it together."

For one terrifying moment, Alexa wondered if she'd left the pill bottle out somewhere, tossed onto the bed or left on the nightstand. She was sure she'd put it back into her duffle bag after the last time she'd looked at it, but...

But so what? she thought. *I'm the only person it means anything to. If somebody were to find it and open the top, it's not like my secrets would come spilling out.*

But still ... her father's name was printed on that bottle. Long-faded and barely legible but still there.

She didn't need anybody finding him. She wanted his memory to stay forever lost and buried from the world.

As if understanding the still-somewhat-strange dichotomy of what might be considered normal and what was happening between himself and Alexa, Ezra added, "Of course, you're free to just take it and go. I don't know what your plans are, but with what's going on, I just figured you might prefer to be here again instead of at the inn, if you're staying in town."

"I'm staying," Alexa said. "At least for tonight. We'll see what I feel like in the morning."

Ezra nodded and poured her coffee and they sat at the table. Barlow trotted off down the hall and disappeared into the living room. "He's taken a liking to the couch," Ezra said.

"He's taken a liking to you, too," Alexa said. The coffee was too hot, so she blew across the brim of the mug.

"He's a good boy," Ezra said. Sipped his own coffee despite the temperature and said, "So tell me what happened with Clara? How bad was it?"

Alexa told him the whole story, everything from the moment she'd left the inn until she'd returned to the farmhouse. Even the bit about Clara's momentary desire for revenge at the middle school, if only to try and illustrate to Ezra that the girl was strong, tough. Ezra sat upright and kept his eyes locked on Alexa's the entire time she told her story. He drank his coffee almost robotically, like he was a computer downloading all the info she was dumping. Analyzing and processing. Like he always seemed to do.

"What are you going to do?" he finally asked. He crossed his arms and leaned back in the chair.

"What do you mean?"

Ezra said nothing. Just stared at her.

"What? What do you think I'm going to do? I've already caused enough trouble as it is. Clara got hurt because of me." She paused, shrugged. "It's not like I can take down the entire mob, even if I wanted to."

He shook his head. "No, of course not."

She studied his face, thought she saw the faintest hint of a grin hiding there. "*What?*"

Ezra stood from the table, took both their empty coffee cups and placed them in the sink. "Come with me," he said, motioning for her to follow him down the hallway. "There's something I want to show you."

CHAPTER 22

A door in the kitchen that Alexa had assumed was a pantry revealed a set of stairs when Ezra opened it. He clicked on a light switch just inside the door, and the stairs went down a few feet before making a hard left and leading away into space unknown beneath them.

Alexa hesitated as Ezra started down the stairs, her mind whirring up again, that fight-or-flight part that had guided her all the years speaking up, shouting again, telling her not to follow him down. Because another scenario was suddenly taking shape, the way you used to stare at those 3-D illusion pictures out on display in the mall, a jumble of colors and computerized swirls that when your eyes focused in just such a way would reveal the true image beneath.

She'd been wondering how the Abatelli family had known about her conversations with Clara, how they'd seemed to have tracked her moves from the moment she arrived in Silent Falls. But now, she realized, maybe it was possible they'd only been tracking her since she'd arrived at the inn. She'd told Ezra almost everything, and each time there seemed to have been a volley returned from the opposing side.

So, what if *he* was the opposing side—funneling information up the chain?

Clara had said it herself, that Ezra was mysterious and nobody in town seemed to know much about him. And then there was the money, too. The cash to buy the old inn and fix it up fancy, then renovate an old farmhouse to isolate himself in—where did it come from? Why here, why now?

Because of secrets, she thought. *Because this isn't who he really is.* There were ulterior motives lying somewhere beneath the Ezra she'd met, motives she could not see, just like she couldn't see what was lying in wait beneath the very floor she was standing on.

Was Ezra a wolf in sheep's clothing? Was he like Tony, a pawn for the mob?

He'd reached the small landing where the stairs made their turn, and he had stopped and was looking back up at her. He seemed to be reading her thoughts—*he's so good at that*—and she thought she saw his face falter for a second, like she'd wounded him. But then he sighed and nodded.

"I get it," he said. "Why would you follow a stranger into the basement of an old house in the middle of nowhere?"

Alexa shrugged, was trapped in indecision. "It's a good question to ask."

"Go get a knife," he said.

"What?"

"There's a butcher's block next to the stove. Grab a knife from there. Get the biggest one, if it'll make you feel better."

"Are you asking me to stab you?"

"I'm telling you there's no reason to. But I don't blame you for being skeptical here. I'm trying to set your mind at ease. Make you feel safe."

They stared at each other. Silent.

From down the hallway, the sounds of Barlow snoring reached Alexa's ears, and with the soft purring her apprehension was suddenly and completely erased. She replayed the moments that Ezra had shared with the dog, how he smiled when he saw him, how he'd taken care of him, talked to him. Had taken Barlow with him on his errands and outings instead of cooping the poor guy up indoors in a strange place.

If there were ever a telltale sign of a good and pure heart, Alexa thought it might be these things.

She started down the stairs, leaving all the knives exactly where they were.

The basement was cozy, yet unremarkable. It had been recently finished, because Alexa could still smell the paint, a dark blue that somehow seemed perfectly Ezra. There was new carpet on the floor and a television mounted on one wall with a love seat facing it, video game consoles beneath the television on a small stand. Behind the love seat, along the opposite wall, was a long modern work desk with two large computer monitors on it. There was a metal rack next to the desk that was nearly as tall as Alexa and housed several pieces of electronics: routers and servers and other things that blinked a seizure-inducing array of colored lights. The basement was also freezing, and Alexa shivered, rubbing at her bare arms again as she followed Ezra toward the desk, again wishing she'd stayed dressed in her Sunday best.

As she reached the desk, she noticed one more thing about the basement: there was absolutely nothing on the walls. No posters or framed art or college degrees or even a calendar. Nothing. Bare. Empty. These walls told no stories, offered no hints of their owner's true self.

Mysterious.

Ezra pulled a chair out from the desk and brought the monitors to life. The screens were so big the light caused Alexa to squint until her eyes adjusted. She stopped just behind him, looked over his shoulder as he started working the keyboard and mouse. More lights started flashing from the rack of equipment in the corner to her left.

"What are you, a hacker?"

He ignored her question. Instead, he clicked on a file and the screen was suddenly filled with a high-above view of a parking lot and the corner of a building, looking out and onto a road that stretched out of view. She recognized the scene. "That's the inn," she said. "From above the office."

Ezra nodded. "I've got cameras all around the building," he said. Then added, "I want to make sure my guests stay safe."

"Remind me to leave that five-star Yelp review."

"Trust me, I will." He hit the Play button on the screen, and the image came to life, a video recording that was as high-definition as anything Alexa had ever seen. "Watch," Ezra said and pointed to the screen. Five seconds later, a black SUV drove along the road, slowing just enough to be noticeable as it passed the inn before driving on.

Before Alexa could say anything, Ezra swiveled around in the chair and she stepped back. "My security software has an image-recognition feature," he said. "When I ran this screen-shot of the SUV through it I got ... well, a lot of results. All within the last two days."

Alexa shook her head. "Ever since I arrived. Son of a bitch."

"And it's like clockwork, for the most part. They make a pass just about every hour or so. Sometimes it's longer. But that might be because—"

"Because they're out following me," Alexa said.

"Possibly, yes."

She had a thought then. She figured she already knew the answer, but she had to ask. "And it's definitely the same SUV every time?"

Ezra turned back to the computer and clicked a few more buttons, and the frozen image on-screen zoomed in. The SUV's license plate was crystal clear. "I ran the plate through the image recognition, too. Same number of results. So, yes. Same SUV, every time."

Alexa no longer had to wonder why the Abatelli family had always seemed to be right in step with her, to know her moves, know about Clara. It was because they'd been shadowing her the entire time. She'd never even noticed.

But she still had to wonder ... why? Why had they started?

She asked, "Is there a hit for the SUV the night I arrived?"

Ezra nodded. "First thing I checked."

"What the hell? Why would they be following me before they'd even killed Tony? At that point, all that had happened was that he'd hit on me at Smokey's and..."

Alexa remembered her first glimpse of Tony again, before she'd even known who he was. The way he'd been standing outside the front of Smokey's and talking on his cell phone. No, not just talking—arguing. She could see the way he was flailing his hands around, the way he was shaking his head back and forth, like he was trying to plead his case and whoever was on the other line wasn't listening.

She now thought she had a good idea who was on the other end of that call. Something had happened that night, some sort of disagreement between Tony and his partners-in-crime in the Abatelli family.

(Tony fucked up, and now he's gone)

And maybe that disagreement hadn't started with just that phone call out front of Smokey's. Maybe it had started earlier. How much earlier didn't matter. But earlier enough that maybe Tony was already being considered a risk, a liability? Earlier enough for a black SUV to already be watching, on standby to take action if action was needed?

And if they were already there, already watching, then they would have seen Tony approach her after his phone call, they would have seen him talk to her and then get angry ... would have seen him slash her tire?

As an outsider—a paranoid and on-alert outsider at that —to her the scene would have been very intriguing. So maybe they had decided to investigate. Keep tabs on her and see if they could find out exactly who this new woman was that had shown up and pissed Tony off enough that he'd committed a crime in a very public place.

(Tony fucked up)

Which, in all likelihood, would have amounted to absolutely nothing. What would they have seen? A woman and her dog walk through town and stop for the night at the local inn. That would have been *all* they'd seen, unless they'd maybe followed her into town the next day to watch her buy a coffee and take in the sights. But, no—then Deputy Colin Wanamaker had had to go try and make a name for himself and piss her off, and then Alexa had gone and let that anger inside of her take over and she'd marched right back to Smokey's to see Clara, and then—this was what would have looked *really* suspicious to anyone tailing her—she'd trespassed in the park and caught their spy red-handed. Chased him. Done worse, later.

This. Was. All. Her. Fault.

"Why did you do this?" Alexa asked, trying to ignore her own guilt.

Ezra looked confused. "Do what?"

She pointed to the frozen image on the screen. "This. Why did you decide to do this, dig into finding out if I was being followed?"

"I told you, I like to make sure my guests are safe."

Alexa stared at him. Said nothing.

Ezra sighed. Looked up at the ceiling and crossed his arms. "It was Clara, okay? You can clearly take care of yourself, make your own choices, but Clara ... she didn't deserve what happened to her. She's innocent. And anybody who can harm an innocent person like that ... well, I don't like it."

"You didn't know the details about Clara until I got back here," Alexa said.

Ezra met her eyes. "It wasn't hard to put the pieces together. I doubt she'd only want to talk to you if she fell off a ladder reaching for the last box of napkins on the high shelf at Smokey's. And you saw how mad her brother was. He knew, too. He knew there was something bad going on."

Now it was Alexa's turn to sigh, and she nodded. She paced back and forth for a few seconds and then walked to the love seat and leaned against the back. Asked, "So now what?"

"What do you mean?"

"What do we do now?"

"We?"

She was tired of him acting like he was still wanting not to get involved in this. The fact that he'd done the digging into the Abatelli family and had now used his super camera system *(and why does he have all this stuff?)* to discover the SUV making its regular passes by the inn was working against the attitude he was trying to outwardly show.

"Yes, *we*," she said. "Why would you take the time to do everything you've done if you didn't think something could be done?"

"What would we even do—take this information to the police?"

Her mouth fell open, shocked. After everything he'd learned and had told her, there was no way he—

Ezra grinned. Couldn't keep himself from laughing. When she realized he'd actually made a joke about taking the information to the police, she was so surprised and relieved she started laughing too. Eventually, the laughter stopped and Alexa said, "I think they were serious, what they told Clara. The score's even. If I just leave this alone, everything will go back to normal. I think they're too smart to take the risk of not keeping their word and causing any more collateral damage. I imagine in the mob world, reputation and respect must mean *something*. Right?"

Ezra shrugged. "Or maybe you've seen too many movies."

She threw up her hands. "Well, what exactly would you suggest?"

Ezra looked up at the ceiling again, and she saw his jaw clenching. Which she knew by now meant he was carefully contemplating his next words, his next choice. When he looked back to her, his eyes had taken on an icy seriousness. "You said upstairs that you can't take down the entire mob."

She nodded. "Correct."

"I agree," he said. "But what if you looked at it at a more micro level?"

"Meaning?"

"What if you didn't worry about taking down the entire mob and instead looked at it as taking down a guy, or a couple guys, I suppose, who hurt an innocent young woman, and in all likelihood have probably done worse."

He wants this, she realized then. *Something inside him, it wants this. Something is waking up.*

And she'd be damned if he hadn't made a fine suggestion.

"Okay, that seems like something I might be interested in. What do you suggest our next steps be, should we chose to do this?"

He turned and pointed to the screen, the frozen image of the license plate. "We start with this."

"You can look up the plate? See where it leads us?"

He shook his head. "I can't. But..."

Alexa groaned. "But you know a guy?"

"I do."

A chill shot through her body and she wanted to say *Christ, why is it so cold in here?* But instead, she said, "If we do this, there could be repercussions. Are we okay with that?"

The answer Ezra gave wasn't really an answer at all. "We just need to do it right."

Alexa shivered again, but it might not have been because of the cold.

CHAPTER 23

After they'd made the decision, they went to bed. Ezra fired off a quick message to whoever his guy was, attaching the picture of the SUV and the license plate number, all while Alexa leaned against the back of the love seat. She was curious, wanted to look over his shoulder and watch every keystroke and mouse click, but she respected him too much for that. Owed him that much and maybe more. He had his secrets, but they were his to keep.

They'd climbed the stairs with Alexa leading the way, and as she reached the top landing, she couldn't believe that only a few minutes ago, she'd stood in this very spot and had seriously considered the idea that Ezra had been about to abduct her, and maybe worse. That maybe he was the final nail in her coffin, the Abatelli family's surprise attack to silence her for good, on this and anything else.

How ridiculous that seemed now. How right that ember in her soul had been. She supposed she should thank Barlow with an extra treat for the gentle hint.

"We'll give it a few days," Ezra said as he moved around

the home and switched off the lights. Alexa waited at the foot of the stairs leading to the second floor. "Then we should have all we'll need to get started."

She had questions, of course she did. *Who are we giving a few days to? What will we get back? What exactly does that mean, to get started?*

She asked none of them. Just nodded her head and said, "Okay."

At the top of the stairs, he told her he'd be heading back to the inn in the morning, said she could come and go from the farmhouse as she pleased. He'd give her a key. "Unless you'd prefer the inn, or want to make other arrangements." He didn't say this sarcastically, was being genuine. Again, she felt he wasn't wanting to assume or push or overstep any boundary she might have set.

Because I have my secrets too, and he's letting me keep them.

"Thank you," she said. "I'll stay here, as long as you're sure we aren't any trouble. If you change your mind, just let me know and we'll figure it out."

He looked at her for a second too long, thinking. "I'm sure you will," he said. "I bet you always do. Anyway, goodnight." Then he headed for his bedroom at the end of the hallway.

Alexa called for Barlow, who lumbered up the stairs sleepily, and the two of them once again found themselves in Ezra's guest bed. Alexa stared at the ceiling in the dark, and as she tried to drift off to sleep, tried to feel safe and content for the time being, she also worked to push down the familiar and rapidly rising urge to jump out of the bed, grab her things, and get her and Barlow the hell out of there. Out of the farmhouse, out of town, out of the state.

Why? Why would I do that?

Because right then, everything felt right.

And that's not a feeling I'm used to. What a broken person I am ... for right to feel so wrong.

Eventually, she did sleep.

And she slept well, because when she woke the next morning, the house was silent and still and the sun was higher in the sky than she'd expected and Ezra was gone, her Oldsmobile alone in the driveway. Ezra had left a note on the kitchen table with both the inn's and his cell phone number on it. Beneath the number, he'd scrawled *Help yourself to brunch.*

She rolled her eyes. If he had drawn a wink-face to go along with the message, she might have groaned.

She found her way around the kitchen and made breakfast. While she ate, holding her bowl of oatmeal on the back porch while Barlow sniffed and explored the backyard, the cold air biting but the sun pleasant on her face, she enjoyed the solitude and the silence and in that moment was almost sick to her stomach at how wonderful and free she felt. It was a giddy feeling that morphed into some sort of emotion that was both wonderfully happy and oddly melancholy. A sadness crept in along with the good vibes, casting a shadow on all the light.

Something warm and wet dripped onto her hand, and when she looked down, she was shocked to see it was a tear.

And she was crying. She set the bowl on the porch banister and her knees buckled and she went down to the ground, the wood cold on her legs and hands. The sobs came hard and fast and sudden, her body shaking in an unexpected purging of feelings that she'd all but forgotten she could still summon. Sorrow and sadness and grief and vulnerability and loneliness poured out with her cries, streamed down her cheeks in the form of tears. She felt dizzy, her mind struggling to find the root cause of this breakdown. She tried to bring herself back to the present, to focus on that cold air and that warm sun on her skin and the look of happiness on Barlow's face as he explored the big backyard and...

Last night again: *What a broken person I am, for right to feel so wrong.*

Because right then, she could be anybody. A woman at home, *her* home, with *her* dog, eating her breakfast on *her* back porch and looking over *her* backyard. A hot shower, *her* shower, waiting for her upstairs. Food in a fridge and in cabinets, television to watch, video games to play, books to read. She could head into town and walk around and be just like anybody else. Pop in for a coffee and muffin before heading over to the hardware store to look at paint samples because she wanted a fresh color in the living room. Ask somebody at the rec center when the woman's softball league might be starting because this was the year she'd finally sign up. She'd stop at the grocery store on the way home and pick up something special for dinner, which she'd cook for her and another—friend, roommate, lover, it didn't matter. They'd eat and they'd laugh and talk about their days, and when it was all over they'd go to bed and wouldn't even think twice about what a wonderful day it had been because in this life it would all seem so—

Normal, she thought. *The life of* somebody, *and I've always been a* nobody.

The crying slowed and then stopped, and when Alexa pushed herself off the porch and stood, she felt like a phoenix rising from the ashes. Reborn with a clear certainty that up until this morning had only been foggy and distant. An idea she'd been kidding herself that she'd been working to achieve, but now was positive to be her only objective.

I will live, she thought as she turned to head back inside, calling for Barlow. *This is where I belong and I will start my life here.*

Lance had shown her the ledge, and somehow, it had been Ezra and his farmhouse that had allowed her to jump.

And jump she would.

But first, they'd take care of the black SUV. She'd come so far after so long. No sense in getting ahead of herself.

SHE SHOWERED and dressed and headed into town, leaving Barlow as king of the castle. She had a suspicion he'd spend most of his time alternating between sleeping on the couch and sleeping on the spot on the floor in the living room where the sun came through the front windows. The life of a dog. She was a bit jealous.

She had no agenda as she headed out, except that she wanted to appear normal—both for herself, to help perpetuate her fantasy of living a normal life, falling into a rhythm and routine of a person who hadn't spent the last twenty-plus years without a permanent address, somebody who started and ended their day in the same place, more often than not, and also to let anybody who might still be watching from behind the tinted windows of a certain black SUV see that she was still here. Still here, but being good. The message had been received and understood. No more worrying about Tony's murder for this gal, no more parking lot fisticuffs, just a few days spent enjoying what the town had to offer.

For the next four days, she avoided Smokey's, just in case a normal trip to the restaurant for lunch might be interpreted by prying eyes as an attempt to speak with Clara or even Big Tony about things forbidden. Even if the conversation had been about things as innocent as puppies and rainbows, she wasn't positive that anyone watching would know that, wasn't sure if they had ears out and about as well as eyes. Why risk it?

But she did go to the café, each of the three days, for a midmorning coffee and pastry or deli sandwich. That FOR RENT flyer taped to the window greeted her each time, the corners starting to droop as the tape began to let go. She'd buy two newspapers, one local and one national, and find a table by the window if one was available and sit and read and enjoy herself. She found that she very much liked the café, she liked the people who worked there and the people who frequented—the regulars. They mostly stayed to themselves, engrossed in computer or phone and tablet screens, newspapers of their own or paperback novels, some with headphones on, staring off into nothing while they listened to podcasts or audiobooks, but they were also friendly, even to her, the newcomer. They would nod and smile or give a small wave or raise their cups in a small recognition when she came in and saw them. They sometimes would offer the normal social pleasantries such as *Good morning, How ya doin'*, and one gentleman in the back who always had all the newspapers spread out before him like each individual one somehow fit together with the others to form one giant story, would each morning tell her which roast she should try. She took his advice each of the four days, and each time, she'd been impressed. He'd watch her take the first sip once she got back to her table, and she'd nod and smile and give him a thumbs-up. He'd nod in return and then he was once again lost in his master newspaper mystery. They were all little things, but they added up to form a sense of inclusion that Alexa had not felt in ... well, a very long time. Not since she was still a kid. *Before.*

That first morning, the local paper did run the story about Tony's murder, but much as Ezra had alluded to, the details were muted. A park jogger had found "the body" on the baseball field. They did add that the body had been "dismembered" but there was no mention of how the parts had been ceremoniously displayed, how the head had been burned, or how such findings were consistent with other reported murders over the years, linking back to one of the state's most prominent crime organizations. Ezra knew, and so did Alexa, but she wondered how many others like the two of them there were. How many other residents of Silent Falls knew the truth?

Sheriff Byrd offered an obviously preprepared statement for the story. "We are shocked and deeply saddened that something as tragic and horrific as this could happen in our county, and we will stop at nothing in our pursuit of Mr. Romano's killer. This just isn't something that happens here. Silent Falls is a safe place, a family place, a place where people never have to worry about locking their doors"— Alexa thought of Clara, pushing right through her family's unlocked front door after sundown—"and enjoy their trips to Collins Park for sports and picnics and fresh air and exercise. With that said, it is the department's opinion that Mr.

Romano's death is an isolated incident, and whoever performed such an egregious act is now long gone from here."

Alexa recognized the last part of the comment for exactly what it was: the subtle admission that Tony's killer would never be brought to justice. Byrd knew the truth, and he knew what he was doing. It didn't make him a bad guy, because who knew just how tightly the screws were wound on him by whoever might be running the show? Alexa thought about Ezra's opinion of the sheriff: *He tries to do his interpretation of what's right.*

Don't we all? she'd said back. Boy, wasn't that the truth.

On that first day, the girl from Saturday who'd been wearing the workout clothes and had the green drink came in and saw Alexa sitting at her table. The girl smiled and said, "Hey, Vintage," and Alexa smiled back and waved and said, "Hey, Tight Ass," and a couple of the folks between them looked up or raised their eyebrows at this exchange but otherwise didn't seem to care. The girl laughed and ordered another green drink and waved goodbye and winked at her when she left.

It had been a good day so far.

After her time at the café, Alexa would walk around town. She checked out the shops, spent more time in Collins Park, which really was very pretty and had lovely walking trails. Each time she passed the baseball field where Tony's body had been found, she instinctively glanced toward the trees, listened for the sound of a camera shutter or searched for the glint of sunlight of a lens. Paranoid, maybe, but she was sure somebody was still watching her. She was actually making a point not to look for anyone, because what would good would it do? All she cared about was getting the point across that she was being a good girl. Falling in line just like everyone else involved in this mess—just like the newspaper and the sheriff and who knew how many others.

That first day, she did see a black SUV parked on a side street a block up from the café. She caught it in her peripheral only, didn't bother with checking the license plate, but she assumed it was them. Which was fine. Let them watch her be normal. She was enjoying watching it play out herself, this whole normal thing. Besides, their time would come. Her own resolution and something that had been in Ezra's voice that night at the computer told her that much was true.

The second day, she couldn't help it and risked a quick text message to Clara. *Hey, thinking about you. Are you doing ok?*

Clara had replied quickly. *Hey! Yes I'm ok. Mom and Dad are curious, but haven't given me trouble. Colin is worse ;-) How are you?*

Alexa tried to remember the last time somebody had seriously asked her how she was doing before she'd arrived in Silent Falls. Was amazed at how much of an impact it could have on your soul when it was asked genuinely. *I'm great*, she typed back. *Let me know if you need anything.*

On the third day, she walked further out of town than on the previous two. She didn't get all the way to Smokey's, of course, but she got close to where the sidewalk ended, passing by the coin laundry and the car wash. She stopped here again, just as she'd done a couple days ago before she'd headed down into the valley and trespassed into the park. She looked at the two buildings on either side of the road and had that funny feeling again, a feeling that the looks of what she was seeing and what Clara had told her about Tony just didn't add up. She turned around and made it back to where she'd parked her car and stopped at the inn before heading back to the farmhouse. Ezra was playing chess with Herb in the office kitchen. They both looked up and greeted her with a smile.

Alexa asked, "Herb, do you love this guy so much you stay here even after your shift?"

Herb moved a pawn forward and nodded. "Ez here is as fine as they come. I couldn't think of finer company. Plus"—he looked up at her—"I live here. Where else would I go?"

Alexa was confused. "What?"

Ezra nodded, not looking up from the board but moving his knight to a square that caused Herb to sigh in frustration and lean back. "Room ten," Ezra said. "The Presidential Suite."

Neither man seemed to have much else to say on the matter, so Alexa let it go.

Their secret. Theirs to keep.

"Ezra, can I talk to you for a second? In private? No offense, Herb."

Herb waved her off, studying the game board. "Lady, I'm the last person on earth t'give a damn about taking offense."

Ezra stood and they went back into the main office. Alexa told him what she wanted and if he knew a guy who could help. Ezra said he did.

"Same guy?" Alexa asked.

Ezra said, "Does it matter?"

He went back to his game, and Alexa went back to the farmhouse. She'd seen a whole chicken in Ezra's freezer and she'd set it out to thaw. She was going to make it for them for dinner that night. Try to, anyway.

Their evenings together, those few days while they waited, had been spent sharing meals and chatting, but never about anything serious, never about the past, and then either reading with coffee or watching television with coffee. Sometimes Ezra would disappear into the basement by himself for an hour or so, and Alexa was always tempted to walk down and see what he was doing but never did. Talk about what they were waiting on, or what they were planning to do, or any words at all about anything that had happened to have led them to this point was nonexistent. It was as though the two of them had simply been dropped into a predetermined, long-existing routine with an old friend. It was strange but wonderful and honestly perfect. For those four days.

Then, on that fourth night, Ezra emerged from one of his trips to the basement and said, "It's here. What we asked for."

This time when he went back down, Alexa followed him, already sensing that everything was about to change.

CHAPTER 24

E zra's computer screens were filled with open windows and applications. Alexa glanced at them over his shoulder after he'd sat down at the desk, but then she focused back on him. It was his show; she'd let him take her through everything at his pace.

Ezra made a single click of the mouse and one of the windows went full-screen. It was a photograph of the black SUV, parked on the street with high-rise buildings on either side—definitely not buildings in Silent Falls. The SUV's driver's-side doors were open. A thick-necked man in a sweater and black slacks was stepping out of the driver's seat, and at the rear, another guy, this one with an even thicker neck and wide shoulders and arms swollen with muscle, also wearing a sweater and black slacks, was holding a to-go box of food in one hand and handing a bottle of water to the third member of the party. The third guy was slim and tall. He was wearing khaki pants and loafers and a button-up dress shirt —what somebody like Griff Ugly Grin would call a *nice shirt*

—and sunglasses that reminded Alexa of Sheriff Byrd's, only these weren't as big. They were sleeker, stylish.

She knew she was looking at the same crew who'd approached Griff in the Lil' Tony's Landscaping parking lot, had been spying on her around town, and had abducted Clara.

The same crew who'd likely killed Tony and chopped his body to pieces and set his head on fire. Hopefully in that order, for Tony's sake.

"Who are they?" she asked.

"Do their names matter?" Ezra asked. He shot her a side glance and waited.

"No," Alexa said, seeing his point. "I suppose not."

"It's who we're dealing with, at this level, for our particular investigation," he said.

Alexa picked up the word *investigation* and filed it away, thought it might mean something about the man sitting next to her. He clicked the mouse and the image remained on-screen, but it was reduced in size, making way for Ezra to slide another window over from the other screen. This was a typed report—no header or identifying information anywhere on it to indicate who'd written or provided the data —and it was broken down into a handful of sections marked off with bolded headings. Alexa didn't bother to read the words. Again, Ezra's show.

"The SUV is registered to V. A. B. LLC," he said. "Listed as a services company and clearly just a shell, one of hundreds the Abatelli family probably uses. On paper they're legit, and revenue isn't high enough to cause any major red flags."

"Because they're spreading it all over all the others, too,"

Alexa said, nodding. "Almost like diversifying their illegal actions."

Ezra nodded. "That's my assumption as well."

"You don't know for sure? Your guy didn't check out the other companies."

"My guy will only look into exactly what I ask him to," Ezra said matter-of-factly and continued on. "Using aggregated data from traffic cameras and other on-network public surveillance systems, as well as other ... not-so-public surveillance systems for image recognition on the plate, plus some geolocation services built into the car, we've been able to establish a pretty regular pattern in the SUV's movement history over the past week."

Alexa said nothing. Turned and looked at Ezra with something that felt like awe. "Your guy can do *all* that?"

"He can."

"Shit, I thought maybe you just meant you knew a guy at the local DMV that could fax you over the registration info."

Ezra twitched a grin. "A guy at the DMV who could also dig into Tony Romano's financial records?"

"Hey," Alexa said, throwing up her hands. "You wouldn't tell me if it was the *same* guy, remember?"

He conceded. "Good point."

He clicked the mouse again and a new window appeared. This document was comprised of several screenshots from different types of maps, some satellite images, some topographical, and a couple that looked like nothing more than Google Street View. They were all marked up with dots and lines and stars marking and tracing paths and locations.

"Basically," Ezra said, "they've been spending most of

their time here in Silent Falls. They make a regular loop around town over and over. They stop to check in on a few local businesses now and again, they take a break for lunch, and in the late afternoon they often head back to East River for roughly an hour or two before heading back." He brought up the picture again of the three men standing outside the SUV parked on the street. "This location is one of the business addresses registered to V. A. B. LLC. They have one there, in Roanoke, and a"—he made air quotes—"'corporate headquarters' in Richmond."

"The big cities," Alexa said. "Just like you thought."

"When they make these evening trips back to East River, they swap out drivers for a fresh shift and the guy in the dress shirt stays behind."

"Night patrol is for the goons, huh?"

Ezra nodded. "Guess so. Anyway, they come back and patrol again, then head back a bit before sunrise, and the cycle repeats most days."

"And they've always done this?"

Ezra held up a finger and pointed to her. "See, that's the interesting part. No, they haven't. My guy went back a little further, and for the most part they were only coming into town once or twice a month at the most before. Only recently have they started the regular trips."

Alexa was about to say something ridiculous, like, "They started coming when I showed up," but of course that wasn't the case. She wasn't that arrogant as to think that her mere presence had summoned the wrath of a crime syndicate. But she'd managed to show up right around the same time that something else had changed. Something had happened to cause concern.

"Tony," she said. "They started coming because of something to do with Tony."

"Considering they killed him, I'd be willing to make that bet."

She heard Griff's voice again, recalling what the man in the nice shirt had told him: *Tony fucked up.*

"And they've stuck around after because of me," Alexa said. "Because they thought I was digging, and that maybe Tony and I were somehow involved in something together because they happened to see us at Smokey's the night I got into town."

"Correction," Ezra said. "You *were* digging, and, yes, I believe that's exactly why they stuck around. The attack on Clara proves that."

It made her feel guilty, that last part. But also refocused her, fueled that desire for retribution. "What about Tony's businesses?" she asked. "Did you get the info on that?"

Ezra nodded. Pointed to a folder on his desktop. He didn't click to open it, however. "It's all in there and it's all very boring unless you get off on spreadsheets. But you were right to bring it up—it was a good thought."

"*Because?*"

He grinned. "Because it was exactly like you thought, and is probably the main reason Tony was in bed with the Abatelli family in the first place. He's laundering their money for them. Nothing huge, mind you, but enough to make him valuable. You'd have to really go into the data specifically looking for it to find the anomalies. And come on, these little businesses in a place like Silent Falls. Nobody's checking for that."

Alexa thought about Clara telling her that Tony had been

doing the books for his father's restaurant. "Was Smokey's part of it?"

Ezra nodded. "Smokey's, and the landscaping business, of course. But your hunch about the car wash and laundromat was spot-on. They were newly acquired and already a ton of cash is being spent, though if you take one look at those places it's easy to see not a lot is happening."

Alexa nodded to herself, felt proud. It felt good to be right. "It was part of the next step. Phase two, maybe? But they never got very far because..."

"Because Tony made a mistake somewhere along the way and they deep-fried his head."

She shot him a look. "Yeah ... that. And we don't know what that mistake was?"

Ezra shook his head. Pointed to the screens. "Nothing here is ever going to tell us that."

Alexa left the desk and went to lean against the back of the love seat. All of this information was good to know and completely validated all the things she and Ezra had been thinking and piecing together on their own, but it didn't really help answer the question now at the forefront of her mind.

"So what do we do now?" she asked. "You said you wanted to do this"—she did not ask for what the definition of "this" would be—"the right way. So now that you've seen all that"—she pointed to the screens—"what's next?"

He had spun around in the desk chair to look at her, and when she'd finished speaking, he waited a long moment, stared at her, almost as if he was running her through his own sort of algorithm the same way his *guy* had run the license plate through all those systems. Or maybe he was reevaluating everything for himself, wondering if whatever decision he'd reluctantly made at the start of this was really the way forward he wanted to go. Whatever he'd been thinking, he apparently arrived at his answer, because he turned back around in the chair and pulled up the picture of the map again.

He enlarged a particular section of it and pointed. "That's next," he said.

Alexa pushed off from the love seat and walked over. Put a hand on his shoulder and leaned in close. It was the first time they'd really touched each other. "What am I looking at?"

"The SUV occasionally makes this detour on their way back to East River. Not every day, but usually every other."

Alexa followed the lines and markings on the map the best she could. "It's away from the highway, and ... well, it looks like it heads away from everything. Just, what? Woods, mountains? What's out there?" she asked.

"The tracking isn't great once they get far enough out, so we don't know the precise location, but we did a search of where the signal seems to drop off and found this." Ezra clicked another window into place, and a new satellite image replaced the map. It showed what looked like a large brick building sprawling over a handful of acres. A towering smokestack punctuated one side. "It's an old rubber factory," Ezra said. "Shut down and abandoned over a decade ago."

The imagery was enough to give Alexa a chill. "And what do they do out there?"

Ezra shook his head. "Regularly? No idea."

"There's a but coming, isn't there?"

"But ... they were there the night Tony was killed. And then they drove back into town. To the park."

It was too obvious. "So that's where they killed him."

"Yes," Ezra said. "Good chance. And it's also where we make our move."

CHAPTER 25

Alexa Shifflett did not put her trust in other people. Well, at least not very often. She couldn't remember how long it had been before Lance that she'd felt on some deep level that a person was inherently good and had her own best interests in mind. But now, Ezra had earned her trust and then some. It had happened so quickly, it seemed, but sometimes the best things happened fast, without you even having had to think about it. Maybe that's why they were the best. They were easy.

She didn't know what his plan was, not exactly. She'd only been left with those words he'd offered last night at the computer in his basement: "And it's also where we'll make our move."

He'd been referring to the abandoned rubber factory where Tony Romano had presumably met his demise, and by "we'll make our move," Alexa could only assume he was planning some sort of ... what? Attack? Ambush? It seemed ridiculous, to think that she would take part in something so comically insane as attempting to take down three mob members at an abandoned old factory. It was something that only happened in movies or crime novels, not to her, not in real life.

But then she thought of Lance again, about the impossible situation that had caused them to meet, and the fantastical feat that had forged their bond. She thought about all he was and what he could do. Which begged the question: What the fuck was real life anyway?

Besides, whatever Ezra was cooking up—and how exactly *was* he able to cook this up in the first place? Who was this *guy* that had provided all their intel? Who the hell was *Ezra?* —Alexa was more than ready. Every time she remembered the image of Clara sitting on that hospital bed in the emergency room, her sneakers dangling off the edge making her look so small and scared, Alexa felt the rush of anger flush through her and she knew that anybody who could chop Tony Romano to pieces and then break an innocent young girl's finger just to send a message was not somebody she should ever think twice about doing something very bad to. Somebody else might tell her that two wrongs didn't make a right, or that the whole "eye for an eye" philosophy was barbaric and uncivilized, but Alexa doubted very much she and those people would get along. They could keep their opinions and she would keep hers. She'd survived just fine on her own opinions for a long time and had come out on the other side to tell the tale.

She was sitting in the café, thinking about all of this, keeping up her normal morning routine, when Big Tony walked through the door.

She'd never met or seen the man before, but his likeness to his son was instantly noticeable. The broad shoulders, the nose and cheekbones. And the eyes—the eyes would give it away from across the street. As his nickname indicated, looking at Big Tony was exactly like looking at Lil' Tony, only aged up to his midfifties, with a little more softness around the belly and a lot more lines around his eyes. His hair was thinning, and it looked as if this morning he hadn't bothered to comb it. He was wearing dark jeans and black shoes with thick rubber soles and a white T-shirt beneath a black windbreaker jacket with "Smokey's" stitched on the back. Alexa realized he was probably dressed to go to work. The newspaper article she'd read about Tony's murder hadn't mentioned anything about a funeral or family visitation, so if and when it had happened, she wasn't sure, but something about seeing this man dressed for work, ready to go in and face the tough reality of a world without his son, made Alexa like him. She respected something she saw there, in those eyes, in those broad shoulders that Big Tony was still carrying high, not slumped, not defeated.

A thought occurred to her, an idea she knew she should probably not chase. But ... she and Ezra had one question that they couldn't yet answer: what had Tony done to piss off the mob enough that they'd decided to kill him? And Alexa still thought of Clara, about how quickly after her lunchtime chat with the girl that day at Smokey's the Abatelli family had seemed to have known about it. Alexa had first assumed there was a possibility that somebody inside Smokey's had tipped them off. And if Lil' Tony had been working for the mob, especially using his father's business as a money passthrough, there was still a chance that Big Tony knew something. Might have been the one to drop the hint about her.

Alexa scanned the café's patrons, looked for anybody who

might be watching her. She saw only the normal morning patrons, and the few folks in line ahead of Big Tony didn't seem to set off any alarm bells in her mind. She glanced out the big front windows and surveyed the street. Checked the parked cars and the meandering traffic, searching for any spot of black that would give away the SUV. She saw none. And then she was moving. She pushed her chair back and weaved through a few tables to just reach the line and jump in behind Big Tony before a young man in a hoodie and with his earphones in that had just pushed through the door could. He looked at her like she was crazy, but the look she gave him back caused him to quickly glance away and pay strict attention to the menu board.

"Very sorry to hear about your son," Alexa said.

Big Tony's big shoulders stiffened just the slightest bit, and Alexa watched as his eyes slitted for just a second, as if he'd been dealt a blow. She felt like shit, instantly. Was already regretting what she was doing. But hey, sometimes life is shitty. She was only trying to learn the truth.

"Thanks," Big Tony grunted. He didn't look at her. Just slid down in line one place. Showed not one bit of recognition of who she was.

"I only met him once," Alexa said. "At your restaurant."

Big Tony nodded. Leaned down to examine something in the glass display case of pastries.

"That's a great place you have there. Smokey's. I've never had a bad meal there. And that waitress you have, Clara, she's really amazing. Friendly and helpful and very bright. That was a good hire on your part."

Big Tony said nothing.

"Great that you're pet-friendly, too."

Nothing. The man was completely uninterested in conversation, and Alexa could understand that. But, unfortunately, this was a time she couldn't accept it. She'd been dragged into a murder investigation and knocked out by a camera-wielding idiot, had received a threatening phone call from the mob, and Clara had been abducted and assaulted. And it had all started with the son of the man next to her.

"Did you know he was mixed up with the Abatelli family? Do you have any idea what he could have done to make them so mad?" It was blunt, probably too blunt.

Big Tony spun toward her so fast the room seemed to move with him, his wide shoulders slicing through the air like a battering ram. "Who *are* you?" He leaned in close, towering over her. Hissed, "My son was *not* involved with the Abatelli family or anything else like that. I don't care what the police might say or the papers might say, I don't care what anybody says, do you hear me?"

And Alexa saw the tears now brimming in his eyes. Eyes that, now that she was up close, appeared very tired and bloodshot.

"My son was *smart*," Big Tony said, losing some of his bite. "He was a businessman. You like Smokey's so much? Guess what? Tony was the reason we've been able to stay afloat all these years. He was a financial genius, always knew the numbers. And he was *thriving*. His own businesses were growing, he was about expand into more areas, he..." The tears came now, spilling down Big Tony's cheeks in fat droplets that looked like rain. His face burned a bright red. "He was my boy."

He left. Pushing past Alexa and out through the door. Hurrying down the sidewalk and out of sight.

Alexa watched him go, then turned to see several of the café patrons staring at her, all with looks of *what just happened?* on their faces. She stared right back at them, kept her face stoic. Nobody said anything, and eventually everyone started looking back down at the newspapers or their computers or anywhere but at her. She left the line and grabbed her coffee from the table where she'd been sitting and then left. Heading, thankfully, in the opposite direction of the way Big Tony had gone. She got in her Oldsmobile and drove away, knowing two things.

One, Big Tony really did have no idea what sort of things his son had been involved in. And two, if anybody had been watching or listening to her conversation just now on behalf of the mob, she'd definitely made things worse.

It had been a risk, and this time it hadn't paid off. All she'd managed to do was upset a grieving father.

Sometimes you're a real winner, Shiffy. A real fucking winner.

SHE PULLED into the inn's parking lot and parked next to a Jeep Wrangler that hadn't been there earlier. She killed the engine and went into the office to confess to Ezra what she'd done like some Catholic do-gooder. But Ezra wasn't there. She found Herb behind the counter talking to an older man who was leaned down and looking at a map that Herb had unfolded before them.

"Those hippie GPS contraptions don't take ya right!" Herb said while tapping his finger on the map. "They don't know 'bout this road, but it's best. Oh, sure, you'll miss those flashy tourist shops"—he waved his hands in the air—"but you can still park and jump on the trails right here. And if you're into fishing, there's another pond here"—he tapped again—"that only locals know 'bout. Trust me, this is the way to go."

The man chuckled and thanked Herb for the info, said he'd head that way first thing in the morning. The men shook hands and then the guy took his room key and nodded politely to Alexa as she left.

Herb smiled at Alexa and said, "I know, I'm not the tall, dark and handsome guy you were expecting, but what I lack in height, I make up for in charm and chivalry."

Alexa laughed and nodded. "I believe it. Honestly. Where's Ezra?"

"Out. Said he had to go check on something a bit out of town, might be gone three or four hours."

He's gone out to that factory, that crazy son of a bitch, Alexa thought. *In broad daylight.* This thought was followed by a sudden pang of worry. *What if they catch him? What if they find him there and tomorrow it's* his *head somebody finds on the ball field at Collins Park.*

She cared about him—that was what this new thought really told her. Not that she was surprised—of course she'd known this before today, had been aware of the bond the two of them had formed. But nothing tells you how you really feel about somebody quite like the fear that something bad might have happened to them.

A glint of light refracted off a picture frame on the wall behind Herb, and Alexa turned and saw a black SUV pulling into the inn's parking lot. Her heart rate spiked and she felt her muscles tense, ready to fight, ready to punch and kick. Ready to run if needed. She was about to warn Herb, tell him bad guys were about to come in for her, but then the SUV parked and she realized it really wasn't black at all but dark blue. And the guy that got out of the driver's seat wasn't one of the goons she'd seen on Ezra's computer but a young guy with blond hair who turned and opened the back door and helped a little girl with pigtails out of the back seat. He held her hand as they entered the office.

Alexa smiled at them and stood back as Herb helped them check in with plenty of charm and chivalry. He reached behind the counter and pulled out a red lollipop for the little girl, and the young dad thanked Herb repeatedly. When they were gone, Herb asked Alexa, "Do you play chess?"

Alexa hadn't played chess since she was a little girl. *Before.* But after the ill-advised confrontation with Big Tony at the café and the paranoid moment of seeing the young guy park his dark blue SUV, she was looking for anything to occupy her mind for a bit. Especially until Ezra returned.

"Let's do it," she said.

Herb looked absolutely thrilled.

CHAPTER 26

Herb beat her two games in a row, fast. But by the third game, she was able to make it interesting. She still lost, but it was a much closer game, taking nearly an hour. When Herb finally called checkmate, she told him she needed to get back to Barlow so he wouldn't pee all over Ezra's expensive floors. Herb chuckled and said to make sure to bring the dog back in soon, that he missed the little bugger. Alexa promised she would.

She drove back to the farmhouse, hoping Ezra would be there, but he wasn't. She let Barlow out and tossed his favorite tennis ball with him in the backyard for a while, and when the sun started to set, she cooked dinner. Nothing fancy, just spaghetti with meat sauce, but as she moved around the kitchen, she found herself constantly glancing down the hallway, looking for any sign of life outside, hoping to see headlights splashing across the front windows.

He's fine, she told herself. *He can take care of himself.*

But how did she know that? She knew nothing about the man.

But ... the confidence. The computers in the basement. His *guy*. The calculated coldness that had been in his voice when he'd said, "We just need to do it right," like he knew exactly what that meant. What moves to make and which not to.

It was just a feeling she had.

Instinct.

Whoever Ezra really was, whoever he'd been before he'd become proprietor of the Silent Falls Inn, Alexa knew it had been a very different life. One that appeared to have been much more exciting.

His secrets to keep.

She trusted him—that was all that mattered.

She looked at the clock, and at seven p.m. she told herself she'd wait five more minutes before eating. She waited three and then he was there, the headlights she'd been waiting for finally doing their sparkle across the front windows, followed by the sound of his truck door opening and closing. Barlow, who'd been seated patiently by the stove and sniffing at the pot of meat sauce, started thumping his tail against the floor and then headed to the front door to great Ezra.

"Smells great," he said when he came into the kitchen.

"Where have you been?" Then she laughed at how stern she'd sounded. "Sorry, I know that I sounded like an angry housewife, but..." She shrugged. "Herb told me you'd gone out of town to check on things, and I guess I sort of know what that means and, yeah, I was getting worried. So what?"

He smiled at her as he petted Barlow. "Well, I appreciate the concern," he said. He stood and washed his hands at the sink, grabbed one of the plates she'd set out. "But I'm fine. I would have been here sooner, but I needed to stop by the inn and talk to Herb about some things." He scooped food onto his plate and sat at the table. She joined him with a plate of her own.

They ate in silence for a minute or two. Ezra ate fast, like he'd been starving, and Alexa again wondered just what the hell he'd been doing all day. Finally, he wiped his face with a napkin and set his fork down and looked at her. "Still want to do this?" he asked.

She didn't need any further clarification. Saw the image of Clara's sneakers dangling off that hospital bed again. "Yes."

He stared at her for a solid five seconds, looking straight into her eyes like he was trying to read her mind. Then, when she gave him nothing, he nodded and said, "I went out to that abandoned factory today, scoped it all out, checked out the perimeter, the land around it, everything. There's lots of fresh tire tracks in the gravel and the mud. Our friends definitely make a regular pilgrimage out there."

"Did they come today?"

He shook his head. "No. That's one of the reasons I went today. Like we saw on the computer, they only seem to go every other day, so the math told me today was probably safe. Still, I parked about a mile further up the road, off in the trees, and then hiked back, just to be safe."

She waited a full minute, watched as he started eating again. Then she sighed and threw up her hands and said, "*And...*"

"And I have a plan," he said. "Way I figure, they'll be back tomorrow. We can hit them then."

A tingle of excitement grew in Alexa's belly, pushing aside that glowing ember of hope that had been taking up residence there.

"I am not intending this to sound patronizing," Ezra said, "but it will likely be dangerous, and there is certainly a chance we could be hurt or killed."

She resisted the urge to roll her eyes. He wasn't trying to talk her out of anything; he was just stating facts, like offering her a verbal safety waiver. "But," she added, "I'm guessing there's a better chance that our *friends* could also be hurt or, you know, killed, should things not go in their favor."

Ezra stood and walked to the stove to scoop more spaghetti onto his plate. He turned back around and licked a small bit of sauce off his thumb. "Oh, that's exactly what I'm betting on," he said.

Alexa got chills.

When Ezra returned to the table, Alexa changed the conversation gear a bit and told him about her encounter with Big Tony at the café. He listened patiently while he ate, and after Alexa had finished talking, he said, "Boy, you really don't stop until you have all the answers, do you?"

She didn't know exactly what sort of response she'd been expecting, but it wasn't this one. She shrugged. "Do you think that's a good thing or a bad thing?"

"Both. Good if you can control it. Bad if you can't. This one is a bit of toss-up."

"Doesn't change anything about tomorrow, does it?"

Ezra shook his head. "I think Big Tony is as ignorant as they come in all this. Right now he's just a dad who's lost a son."

Alexa thought for a minute. "But that might change, right? They might come for him later—you know, because of Smokey's. Are they just going to stop using it for their money laundering? I mean, it's got to be one of the busiest places in town, right? It's *prime* for that kind of thing."

Ezra didn't seem very interested in this line of questioning. "Let's just wait and see how tomorrow goes," he said. "That's our only priority. Not Smokey's, not Big Tony. Nothing else."

Alexa sat back in her chair. That coldness had crept back into Ezra's voice, the one from a few nights ago. *He's out for blood*, she realized—or maybe she was just confirming it once and for all.

"Okay," she said, crossing her arms the way Ezra did so often. "Tell me this grand plan of yours."

So he did.

CHAPTER 27

At five a.m. the following morning, before Alexa headed outside to join Ezra in his truck, she pulled her phone from her jeans pocket and sent a quick message to Clara: *Thank you for being kind to me and Barlow. I think you're a very bright young woman and am happy to have met you. Sorry I dragged you into such a mess. Tell your brother I'm sorry too.* —*Alexa*

She hit Send.

Then she leaned down and scratched Barlow on the top of the head, which turned into a full-on hug. He licked her face and she breathed in the scent of him, got lost in his soft fur. She pulled back and took his head in her hands and said, "I love you. You've saved me, if only for a short while, and I will never forget that."

She stood and stepped outside and closed the door and walked down the porch steps toward the truck. She did not look back, did not want to see Barlow's face in the window watching her leave.

I'll be back, she told herself. *We'll both be back.*

Because Ezra is confident and I am who I am. Change be damned. I'm a survivor. This will not be the end of me.

But now was not time to think about the future and whatever it might hold.

Now, there was only today. It would define whatever came next.

If anything came at all.

CHAPTER 28

They arrived before the sun came up, the headlights of Ezra's truck splashing across the overgrown field and faintly illuminating the deserted factory that lay in its depths, as if it were rising from the earth with the fog. An access road, asphalt broken and crumbling and spotted with weeds, led off the county road they'd been driving for the last twenty minutes, the only indication that it existed being the two wooden posts left behind in the ground, posts that had presumably at one time or another held a sign advertising the factory. Ezra turned onto the access road and parked the truck just beyond the skeleton of the sign. Pushed the door open against the reaching overgrowth from the field and walked around to the back of the truck. Alexa twisted around and watched as he, glowing red from the truck's taillights, squatted down to the ground for a couple seconds and then popped back up. He got back in the driver's seat and they drove on.

"What was that?" she asked.

"Motion sensor. It'll alert us as soon as anyone heads this

way. I timed it yesterday. Even if somebody floored it—which they won't, not on this road with all the holes and asphalt chunks—it'll give us roughly a minute's head start to get ready."

She turned and looked at him. A front tire dipped into a hole, and despite the truck's fancy suspension, they were still jolted in the cabin. "You didn't tell me about the motion sensor."

Ezra gripped the wheel and slowed the truck down a bit. "You're right. Sorry. I usually try to make sure my team has every detail. It won't happen again."

"Anything else you're forgetting to tell me?"

He shook his head. "No, ma'am. You know the script. Stick to it, and we'll be fine. These guys are just goons, remember that. Hired hands used to using their puffy muscles and reputation to scare people. That won't work on us. We know they're just bullies, and when they come out here, they'll be all alone."

"Puffy muscles and reputation killed Tony and chopped him to pieces and turned his head into a piece of charcoal. Puffy muscles and reputation can apparently do a lot."

"Not to me," Ezra said. Then quickly: "Us. We have a tactical advantage."

"Which is?"

"The good ol' element of surprise."

"You sounded a lot like Herb just now."

Ezra nodded. "Herb would agree with me."

The factory was two stories, and while it wasn't very tall, it sprawled out across the land, stretching its arms. Most of the windows were either missing or broken; a big metal door near the front was hanging sideways, only one hinge remaining. One of the large smokestacks on the far end from them stretched high into the sky, but it had an unnatural lean to it, along with several dark spots that looked like missing chunks of brick, like the world's tallest Jenga game. In the glow from the truck's headlights, Alexa could see the deep red of the building's exterior. It reminded her of blood, like a solidified version of what had come flowing out of the elevator in that scene from Kubrick's *The Shining*. She shivered at the thought.

Ezra bumped and rumbled the truck along the access road until they reached a parking area, a wider, flatter sea of asphalt that had held together a little better than the road did but was still being taken over by the wild. It stretched nearly as long as the building, probably where all the workers had parked back when the place was still booming. If it ever had been booming. Looking at it now made that very hard to believe. Dilapidated and long-extinguished light poles sprouted from the parking lot like lonely trees. Like the smokestack, several of them were leaning, too, like a particularly strong gust of wind would finally send them falling to their death. Ezra passed by the parking lot without slowing, continuing on toward the factory, following the access road as it took a wide arc around and then led behind the building. There were big bay doors here, places for trucks to deliver and pickup. A loading dock stretching for what seemed like nearly a third of the building's length. There was a row of old dumpsters in the far back corner, rusted out, their lids ripped off and scattered on the ground around them.

Alexa saw what Ezra had meant about the tire tracks. Back here, nature really had started to win the war. Most of the parking lot had crumbled and given way to tall grass and dirt, muddy still from the last bit of melted snow. But swaths of the high grass had been pushed over by something big and heavy, forming multiple snakelike paths coming and going.

"You think all of this was them?" she asked as Ezra turned and headed toward the dumpsters, the cabin shifting and shaking across the uneven ground.

"Them and whoever they meet out here."

Alexa looked at him, waited for more.

"I don't know who, but I don't know why else they come out here so regularly if not for some sort of rendezvous. They're not chopping people to bits every other day. That would have to be exhausting, even for them."

Alexa honestly wasn't sure if he'd meant that last part as a joke or not. "What if whoever they meet here comes while we're, uh, fulfilling our plan?"

"We'll be gone before they do."

She sighed. "And how exactly do you know this?"

"Tactical advantage again. Our guys will want to be the early ones, be here and ready, waiting. They won't want surprises. Plus," he added, "it's good they're meeting somebody."

"Why?"

She was watching him as she spoke, and in the faint glow of the dashboard lights she saw a small grin on his lips. "Because there's a good chance they're going to get blamed for the mess we make."

"Oh," Alexa said. "I suppose that's a good point." And she wondered what this mess would look like, when it was all said and done.

Ezra reached the dumpsters and swung the truck around in a semicircle and backed up between two of them, leaving the cab of the truck protruding like a tongue sticking out. He cracked the windows and then killed the headlights and the engine. After a few moments, the cabin went dark, and Alexa could barely see the grayish-blue tint of the very first rays of the sun creeping in.

"This is the waiting part?" she asked.

"This is the waiting part," Ezra agreed. "According to the data we saw, they probably won't be here till late in the afternoon, so we have some time. You can try to sleep if you want."

"Are you kidding me? No way I could sleep right now. I'm not like Barlow." The thought of her dog pricked a quick pain in her heart.

"I brought my Kindle," Ezra said. "You're welcome to read something."

She stared at him.

"What?" he said. "Would you rather play the alphabet game?"

"Is this *fun* for you?" she asked. "Like, are you genuinely enjoying yourself right now, with what we're about to do?"

He'd been grinning at her, but now his face fell. It hardened in that way she was getting used to seeing, his mind working. He looked away from her, out the window and toward where the ground sloped up and away from them, a hillside beyond lined with a thick crop of trees that were growing lighter in the morning sun. When he looked back to her, he was still serious, but his eyes were softer. "We're about to stop some very bad people from hurting anyone else. They deserve what's coming to them, and if we're the ones to deliver that justice, then, yes, I think that's a fine way to spend my time. I won't lose any sleep over it." Then, "Will you?"

Alexa took a long, deep breath. Let it out and shook her head. "No. I suppose I won't."

He nodded. "Alright, then. I went to the store and bought an avocado."

She rolled her eyes. "Jesus. Fine. I went to the store and bought an avocado and..."

THEY FINISHED the game just as the sun was fully cresting the trees to the east, its rays sloping down the hill and warming the truck's cabin and sparkling off the morning frost. They were quiet after, not sure what else to say. Ezra pulled out his Kindle from the truck's center console and, despite her earlier protests, Alexa leaned her head back, reclined the seat slightly, and closed her eyes.

She woke with a start, a noise jerking her back to reality. She sat up fast in the truck's seat, looked left and saw Ezra was gone. *Shit! He didn't wake me up when they got here! Where is he? Did they take him?*

No, that was silly. Of course he'd wake her up. They were a team—he'd said as much when they'd been driving toward the factory after he'd set up the motion sensor. She was part of the plan. Ezra might be confident, but she didn't think he was so cocky and stupid as to try and take this all on by himself.

Movement from the back of the truck. She spun around and breathed a sigh of relief at the sight of him. He opened the door and must have seen the look on her face. "Sorry," he said. "Had to use the facilities."

Alexa slumped back in her seat. "Oh," she said. "For a second I thought..."

"I was off getting chopped to pieces?"

She glared at him but then felt herself smile. "Stupid, I know."

Ezra shrugged. "Not really. It's normal to be scared, or paranoid, or ... anxious. When you haven't done stuff like this before. Some of those feelings never go completely away, even when you have."

Maybe it was the moment, the day, the entire crazy scenario, but Alexa saw this opening as the best one she'd had since meeting Ezra. She couldn't let it pass by. He'd showed her the cracked door, and she was going to try to nudge it open. "And you have?" she asked. "Done things like this before?"

He must have instantly seen what had happened. Replayed the previous seconds of conversation in his head and realized he'd set himself up. He didn't answer, just clenched his jaw and turned and looked out the window, up the slope to the trees.

She regretted asking. Felt guilty. After all this time of Ezra respecting her privacy, ever since that very first night at the inn, she couldn't reciprocate. Plus, she knew the answer to her own question—*of course he's done stuff like this.* Any idiot could see that. The ability to get their intel from his *guy*, the computer equipment in the basement, coming up with this plan like it was nothing more than planning a picnic lunch and a hike ... his apparent indifference to ending the life of somebody bad.

These were not things normal people could do or would

do. He'd might not have told her his truth, but he'd *shown* it to her. She should have accepted that.

"I'm sorry," she said, because she could think of nothing else.

She looked at the clock on the dash and saw it was nearly noon. She hadn't realized she'd slept so long. She needed to get out of this truck, now. "Which way to the facilities?" she asked, trying to sound chipper, pleasant. Trying to take back what she'd said before.

Ezra used his thumb to point behind him. "I just went a few yards into the grass behind the dumpsters. Oh," he said, remembering something, "here." He turned and reached into the back seat, where he had the bag with their supplies, all of which he'd picked up on his way home last night. Another reason it had taken him so long to return. He unzipped it and fished around a bit before pulling out a roll of toilet paper. "Thought you might want this."

She took it from him. "Thanks. You really did come prepared." She smiled, but he'd already turned away again, staring back to the trees.

When she'd finished her business, she risked a short walk up and back down the factory's loading dock, kicking at discarded beer cans and chunks of concrete and a few stray bricks. She figured if the motion sensor triggered, Ezra would do something to get her attention—honk the horn or maybe just stick his head out the window and yell. The air was cold but the sun felt good, and it helped to clear her head after sitting in the truck for so long.

She made her way back and climbed inside the truck. Shut the door and was about to launch into another apology, trying to impress upon Ezra that she understood he had secrets and she was rude for prying and she felt terrible and—

"I have," Ezra said. He was gripping the steering wheel and looking out the windshield. "I have done things like this before."

Alexa said nothing. Sat frozen with her hand still on the door handle. Afraid to move, as if she might scare away whatever revelation he was about to offer.

"Lots of times," Ezra said. He paused, seemed to be struggling with where to start. She let him struggle, didn't dare offer a word of encouragement or ask any questions. It was his secret to tell. Only his.

"I've always had money," he said. "Well, my family has. My grandpa was in banking and my father followed him. Made some great investments in Silicon Valley, back in the *early* days, back when the companies everybody knows now were just breaking out of their garages. Anyway, we were rich, no other way to say it. I was smart—*am* smart, I guess—and graduated high school a year early before heading to college at the University of Maryland. My junior year, both my parents died." He stopped here for a second, and Alexa saw his hands grip the steering wheel a little tighter, heard the leather crackle.

"I'm sorry," she said, again because she didn't know what else to say.

"Mom had lung cancer. Never smoked a day in her life. They thought they had it under control, but then ... well, it got bad real fast. She died during fall semester exam week. I never even got to say goodbye." He swallowed hard, his Adam's apple bobbing up and down. "Dad killed himself three months later."

Alexa felt her heart sink. For so many reasons.

"Ninety days," Ezra said. "That's how long my dad was able to pretend everything was going to be okay. That's how long he could stand to live on this earth without my mama."

Alexa wanted to reach out and lay a hand on his, wanted to do *something* to show some sympathy, but remained still. Somehow felt this was the way he'd prefer it.

"So I was alone," Ezra said. "I went into my senior year basically an orphan, and I'd inherited more money than I'd ever need. I think about that time a lot, and I ask myself why I stayed in school, why I kept going after my degree. Why I did any of the things that suddenly didn't matter at all. If I'd left, maybe things would have turned out differently." He shrugged. "The only answer I can come up with is that school was all I had left, those friends I had there were my family now. Anyway, I finished up my degree in computer science but had also minored in foreign policy—a weird combination, I know. But that came from my dad, the financial side of him. Always told me that if you understand the way the rest of the world works, you'll be smarter than most everybody else you'll meet. Plus, it wasn't that hard. Like I said, I'm smart." He didn't say it with humor or arrogance or even that sly grin. To him, it was just a fact.

"Anyway, that combination must have attracted some eyes in the government recruitment offices. Because one day just before graduation, I get back to my apartment off-campus and there's two guys in suits waiting for me."

"CIA?" Alexa asked.

He turned his head slightly, just enough to give her a sideways glance. "Nobody you've ever heard of. But they exist, in a big way. Just one of the many secrets our government keeps from its people. But if you want to call them the CIA, then, yeah, go ahead. It doesn't change the story any.

"They made their pitch, promised me the world because of how bright I was, how full of potential. How I could use all my skills to make our country a safer place, to help change the world for the better. But I think they obviously knew about my parents, too, figured here's a guy with nobody to turn to, let's make him one of ours." He shrugged. "Well, it worked. I basically signed my life away right after school."

He stopped here and ran a hand across his head, back and forth back and forth, like he was trying to ruffle away the memory. "Nonstop training for the next two years," he said. "The outside world stopped existing in those twenty-four months, and I became exactly what they wanted me to be."

Alexa waited. The truck's cabin was silent. It almost seemed like he was waiting for her, giving her permission to ask the question herself. "Which was what?"

He turned and looked at her now for the first time. "An assassin."

You could have heard a pin drop in the truck. A beat of absolute silence followed that revelation.

But then Ezra started to grin, and that grin got bigger and eventually morphed into a smile that accompanied a short, soft laugh. "Sorry," he said. "That was quite melodramatic, wasn't it?"

Alexa was confused. There was no way he'd been bull-shitting her about all that, was there?

He cleared his throat and kept going. "I wasn't an *assassin* —officially, that is. But I was trained to kill. Well, to defend myself and those around me, technically. But by the time I got into a place where that sort of self-defense was required, well, only one person in the fight was going to walk away. Name a type of hand-to-hand combat, I probably know it. Guns, blades, I'm decent enough in all of them. I won't bore you with all the technical details; I think you get the picture. I spent a lot of time at a desk behind a computer screen, don't get me wrong there, they really did want me because of my brain, but the other half of the job, well, it was inevitable. Couldn't have one without the other. They needed versatility. Nature of the job. I spent the next several years traveling the country and the globe on missions the public has never and will never hear about."

Alexa had thought that Ezra's truth would answer her questions, put to bed the mystery of who he really was. She was wrong—the truth he'd told her so far had only prompted more questions. She was now sitting in a truck with a guy who could probably kill her with two fingers, which does change your perspective a little. The quickness and confidence with which he'd thrown together their little plan to take down a handful of mob goons now made a lot more sense. This sort of job was probably like playing peewee T-ball to him compared to what he'd done in his past life. But wait … was it his past, truly?

"So what happened?" she asked. "How did you go from Mr. Top Secret Government Agent to the proud and polite owner of the Silent Falls Inn?"

He gripped the steering wheel again, as if bracing for impact. Swallowed hard once more. "Cheyenne happened. She changed everything."

Ezra stared out the windshield for a long time then, as if the mere mention of this woman's name had sent his brain spiraling down memory lane, completely engrossed in the past. *His* before, Alexa thought. "Your wife?" she asked softly.

He came back to the truck then. Put on another small grin, but it looked pained. Shook his head. "We were going to get married, yeah. That was the plan. But, no, not even engaged yet. We met at some fundraiser event in the city. Stuff they sometimes forced guys like me to attend to try and make us feel like normal people again. As if sticking us in an uncomfortable tuxedo in a room full of actual normal people talking about their actual normal lives was going to help instead of make things worse. It was a joke, but it was part of the job. Cheyenne was working at a law firm that was one of the night's big sponsors. I saw her across the room, wearing this black dress that made my heart flutter. She saw me, came over, we started chatting ... well, you can imagine the rest."

"You hit it off."

He laughed. "We hit it out of the stratosphere. She was perfect. We fell in love. Talked about our future." He fell silent again, trailed off.

"Did she know about what you did? What your job was?"

He shook his head. "No. That was forbidden. Obviously. Liability and all that bullshit. She knew I worked for the government but thought it was just as an intelligence analyst in a cybercrime division. But ... I was going to tell her. I kept telling myself that. If she was going to spend the rest of her life with me, I needed her to know. Needed her to see all the cards before placing her final bet, ya know? What kind of person would I be if I didn't? Our entire future would be based on a lie."

"But you never did?"

He squeezed the steering wheel so hard his knuckles

cracked. "Never got the chance to." He took a deep breath, as if trying to bring himself back down, get his emotions under control. Alexa found it painful to see him like this, a guy who normally seemed so carefree and at ease with life. "She got pregnant," he said, "about eight months after we started dating. It wasn't anything we planned, obviously, and even though I was scared shitless, for so many reasons, we were both thrilled. God, you should have seen the way her face lit up when she told me. Anyway, we were baby crazy after that. Believe it or not, work was making it about as easy as it could be for me, keeping me stateside for the majority of the time, so I was able to go to most of the doctor's appointments and whatnot. For a while, things were good, really good.

"But then one afternoon we had a doctor's appointment that we'd already had to reschedule once because of Cheyenne's boss needing her for some extra hours, and this time it was me who couldn't leave. We'd picked up a hot tip on the location of a small terrorist cell rumored to be working on weapons smuggling in South America. My team got called in to run some intel, pull apart the pieces and figure out what was worth pursuing and what wasn't. We'd been chasing this one for months, and there wasn't even an option of me getting out of there."

He stopped, pinched the bridge of his nose and then cleared his throat again. "She was pissed. That's the thing that makes the whole fucking thing even worse than it is," he said. "She was pissed because I couldn't leave work and she'd have to drive herself into the city for the appointment. The last time I talked to my girlfriend, she was angry with me. See, it was pouring down rain that day, like a full-on monsoon type rain, and Cheyenne hated driving in the rain.

Especially on the highway headed into the city. I told her we could reschedule again, that the doctor would understand, but she wasn't having it. She was thinking about the baby, you see? I think she felt that if she couldn't even get to her appointments on time *before* the kid was born, how was she ever going to be a good mother after it came into the world?"

That's ridiculous, Alexa thought. But then again, she'd never been a mother. Had never even known hers.

"So she went by herself," Ezra said. "When she was half an hour late for the appointment, the doctor's office called me and asked if there was a problem. I knew right then and there. I knew something terrible had happened. And I was right."

Oh God, this poor man.

"Police report says her car hydroplaned around a curve and skidded sideways. Hit the median and flipped over it, landing in the way of oncoming traffic. A red Jeep Grand Cherokee never even had a chance to slow down before slamming into her."

He didn't go into more detail. Didn't need to. There was no question of the outcome.

"I quit my job the next day," Ezra said. "Because, you see, it was so ironic. I had been so worried that I was going to be the one my job ended up killing, and in the end it was Cheyenne who had her life stolen by it. I had put one evening of work above the life of my future wife and baby."

"You don't know that things would have ended up any differently if you'd been driving," Alexa said. "For all you know, you'd be dead too."

Ezra shrugged. "Still seemed like the better alternative. For the first time in my life, I got a taste of understanding what it must have been like for my dad, why he killed himself. I forgave him then, in those days after. But I couldn't forgive myself."

Alexa couldn't help herself then; the human part of her that was grieving right along with Ezra as he told his story would not allow her to just sit there. She needed to share in this moment with him, let him know she was there, whatever that was worth. She reached out and gently laid a hand on top of one of his. He didn't look at her, but he didn't pull away.

"Thing is," he said, "quitting that job wasn't exactly as straightforward as putting in a two-week notice via email. Once you're in that system, as deep as I was, they don't just let you back out free and clear. You can leave, but it's a complete reboot of life. A slate wiped clean. The old you is erased, the new you is built from the ground up. Completely new identity, new home, new world. For a lot of people, that's a problem, enough of a hurdle to jump that they stay in. It would be too much of a disruption. Because a lot of the guys I worked with, they *did* have families. But me ... I had nothing. No parents, no siblings, and a recently deceased girlfriend who'd been pregnant with my unborn child. I still had money, worked fixed all that for me, making sure all the assets my parents left me would transfer to my new person, but..." Another shrug, this one the heaviest. "Money was about as relevant as confetti to me at that time. Though now, I'd be crazy not to see it certainly helped with all that's come after."

She nodded. Thought about the inn, the farmhouse, a new life paid for.

"I sold everything I had and started driving. I bounced around, like a zombie. Town to town, no agenda, just..."

"Running," Alexa said.

He nodded. "Running, yes. Exactly. But see, it didn't do any good. My demons weren't the kind you could get away from. They were riding shotgun. Guilt, depression, sorrow. You can't outrun those things. Anyway, it had been about three months, which I can't help but think played some sort of significance in my decision—being that it was the same amount of time that it took for my dad to make his choice to end his life. It was late one night and I rolled into Silent Falls. Something about it just seemed, I don't know, comfortable. I came in on the Smokey's side and drove until I found the inn. Which was closed. Had been foreclosed on by the bank about six months prior, I learned. And for reasons I'm not sure I'll ever be able to explain, I couldn't take my eyes off the For Sale sign in the office window."

The same way I stared at the VACANCY sign...

"I made a choice that night. A choice to not be my father, and to live. To spend the rest of my life living on my own terms, doing good for others, and try to find some inner peace within myself in the process. I bought the inn, found the farmhouse and the land, spent a fortune on both. Poured my heart and soul into it all. And you know what? It's all sort of worked. I've met a lot of great people. I live a simple yet fulfilling life. I'm spending more time trying to enjoy the present than I am imagining about the happiness I missed out on because of my past."

He seemed to be finished then. He let go of the steering wheel and reached around the seat and pulled a bottle of water and a protein bar from the bag of supplies he'd brought. Offered her one of each, which she took. Now that his story was out, the cabin air felt lighter, like a tension between them had been finally released. She wanted to offer more sympathy, wanted to dive into the similarities of their first nights in town, wanted to talk about the Universe and how things apparently have a very unique way of working out exactly how they're supposed to. But all of those things just seemed wrong, the moment off. It was almost as if they'd both been in a trance while he'd told his story, and now that it was over, they'd slipped back into the regular familiarity with each other. A casual comfort.

"So here you are," she said, taking a gulp of water, "minding your own business and trying to live the simple life, and then I walk in and the next thing you know you're on a stakeout waiting for the mob. I feel like I need to apologize."

He ate nearly half his protein bar in a single bite. Shook his head. "You can never fully outrun your past," he said. "And there's one part of mine that hasn't changed anything about my life now. You know what that is?"

She shook her head, clueless.

"Taking down the bad guys still feels really fucking good."

She held out her water bottle. "Amen to that." He smiled, a real smile then, and clicked his bottle against hers.

"So Ezra's not your real name?" she asked through a mouthful of protein bar.

He shook his head.

"How'd you pick that one? Or did they assign it to you during your, how did you say it, reboot?"

"Cheyenne and I had picked out baby names already. Well, she picked them out. I agreed to them without question. If it had been a girl, we'd name her Erica. If it had been a boy ... Ezra."

Alexa didn't get a chance to respond, because just then

Ezra's cell phone chirped a noise she'd not heard before. He sat up quick and pulled it from his pocket and checked the screen.

"Looks like they're early," he said. "Time to do this."

He sounded excited.

CHAPTER 29

They hadn't rehearsed anything, but they moved fast and with silent efficiency, the plan playing out in their minds. Ezra pulled one of the white hard hats from the bag in the back and handed it to Alexa before pulling out his own and placing it on his head. Then he grabbed the two bright orange safety vests and a clipboard. Handed a vest to Alexa and kept the clipboard for himself. Finally, he reached in the bag and pulled out a small pistol, a light and sleek nine-millimeter, and gently set it in Alexa's waiting hand.

"Remember," Ezra said, "you won't have to use this. It's just for looks, for intimidation. Like all their puffy muscles, right? Stick to the plan."

"And if the plan doesn't work?"

Ezra looked offended. Shot back, "Then by all means, pull the trigger. Safety's on."

They jumped from the truck and Alexa tucked the gun into the waistband of her pants and headed toward the loading dock. Climbed onto it. One of the old bay doors was partially ripped away from its place, forming a small cave-like entrance into the factory. She hunched down and slid through, the smell of rusting metal and sawdust and something dead and rotting all invading her nostrils. She coughed once and then covered her mouth quickly, as if she might have given away her location. She squatted down and perched by the small entrance she'd climbed through, looking out onto the open, weed-filled parking area.

Ezra had grabbed one last item from the truck bed, an old tripod, and had set it up slightly in front of him. He had mounted an iPad to the top, but it was all just for show. A prop, just like the hard hats and the safety vests and clipboard.

Just like the gun, Alexa thought. *Unless the plan fails.*

Ezra had added a pair of dark sunglasses to his outfit, and he was standing behind the tripod setup with his head bent, staring at the blank sheet of paper on his clipboard when the soft purr of a strong engine began to echo around Alexa and then the black SUV slid slowly into view from her right.

The tires dug through the mud, the undercarriage of the heavy vehicle pushing through the high grass and growth, moving forward slowly, inch by inch, like a predator stalking its prey. Alexa could only imagine the conversation taking place inside the SUV right now, the confusion, the questions, and hopefully the concern. She wanted them afraid, wanted them worried. Wanted the worst.

The SUV stopped and Ezra was on. He had looked up from the clipboard and was waving a friendly wave, smiling big like he was about to greet friends he'd not seen in ages. Then he tapped his watch and gave the SUV a thumbs-up, like he was congratulating them for being right on time.

For what felt like an eternity, nothing happened, and

Alexa's mind starting spinning tales of horror. Saw the men in the SUV all pulling out weapons and discussing who would shoot which part of the strange black guy that had no business being out here. She gripped the gun in her hand tight, was surprised to find that she found no comfort in it.

Ezra tucked the clipboard under his arm and then raised his hands up in a *what-gives?* gesture.

The driver's side front and back and the rear passenger door opened in unison, like a choreographed move, and three figures stepped out.

The same three figures from the picture on Ezra's computer.

Well, Alexa thought, *at least we've got the right guys. Plan's working so far, I guess.*

The doors were pushed closed and the three men moved to step around to the front of the SUV's idling engine. The two meatheads in the sweaters and black slacks took the lead, staying just a couple steps ahead of the tall guy in the nice shirt and the sunglasses.

They stopped together five feet from Ezra. The two sweater goons crossed their arms over their big chests, their biceps popping. Showing their puffy muscles.

Ezra acted like he didn't even notice, acted like he had no cares in the world. Which was to say, he acted remarkably normal. "Glad you guys made it!" he said. "This is always so much easier when the owners are actually here, so we can go over the report on-site instead of having to send emails and wait and all that back and forth bullpucky."

Bullpucky? Oh boy.

The man in the nice shirt put a hand on the goon standing on the right and stepped around him. He was nearly as tall as Ezra but looked stiff like cardboard. "Who the *fuck* are you?"

Ezra actually laughed then, like he thought the guy was joking. "You know who I am. Mark Weston. I'm the inspector from the county."

He got nothing but blank faces in return.

"We're here surveying the land, calculating the effect of the blast radius."

These words got Nice Shirt's attention. "Blast radius?"

Ezra laughed again. "Come on, are you guys messing with me? Yes, blast radius. You know, for the demo day?"

"Mr. Weston," Mr. Nice Shirt said, "you have three seconds to get in your truck and leave before we are going to have a serious problem on our hands."

Ezra acted unimpressed. "No, we're going to have a problem if we demolish this building and any debris causes damage to any surrounding structures or people. Or, God forbid, wipes out, say, a den of foxes and then we have PETA all over our butts." He shrugged. "You know how it is. Red tape and all. I just need you to look at my findings and sign off on it and we can all be on our way."

What a bunch of crazy, Alexa thought, smiling. *If these guys fall for that, they're even dumber than they look.*

Mr. Nice Shirt took a step closer. But when he spoke, his voice carried a new wave of concern. Not much, but enough to indicate he was realizing there was a real possibility he might be missing something here. "What do you mean 'demolish' this building?"

"Boom!" Ezra shouted, and all three of the men jumped back, the two goons reaching behind their backs, presumably for guns. But Ezra's laughter that followed seemed to confuse them all enough for no bullets to fly just yet. "We're tearing it down to make way for the new factory, right? Isn't that what you guys wanted?"

"Mr. Weston, I can assure you that you are mistaken. Go back to your office and check with your boss. You're in the wrong place."

Ezra's voice stayed jovial, and he didn't back down. "All due respect, sir, maybe you should check with *your* bosses. They're the ones that put in the work order and informed us it would be *you* coming out to oversee our work and sign off on everything before the big day."

"Bullshit," Mr. Nice Shirt hissed. He took another step back and nodded to his goons. But before they could move more than a half-step, Ezra said, "Are you not Peter Carimi?"

The two goons stopped. Mr. Nice Shirt's head cocked to the side, as if gently slapped.

Alexa grinned and shook her head. She'd asked Ezra what the three men's names were that night in his basement. He'd asked if it mattered. She'd said no. Apparently it did for his purposes.

"How do you know my name?" Mr. Nice Shirt aka Peter Carimi asked. His voice was ice.

Ezra looked to the sky and sighed as if exasperated. He held up his clipboard. Tapped it with his finger. "It's right *here.* Like I said, your boss put in the work order and you're the contact we had assigned to sign off on the work today. Did they really not tell you any of this?"

And then Alexa felt all her muscles tense, because Ezra started moving forward and she knew this was it. The next few seconds would define the rest. He'd not given her many specifics on what he was about to do, said he would *improvise* and that as soon as the two goons' backs were turned to her she would make her move. She didn't know how exactly he would get them to shift their positions, but that wasn't her problem. She trusted him.

Ezra had estimated a fifteen-minute window between when the mob boys would show up and when whoever they were meeting was scheduled to arrive. So, with a few minutes already off the clock, Alexa knew it was about to be crunch time.

Ezra laughed again and held out the clipboard in front of him like a serving tray. He tapped it again with his finger and said, "See, right here? Peter Carimi." Because he'd walked toward the men and stepped more left, toward the man now known as Peter Carimi, he was now positioned more to the two goons' right, and, like any good pair of protectors, they shifted their feet just slightly, angling themselves to keep Ezra in front.

That was when Alexa saw the guns tucked into the waistbands of their pants. Their sweaters pulled up and tucked behind the grips for easy access. The sight of this, along with the three-against-one situation in front of her, suddenly caused her to cast a lot of doubt on Ezra's grand plan. She started to stand and move forward. Gripped the gun in her own hand and held it out, flicked off the safety, aiming at the goon on the left's back. Center mass. Just like she'd been taught. A thing she'd honestly hoped she'd never have to put into practice.

She'd taken half a step out of the cave-like entrance in the bay door when Ezra said, "Here, look," and handed the clipboard to Peter Carimi, who took it instinctively, and then Ezra dropped his pencil to the ground and said, "Oh, whoops," and bent down to pick it up. Only he didn't go for the pencil. In a flash of speed that made Alexa feel as though she was temporarily suspended in time, Ezra lifted the end of his pantleg, fingered free a small knife, and then stood and simultaneously flicked it through the air like a dart. It struck and embedded itself into the right goon's throat, causing the man to let out a half-scream that was instantly cut off and replaced with a gurgled whistle as he fell to his knees and clawed at his neck.

At the same time, Ezra punched Peter Carimi once in the face and then moved behind him and wrapped his arms around the man's neck and head in a grip that instantly immobilized him and, by keeping him upright, forced him to play the role of human shield.

The one remaining goon, to his credit, ignored his now-dead comrade splayed out on the ground next to him and had reacted as quick as somebody as big and dumb as he was could react. He'd pulled his own gun from his pants and had it aimed at Ezra. Only it wasn't really aimed at Ezra, it was aimed at Peter Carimi, who had blood pouring from his nose and was cursing and trying to buck himself free from Ezra's grip.

Ezra looked like he wasn't even trying. Like he was doing nothing more than holding on to a balloon that was trying to float away.

This was Alexa's time now. She stepped out onto the loading dock and crept forward.

"My partner has a gun aimed at your head," Ezra said. "She's right behind you, and if you even think about turning around, she'll end you."

"Hi, asshole," Alexa said, jumping down from the loading

dock. The sound of her boots hitting the ground caused the goon to flinch and duck his head. She smiled. She'd liked that. She liked his fear.

"Put the gun down," Ezra said. "Slowly. On the ground in front of you."

"Don't do it!" Peter Carimi yelled to his bodyguard.

Ezra did something, just a subtle flick of his hand, and the man cried out. "Hey," Ezra said, getting the goon's attention. "You don't listen to him anymore, okay? You want to live, you listen to me. Gun on the ground."

The goon hesitated a second too long.

"Fine," Ezra said. "Shoot me. Or try to. If you think you can miss hitting your boss here. But, if you do that, my partner still shoots you. So really, what's the point? You willing to take that risk?"

The goon, apparently, was not a risk taker. He set the gun on the ground. Slowly. Just like he'd been asked.

"Good," Ezra said. "Now walk slowly to the SUV and put your hands flat on the hood."

The goon didn't like that. Stayed put. Ezra sighed. "Okay, shoot him."

"Wait!" It was the first word the goon had spoken. His voice was comically high. Maybe fear, maybe steroids. He cursed under his breath and started moving. Faced the SUV and put his hands on the hood.

"Good," Ezra said again. "I don't care if you have to sneeze, or if a bug flies into your mouth or anything, if a single finger lifts off that hood, you're dead. Game over. Got it?"

The goon grunted something that Ezra apparently interpreted as mutual understanding, because he turned his attention back to the man within his grip. He loosened one of his arms from around the man's neck and then darted a kick to the inside of the man's right ankle. The leg buckled and the knee bent and then Ezra repeated the process on the other ankle and the man plopped down onto his knees in the mud and weeds.

"Question time," Ezra said, adjusting his position and wrapping one arm around the man's neck and placing the other hand atop his head. "One wrong move and I'll snap your neck. You won't even know it's happened."

Alexa moved in then, walked right up to the guy on his knees. The guy who had gotten Tony Romano killed, the guy who'd sent Griff into the woods at Collins Park, the guy who'd had Clara taken, her finger snapped. All the problems Alexa had encountered or been a part of since arriving in Silent Falls were because of Peter Carimi.

When she was ten feet away, he recognized her. Groaned. "Are you fucking kidding me? This is because of you? You stupid, crazy bi—"

Ezra squeezed and the man's eyes bulged and his voice was choked off.

Alexa stood directly in front of him, got down on one knee of her own. Reached out and pulled off the man's sunglasses. Tucked them into her own pocket. The man's eyes were a dull green. "Yes, all because of me," she said. "You fucked with the wrong bitch, wouldn't you say?"

Peter Carimi's eyes narrowed to slits, his face was boiling with anger—or maybe that was just the pressure Ezra was applying to his windpipe.

"Two things," Alexa said. "First, hold out your hand."

Peter Carimi didn't move. Glared at her. Then he spat in her face.

Alexa whipped the barrel of her pistol across his face. It connected just below his right eye and opened an ugly gash. Blood flowed fast and freely. Peter bucked against Ezra, trying to wiggle himself free, but again, pointless.

"Hand," Alexa said. Cocking the gun back, preparing another blow.

Peter Carimi's eyes darkened, a spark extinguished. It was the image of a man accepting defeat. He held out his left hand. Alexa didn't waste a second. Reached out and grabbed his pinky finger and snapped it as hard away from the man's hand as she could, put all her strength behind it. She felt the bone snap in her palm. It was followed by a primal scream of pain from Peter Carimi. She stood up and stepped back, watched as the man flailed and writhed against Ezra's grip. "That's for Clara," Alexa said. "There's a special place in hell for people who harm innocent young women."

Maybe you'll meet my dad there...

Eventually, Peter Carimi calmed down. His broken finger hung limply from his hand and he cradled it against his chest like he was protecting a baby bird.

"I only have one question, though," Alexa said. "Why did you kill Tony Romano? We know he was laundering money for you guys, so what went wrong? Because whatever led you to that decision is exactly why you're here with us right now. I want you to think about that. Killing Tony Romano is what got *you* killed. So"—she shrugged—"I'm just curious what that thing was, because clearly it wasn't worth it, right?"

Peter Carimi spat at her again. "Fuck. You."

And Ezra snapped the man's neck.

The sound was unlike anything Alexa had ever heard, a quick sickening crunch that was a million times worse than the noise Peter Carimi's pinky had made. The suddenness of the whole thing shocked her, and the ease with which Ezra had ended the man's life froze her brain for a second.

Which was all it took.

Because as the sickening sound faded from her ears and Peter Carimi's body slumped forward and landed facedown with a *thud* into the tall grass, the goon by the SUV must have also heard the sound and realized that with his boss now dead, the odds were very good that he would not be making it away from the old abandoned factory alive. He should have gone for the driver's door, should have made a run for it. Maybe it was loyalty leading to a desire for vengeance, or maybe it was stupidity, but whatever the cause, the goon did not go for the driver's door and instead he pushed off the SUV's hood and spun around and took three long strides toward where he'd dropped his gun in the grass.

"Get down!" Ezra called to her, and she saw him hit the ground himself. Falling to his knees. Alexa did not get down, however. Instead, something about the image of this muscle-bound waste of life bounding across the earth toward her—toward his *weapon*—sparked that fire of rage in her. She raised her own pistol and aimed. Just as the goon stopped moving and reached down to search for his gun, she squeezed the trigger. Once. Two times. Three.

Click. Click. Click.

Nothing happened. The gun did not fire.

The goon found what he was looking for. Scooped it up and was just beginning to point it at Ezra when a gunshot cracked through the air and echoed like thunder. A burst of red bloomed in the center of the goon's sweater and his face went wide with surprise and his eyes bulged. He collapsed, swallowed by the weeds.

Alexa spun and looked at Ezra, who was just pushing himself from the ground. He didn't have a gun in his hands. She looked down at her own pistol again. Pointed it at the ground and squeezed the trigger.

Click.

Ezra walked slowly over to her and gently removed the weapon from her hand. "It's empty," he said. She looked at up him, somewhat miffed. He gave her that small grin. "You're a lot of things," he said. "But you're not a killer."

"But..." Alexa looked back to where the second goon was lying dead. "How?"

"Y'all alright?" a familiar voice called from somewhere far off. "Still got all your fingers and toes?"

Alexa twisted and looked toward the crest of the hill, high up where the trees were. Saw a short and stocky figure begin to make his way carefully down the hill. A rifle was slung over his shoulder.

"Let me introduce you to Marine Corps Corporal Herbert Little, 0311 ... Grunt," Ezra said. "The third member of our team."

Alexa watched as Herb made his way slowly down the hill and approached them. Ezra shook the man's hand. "Nice shot."

"Only way I shoot," Herb said. Then he nodded a greeting to Alexa. "Ma'am."

Alexa glared at Ezra. "I asked you if there was anything else you were forgetting to tell me, remember?"

"And I answered honestly," Ezra said. "I didn't forget to

tell you about Herb being our third. I chose not to. Element of surprise, remember?"

Alexa wanted to protest, wanted to get mad, but the simple truth was the three of them were standing tall and alive while three members of the mob were now dead on the ground.

"Come on," Ezra said. "Job's not done yet, and we're getting low on time."

They did a quick search of the SUV and found a small briefcase full of cash in the back seat, and in the spare tire well in the far back they found a duffle bag full of guns. Presumably, one or both of these things were why the goons had their regular rendezvous at the factory. A pickup or drop-off. Ezra left all the cash and guns where he'd found them and he and Herb piled the bodies into the SUV, and then Ezra pulled two cans of gasoline from the back of his truck and he and Alexa doused the entire thing. Herb pulled a pack of matches from his pocket and handed it to Alexa. "Wanna do the honors?"

She did.

She lit the match and let it flicker in her fingertips. Tossed it into the opened window of the SUV. It landed on Peter Carimi's lap and the blaze instantly caught.

The three of them got the hell out of there.

Ezra dropped Herb off where the man had parked a small and worn-down two-door pickup truck that looked like it had shared a life with Alexa's Oldsmobile. It was about a mile before the factory, hidden deep in the trees near what looked like a fire road. "Get going," Ezra said. "We were never here."

Three minutes later, as Ezra's truck roared down the rural

county road away from the abandoned factory, a different black SUV passed them, heading toward it.

"Just in time," Ezra said. "Just like we planned."

Alexa watched in the sideview mirror as black smoke began to climb into the sky.

CHAPTER 30

Alexa did not feel bad, exactly, and certainly not remorseful or guilty for what they'd done. Three bad men had died, and just like Ezra had told her, taking down the bad guys felt really fucking good.

But, no, she didn't really feel good, either.

She felt ... numb. Empty.

Cold.

She and Ezra and Herb had achieved exactly what they'd set out to—they'd gotten their retribution on men who had murdered and abused and had likely gotten away with it for what was likely far too long. Alexa had fought back against them for Clara ... and for herself. She should feel better, should feel triumphant, right? The chains that the events from the last few days had used to bind her should have fallen free by now, should have clanged to the ground in her mind and allowed her to set off on the new life she'd been dreaming of.

But something didn't give. One chain seemed to hold strong.

The cabin of the truck was silent except for the hum of the tires over the asphalt. Ezra had slowed his speed back down to the speed limit and his face was blank and unreadable. His eyes still hidden behind the sunglasses. His story of loss and grief had been immense. He'd bared himself to her, a man who appeared so invulnerable. She had sensed that his past had been dark, but the tragedy he'd lived through made her own secrets seem almost...

No, she told herself. *Not incomparable. Just different. We all have demons. Nobody can really feel them but the ones they belong to.*

And that's when the chain that had remained in place began to loosen. Alexa felt a great rush of anxiety begin to fill her lungs, pushing out the oxygen, a debilitating fear that threatened to overtake all her other senses. But just like she'd done her whole life, she fought back, she closed her eyes and searched for that glowing ember in her soul, and when she found it, she grabbed hold tight and the anxiety began to melt and the words started forming on her tongue and then she was talking.

"When I was twelve, my father molested me," she said.

Ezra did not make any indication he'd heard her. Hands on the wheel, eyes straight ahead.

"He was a police detective on a special task force meant to track down and arrest pedophiles. He was good at his job, got a special award from the mayor and everything. Turns out the reason he was so good was because he was exactly the same thing that he was hunting. I didn't understand all of this then, but I started putting the pieces together as I got older. After everything happened."

She thought she might start to cry, speaking to life these

memories that she'd kept buried away for so long. But she didn't. She felt calm. Was surprised at how good it felt to share her secret with Ezra, to release the great weight that had been on her chest for all these years.

"I was on his computer one day in his home office. I wasn't supposed to be in there, but I guess my instinct—"

(The Universe)

"—must have started to realize there was something off about my dad. I guessed his password—it was his nickname for me—and found all these pictures of nude children. Myself included."

Nothing from Ezra. It was almost as though he wasn't even breathing.

"He caught me," Alexa said, that horrible image of him standing in the opened doorway of his home office flooding into her memory. The way he walked toward her. The way he discovered what she'd found and had tried to soothe her, calm her. She could still smell him, the whiff of deodorant and cologne she'd gotten when he'd pulled her into that hug ... the hug that became more than a hug. It had been a trap she could not escape. A grown man's strength restraining a small girl while his hands touched her in all the places she'd been taught to protect.

She told Ezra all this. Left nothing out.

"After, he knew he'd messed up," she said. "He basically kidnapped me and we hit the road. Drove for what felt like days. He knew that if he let me out of his sight I was going to tell someone. He knew his life would be over if he ever let me go. He was scared," she said. "He didn't know what to do."

She paused for a second. Watched out the window as

trees blurred by. Remembered the motel. The night it had all changed.

"We found an old motel out in what felt like the middle of nowhere," she said. "He died there our first night. Overdosed on a bottle of his migraine medicine. Choked on his vomit. I woke up and found him in the morning."

Her father's overdose was easy enough to believe. Most folks would just assume suicide. But the next part of the tale was the gray area, the part that was hard to explain to somebody who had both feet firmly planted only in the earthly reality that most common people understood to be absolute. She could try to explain but decided against it.

That was a different story altogether.

She settled on just stating that the motel owners and their nephew Quinten had helped her. Taken care of her in the days that followed. But she would never go back home. Never go back to the life she lived before, the person she'd been.

"Honestly," she said, feeling the rush of her story come to an end, "it's like I've not been fully alive since that night. I've just been drifting along. Alone. Clawing out an existence."

They were back at the farmhouse now, and Ezra pulled the truck up to the front porch and got out without a word. Alexa didn't know what sort of reaction she was expecting, but she'd anticipated more than being completely ignored. He was walking around the front of the truck and she pushed open her door, feeling anger start to build. What she'd just done had taken her over twenty years to build up the courage to do, and she *would* be heard. She jumped out of the truck and—

And Ezra wrapped her in a hug.

She stiffened at first, thought she was going to push him

away. But then he laid a hand atop her head and pulled her closer and she smelled *him* now, not the memory of her father, and her body relaxed and he stroked her hair and whispered, "I'm so sorry that happened to you."

The tears did come then. Hot and heavy and accompanied by great sobs that she didn't know she even had inside her. This ... this comfort, this compassion, they were like warm blankets wrapped around her after an eternity in the cold. She felt the life coming back into her. Felt her future brightening.

When she'd finished crying, Ezra pulled her gently away from him and took off his sunglasses and looked her in the eyes. "I don't know everything," he said, "But I know you're strong. You are a *survivor*. Don't ever forget that." He winked at her. "I think you're just getting started."

He turned then, and together they walked up the porch steps, Barlow's happy face greeting them from the other side of the window, tongue hanging, tail wagging.

CHAPTER 31

Three days went by. Alexa stayed at the farmhouse, playing with Barlow, reading books she would pluck from Ezra's shelves, napping, cooking, enjoying herself—maybe for the first time fully since she was twelve. Ezra went to work at the inn, said he was monitoring the situation with the abandoned factory, and so far everything seemed fine. Just as he'd suspected. Alexa didn't know what exactly he meant by "monitoring the situation," but she'd grown to just accept that he had his methods, his connections, his ways of doing things, and she would trust them all.

On the fourth day, she headed out, needed a change of scenery. Plus, she had something she needed to do. She stopped at the inn first, found Herb behind the counter instead of Ezra.

"Just a lunch break," Herb said, "no need to worry. He's not out causing more trouble." Herb grinned and Alexa grinned back.

"I never got a chance to thank you," Alexa said. "For what you did to ... you know, help us."

Herb waved her off. "Think nothing of it. Old man like me won't lose any sleep over causing the world to have one less asshole. I saw my share of nightmares overseas, and I don't need those wannabe thugs causing trouble in my own damn country. No place for it, I say."

Ezra had told her some of Herb's story. Vietnam veteran who'd returned home and, after a battle with PTSD had become a drifter. Just like Alexa and Ezra had drifted. Only Herb's drifting had lasted forty years. He could never seem to keep steady work, and his mental and physical health went up and down like the sun. He tried to get help, tried to get back on the straight and narrow, but in the end, just like the fate of so many of America's finest heroes, it seemed like the system failed him time and time again. He'd eventually ended up back in his hometown of Silent Falls and had worked out a deal with the previous owner of the inn to do odd jobs in exchange for a room to stay in. When the inn had gone under and the bank had taken the keys, Herb had been out of options. So, he'd squatted. Nobody had seemed to notice or care. The inn was likely going to be demolished anyway.

But then Ezra had shown up. Bought the place, and found Herb one day while he was inspecting the rooms. And in true Ezra fashion, after hearing the man's story, Ezra agreed not only to reinstate the previous owner's deal but also to offer Herb a full-time salary.

"He's the only other person besides you who knows my full story," Ezra had told her one night over dinner. "From what I gather, he was a hell of a soldier, and he's a hell of a man. I trust him implicitly. We share a lot of the same ideas and values. I don't think ... I don't think it was an accident he and I ended up meeting."

Alexa had smiled. "Me either."

She turned to leave the inn's office now and said, "Hey, chess later?"

Herb's smile warmed her heart. "I'll never say no to chess. You like losing that badly, huh?"

She laughed. "Bring it on! I need to run an errand, then I'll be back."

She drove the Oldsmobile into town, made the right turn near the café, took the left that would take her past the middle school, and then she pulled into the lot of Lil' Tony's Landscaping. There were a few cars in the parking lot, and as she'd pulled in, she saw the front end of one of the work trucks around back of the building. She'd already called ahead to ask if he was working today.

Inside, a pleasant woman who Alexa assumed was Janis sat at a makeshift reception desk. She was typing on a computer keyboard with blazing speed and didn't even look Alexa's way as she asked, "Help you?"

"Hi," Alexa said. "I'm looking for Griff? I needed to drop something off for him."

Janis pointed to a door across from the desk marked STAFF ONLY. "Go ahead in. He's tinkering with something out there. Hard to tell what with that bozo."

Alexa liked Janis. "Thanks."

She pushed through the door and entered a large open space with high ceilings that smelled of oil and gas and earth. The big roll-up bay door was to her left, and she was hit with a sickening realization that this was likely the exact place that they'd brought Clara the day they'd snapped her finger. The image of Peter Carimi lying facedown in the mud helped to alleviate some of that sickness.

Griff, as promised, was indeed tinkering with something. He was bent over the opened hood of a large tractor and was elbow-deep into the machine's guts. His pants were sagging and a third of his ass crack was showing. Alexa looked around the room, saw they were all alone, and then took three quick strides across the floor and planted a kick between the man's legs, once again pulverizing his unsuspecting testicles.

Griff yowled and dropped like a bag of sand, banging his chin on the front bumper of the tractor on his way down. His teeth clacked together hard, and when he rolled over there was blood on his lips. He was grunting and huffing and puffing and staring up at her in complete surprise and confusion. The surprise and confusion were replaced with fear when he recognized her.

Alexa lifted one boot and stood on his chest. "So, you like hurting young girls?"

It only took a couple seconds—as fast as poor Griff's stunted brain could compute—for the man to realize what she was talking about. He started protesting immediately. "I had to! I had to! I told you they were bad people! I told you they were going to kill me!"

"You look alive to me," Alexa said, pressing harder with her boot. Griff squirmed but went nowhere.

"That's because I did what they said. They gave me a second chance! God woman, what's wrong with you! Didn't you get the message? Jesus, do you have a death wish?"

Alexa reached slowly and deliberately into her pants

pocket and pulled out Peter Carimi's sunglasses. Griff's eyes focused on them and went wide with shock.

Alexa bent down and tossed the sunglasses into Griff's face. "You work for me now," she said. "You do what I say, or I'll turn you into just one more body they'll never find."

She didn't wait for a response. Walked back through the side door and gave Janis a pleasant goodbye and got in the Oldsmobile and headed back into town.

She felt good, empowered. Rolled down the windows as she drove and let the cold air fill the car with a fresh breeze. She tugged up the collar of her leather jacket and turned on the radio and sang along to a song she recognized and decided she would celebrate her recent idiot beatdown with a coffee and maybe a muffin from the café.

She found a parking spot on a side street about two blocks away and killed the engine. Stepped out of the car and was still humming the song from the radio when she heard the engine come up behind her. Then there was a blur of black beside her. The SUV drove past her about five yards and hit the brakes. Stopped. The rear passenger window rolled down just as she was in line with it. The gun pointed directly at her.

"Get in," the man holding the gun said.

CHAPTER 32

Running would do no good.

Alexa wasn't positive they'd shoot her right in the middle of the street, but when you were dealing with a group that chopped body parts off and set them out on display for the world to see, it was wiser not to take any chances. The way she saw it, two things were going to happen if she got into the back of the waiting black SUV: they'd either take her somewhere and torture her, another message perhaps, or they'd take her somewhere and kill her. Both options bad, sure, but there was one big question that needed to be answered. Her curiosity, in this case, might very well kill the cat.

Did they know she and Ezra had killed Peter Carimi and his goons?

"Get in. Now, please," the man holding the gun said. Like Carimi, he was wearing a nice shirt, though he wore his with the top three buttons undone, exposing thick black chest hair. His sunglasses looked exactly like Carimi's, too, and Alexa suddenly wished she had kept the ones she'd just thrown into Griff's face, so then they could have been twinsies.

Get it together, Shiffy.

Hey, the guy did say please, didn't he?

She looked up and down the block. There was nobody. She sighed, nodded, and stepped off the sidewalk and into the street. The back passenger door was pushed open and the man holding the gun slid across the back bench seat to make room for her. She climbed in and closed the door, oddly at ease with the idea that today would be the day she died. Maybe the moment in Ezra's driveway had been even more cathartic than she'd realized. Maybe the execution of Carimi and his goons had been her last good deed, her final payment to the Universe. Couple that with the release she'd felt in telling her truth to Ezra, and maybe she was finally free. Her purpose served.

It was an odd feeling, not to care if she was going to die. Especially when, for the last few weeks, all she'd thought about was finally getting to live.

What was the saying? Man plans and God laughs.

Fucking-A.

The window was rolled up and she heard the click of the door locks. The inside of the SUV smelled of too much cologne and cigars. The driver, who was a carbon copy of one of Carimi's goons—*Where do they get these guys? Is there a factory? (Oops, is it too soon for a factory joke?)*—put the SUV into gear and they started moving.

Based on Clara's story of her abduction, Alexa was expecting a black hood to be placed over her head at any moment now, and maybe a solid punch to the gut. But neither came. The man next to her wasn't even aiming the gun at her anymore, just had it sitting casually in his lap like he'd forgotten about it.

The man in the front passenger seat spoke then. He was tall, with his head nearly hitting the SUV's ceiling, and his massive frame was surrounded with massive amounts of fat. He looked like an NFL lineman who'd retired and had stopped working out. He was balding, and his olive-complexion scalp was covered by a comb-over that was about as effective as using a screen door for privacy. He wore a black windbreaker that could have doubled as a car cover. A thick gold chain rested around his collar.

"Do you know who I am?" he asked.

Alexa thought for a moment. "Weren't you in *Star Wars*? Hutt something?"

If she was going to die, might as well have some fun. Get out a few last jabs, just to make herself feel good.

To her surprise the man started to laugh, his shoulders rising and falling like mountains being rocked by an earthquake. "Funny," he said. Then, "Cocky."

"No," Alexa said. "I don't know who you are." But she had an idea. The guy's presence exuded power, authority. You could practically see it in the air, taste it. Whoever he was, he was very high up in the Abatelli family food chain. Maybe the very top.

"Three of my men were killed," he said, as casually as if he were declining to supersize a fast-food meal, which, let's be honest, he probably never declined to do.

"How many does that leave you with?" Alexa said.

This answer caused the man with the gun to shift in his seat, as if her attitude was making *him* uncomfortable.

"I think you had something to do with their deaths," the big man said. "I think you might have killed them yourself."

"Little old me?" Alexa asked. "How? Why? Like I said, I don't even know who you are."

She thought of Barlow, back at the farmhouse. She wished she'd gotten the chance to tell him goodbye. These men were definitely going to kill her.

"Whoever killed them did us a favor," the man said. The driver flicked on the turn signal and then made a left turn down another side street.

Wait, what? A favor?

"Well, that's nice," Alexa said.

"Carimi was a problem," the big man said. "He thought he was smarter than us, better than us. He stepped out of line. The thing with the Romano kid—never should have happened."

Alexa thought of the look on Big Tony's face that day in the café, those bloodshot eyes. "I'm sure Tony's parents will be very happy to hear that. It'll be just the same as bringing their son back."

The man ignored her. Alexa couldn't tell if this was a good sign or bad one.

"Carimi was the Romano kid's handler, kept the money flowing here. The kid was smart. Good at what he did," the man said. Alexa was noticing that the fat roll on the back of his head bobbed up and down when he spoke. "Carimi was well compensated, but he felt he deserved more. He'd asked for additional responsibility, wanted to be more important than he was. I told him no. Never really liked the guy. But it was business. You have to separate the personal. So, he thought he'd carve out his own slice from somewhere else.

Decided to try and start selling drugs, using the Romano kid's businesses as distribution points."

This time, Alexa said nothing.

"We don't sell drugs," the big man said. "Never. We will transport it for whoever needs it moved, but that's it. Selling drugs is for the cartels and street thugs, not us. We are above that. Plus, too much risk. Not good for business."

The absurdity of what the man was saying made him seem borderline delusional.

"Carimi went behind our backs and tried to force the Romano kid to comply with pushing drugs. The kid said no. Pushed back. Said there was no way he was going to spoil his father's restaurant with drugs. I respect the kid for standing his ground. Family is everything, after all. Right?"

Alexa nodded. "Sure."

"Carimi did not react well to being told no. His temper ... well, it was not good. The Romano kid learned that the hard way. Afterward, Carimi came to me, tail tucked. He knew he'd made a mistake, asked for help and forgiveness. So, we did what we do. Needed to protect our name. But ... plans were in the works."

"Plans?" Alexa asked.

"To make sure Carimi didn't cause any more trouble."

"You mean you were going to kill him."

"Yes."

Honesty. There was something to be said for it.

But not from her, not right now. "So it's *you* guys who've been threatening me? Are you the people who hurt that poor girl from Smokey's?"

"Business...," the big man said again. "Not personal."

Alexa said nothing.

"So..." The man shrugged, and Alexa would swear the car bounced. "Like I said, you did us a favor."

"I don't know what you're talking about."

The big man nodded, as if he was actually about to believe her. But then he dropped the bomb, let her know that despite his patience, he was not playing around. "I am curious, whatever happened to your father, Alexa? Robert Shifflett? The two of you went missing quite some time ago, yes?"

Alexa's blood ran cold. Her heart seemed to stop for several beats before kicking back up again in a burst that made her dizzy.

The big man pointed and the driver made another left turn. They were right back on the street where they'd started, Alexa's Oldsmobile coming into view ahead. The driver pulled the SUV alongside it. Parked. The big man still did not turn around, but his words struck her deep.

"Staying in town?" he asked. "Plan on making Silent Falls your new home?"

Alexa's focus was returning, the fighter in her regaining strength. That glowing ember in her soul flashed a warm blast through her veins. Ezra's words echoed in her mind: *You're a* survivor. *I think you're just getting started.*

"Yes," she said. "That's the plan."

The big man nodded appreciatively. "Wonderful. It's a very nice place. I've always enjoyed my visits here." He nodded again and the driver reached down and hit a button and the doors unlocked. As Alexa reached for the handle, the big man said, "You're a part of this now, you understand that, yes?"

Alexa was silent.

"Please answer me," the big man said.

"Yes," Alexa said, because what else could she say? She was seconds away from freedom.

The man nodded again. "Good. I'm glad to hear that. Remember, it's not personal, just business. You *made* yourself a part of this. We are only asking you honor your debt."

"Debt?"

"We may call on you, you know, from time to time. You seem to be very resourceful."

Shit.

"Otherwise," the man said, "forget you ever saw us today. And don't worry, we're very good at keeping secrets." He paused, and Alexa thought this was when he'd finally turn around and show her his face. But he did not. "Just like you are."

The man next to her with the gun jerked it once toward the door. She didn't hesitate. She pulled the handle and stepped out onto the street. The SUV drove away just as slowly as it had arrived, leaving her alone by her car.

She stood there for a long time.

The two parts of her raged a battle inside her mind. Stay or leave?

Many signs pointed toward leaving, to falling back into that old familiar comfort of being nobody and living nowhere.

But she thought of Barlow, of Ezra and Herb's story and how the inn had seemed to bring the three of them all together. She thought of Lance, recalled something he'd mentioned to her shortly before they'd parted ways. Something about how there's lots of devils in the world, and you can't beat them all at once. You can only face down the one directly in front of you.

A person rounded the corner from the main street and started walking up the sidewalk toward her. It was the man who always had all the newspapers at the café and always recommended which roast to try. When he reached her, he nodded once and did not stop but only said as he passed by, "Colombian today. The fruit tones are nice."

Alexa Shifflett knew then. She was going to stay. Going to live.

She would run no more.

CHAPTER 33

(Four Months Later)

The balding man with glasses and the pointed nose whose headshot had been on the FOR RENT advertisement taped to the café's window turned out to be very friendly. His name was Steve, and when Alexa had called to ask more about the two floors that were for rent above the café, he said he could meet her there that very day for a tour.

The floor directly above the café was empty and wide open and would be perfect for an office space. The third floor was a studio apartment with big windows that let in a lot of light. It wasn't as grand as the farmhouse, but the moment she'd stepped through the door, she could imagine it all, grew almost giddy with excitement at the prospect of something being hers for the very first time.

She'd pitched the idea—which had really been sparked by something Clara had said to her that day at Smokey's, when Alexa had been asking her questions—to Ezra a couple weeks after the incident in the street with the black SUV, which she'd never told him about. She didn't know how he'd react, and she didn't need him worrying about her or going off and trying to plan some kamikaze mission to take down the entire mob. They'd been having dinner together, and when she'd told him what she was thinking about doing, he had leaned back in his chair and crossed his arms and she had watched his jaw work as he thought. The anticipation was excruciating. She wanted his approval on this. He was smart, very smart, and if he thought it was a good idea, then she'd know that she wasn't crazy for thinking such a thing.

Finally, he smiled and stood from the table and pulled a bottle of wine from the rack on the counter. Opened it and poured two big glasses. All without saying a word. He offered her a glass and she took it and he raised his own glass in a toast. "I think it's a great idea," he said. "Perfect, in fact. You're meant for this."

She laughed and clinked her glass against his.

Then he offered to fully fund her for the first year and she rushed around the table and kissed him on the cheek. "Thank you so much," she said. "Because here's a secret. I'm sort of broke."

They laughed again and drank more wine and it was one of the best nights of her life.

So now here she was, sitting at her own desk, in her own office, with her own window open to let in the spring breeze. Smells from the café were constantly wafting up to her, which was a built-in perk of the location. Barlow was curled up on his bed next to her desk, and his ears perked up at the sound of footsteps on the stairs. Somebody knocked softly and then opened the door and stepped inside.

The girl in the workout clothes and the green drinks, as it

turned out, was a fitness instructor online and had a YouTube channel with over six million subscribers. She was twenty-seven. Her name was Piper, and Alexa wouldn't go so far as to say they were in love, but they sure as hell liked each other. It didn't make sense, really, that somebody as private and secretive as Alexa should find herself falling for somebody whose entire livelihood literally required her to film and broadcast her life to the entire planet, but hey, what exactly made sense, anyway? What exactly was reality?

"Hey, I can't stay. Got a livestream in thirty minutes, but I wanted to bring you this." Piper held a green drink in one hand and a coffee in the other. She set the coffee down on Alexa's desk. "And this," she said as she kissed her on the lips. Just a quick one, but it got the job done. "Dinner here tonight?" Piper asked.

Alexa took a sip of the coffee. "Sounds great."

"Cool, I'll pick something up on the way."

And then she was gone, leaving Alexa to sit and enjoy her coffee and look around the room and marvel over just how far she'd come so fast. Was this happiness? If it wasn't, it was damn close enough.

The phone software on her computer gave off its soft chime that meant somebody was calling, and Alexa sat up fast, butterflies in her stomach. She was still getting used to this part. She put on her headset and clicked the button on the screen and the call connected.

"Shiffy PI, Alexa speaking. How can I help you today?"

AUTHOR'S NOTE

Thanks so much for reading **RUN NO MORE**. I hope you enjoyed it. If you *did* enjoy it and have a few minutes to spare, I would greatly appreciate it if you could leave a review saying so. Reviews help authors more than you can imagine, and help readers like you find more great books to read. Win-win!

While the Shiffy P.I. series can stand on its own, Alexa first appeared in a couple books from my Lance Brody series. If you like supernatural mysteries and want to learn more about this guy named Lance, I hope you'll give them a read.

If you'd like to stay up-to-date on what I'm working on, there's a link on the following page where you can sign-up for my newsletter, and as a thank you you'll receive a free book starter bundle. And...

If you'd like to check out my Patreon page (patreon.com/ mrobertsonjr), I'm offering lots of perks, early-access to projects, and behind-the-scenes content to supporters.

THANK YOU to the following Patreon members for your support:

Chris Cool, Debra Kowalski, Diane Benson, Judi Josephson, Karin Anderson, Kathy Oudinot, Linda Crisp, Lisa Fazalare, Martha Gilmore, Mike Gagliardi, Raven Morgan, Rebecca Curry, Steph, Tami, and Tanya Wolf.

You guys rock!

-Michael Robertson Jr

For all the latest info, including release dates, giveaways, and special events, sign up for the Michael Robertson, Jr. newsletter. (He promises to never spam you!)

https://mrobertsonjr.com/newsletter-sign-up

Follow On:

Facebook.com/mrobertsonjr

Twitter.com/mrobertsonjr

Instagram.com/mrobertsonjr

Patreon.com/mrobertsonjr

More from Michael Robertson Jr

LANCE BRODY SERIES

Dark Holiday (Book 6)

Dark Rest (Book 5.5 - Short Story)

Dark Woods (Book 5)

Dark Vacancy (Book 4)

Dark Shore (Book 3)

Dark Deception (Book 2.5 - Short Story)

Dark Son (Book 2)

Dark Game (Book 1)

Dark Beginnings (Book 0 - Prequel Novella)

OTHER NOVELS

Cedar Ridge

Transit

Rough Draft (A Kindle #1 Horror Bestseller!)

Regret*

Collections

Tormented Thoughts: Tales of Horror

The Teachers' Lounge*

*Writing as Dan Dawkins